TANTRIC COCONUTS

TANTRIC COCONUTS

A Novel

Greg Kincaid

CROWN PUBLISHERS

New York

Copyright © 2014 by Greg Kincaid

All rights reserved.
Published in the United States by Crown Publishers, an imprint of the Crown Publishing Group, a division of Random House LLC, a Penguin Random House Company, New York.
www.crownpublishing.com

CROWN and the Crown colophon are registered trademarks of Random House LLC.

Library of Congress Cataloging-in-Publication Data
Kincaid, Gregory D., 1957–
Tantric coconuts / Greg Kincaid. — First edition.
  pages cm
  1. Grandsons—Fiction. 2. Grandfathers—Death—Fiction. 3. Life change events—Fiction. 4. Voyages and travels—Fiction. 5. Psychological fiction. I. Title.

PS3561.I42526T36 2014
813'.54—dc23   2014001497

ISBN 978-0-307-95199-1
eBook ISBN 978-0-307-95200-4

PRINTED IN THE UNITED STATES OF AMERICA

Jacket illustration: Charlie Lewis

10 9 8 7 6 5 4 3 2 1

First Edition

To teachers—whose words and inspirations
fill these pages

The first thing to do with a coconut, of course, is to get at it.

—IRMA ROMBAUER, *Joy of Cooking*

1

Ted Day

Crossing Trails, Kansas

Ted Day turned the key in the ignition of the old silver and black Winnebago 32RQ Chieftain. The battery was strong. The worn and rusted engine sputtered and hesitated but, after several cranks, started. This ruined the first excuse that had crossed Ted's mind. After the engine smoothed out, he climbed down out of the cab and faced the crustiest old man he would ever love. His grandpa, Wild Bill Raines, was proudly smiling from the perch of his mechanized scooter. "Like I said, she always starts." Grandpa Raines pointed to the highway that flanked the north edge of Crossing Trails, Kansas. "Take her to Colorado, California, the Rockies." As if the advice came from personal experience, he added, "It'll do you good to get the hell out of Crossing Trails." His voice softened. "Ted, you need to enjoy life. I can cover your office for a few weeks." Ted cocked his head to the right, so Grandpa Raines got out ahead of his skepticism. "I ran that law office for sixty years. I'm betting I can cover it for another week or two."

Ted couldn't help sounding annoyed. "Grandpa, you can't drive. Remember?"

"To hell with them! I'll be dead and buried before any man in this county can take me to court."

"Grandpa, this isn't New York City. Crossing Trails only has two cops and you're the only guy in town driving a 1982 Cadillac on a suspended license." Ted moved his hands through the air like a fish swimming in the sea and added, "With a personalized license plate, SHARK. What do you think? You're going to take that case to the Supreme Court?"

"Logistics. That's all it is. We'll work it out." Grandpa Raines rapped his knuckles on his scooter's chrome wheel guard to distract Ted from his train of thought. "One day you'll be old too. It happens faster than you think. When it does, you'll look back and wonder if you lived your life right. Don't wait until you're an old fart to slow down and set your course straight." He pointed his cane at the side of his cherished RV. "Being on the road allows you to clear your head and set your priorities."

Ted had no interest in spending his little vacation time sequestered in a tin house on four wheels. "Road trips sound good in theory, Grandpa, but in practice they're not that fun. I don't like to drive and I get carsick. The interstates are a breeding ground for strange people and awful food."

"Ted, you're sounding wimpy. Just take the back roads and cook your own chow."

Deciding that the argument would go nowhere, Ted capitulated. "Okay, Grandpa, I'll think about it."

"Do you realize that since you came to work for me five years ago, you've barely left the office? A good-looking kid like you should be enjoying life."

"Grandpa, I enjoy working. I don't need any time off. Not now, when I'm trying to get established."

Grandpa Raines inched the scooter half a foot closer, leaving Ted no escape route. He looked hard at his grandson. "I gave you my law practice. I didn't sell it to you. Do you know why?"

Ted shrugged. "Because you're generous?"

"Nope. I'm not that generous. I gave it to you because that's what it's worth. Nothing."

Ted tried to straighten him out. "Grandpa, there are a lot of people in Crossing Trails that would line up to make the living we've made from that practice."

"Sure, Ted, it's a good practice. But the problem, as I see it, is that you're not building much of a life to go with it. That's why that little blonde girl left you last year."

Ted tried to track his point. "You mean Lisa, my wife?"

Grandpa Raines nodded.

This one still hurt.

Ted told his grandfather the same story he had been telling himself. "Lisa left me for Thor, Grandpa. He was tall, blond, handsome, and rich. If he'd asked me, I'd have left too."

Wild Bill Raines pointed in the direction of his modest house and the old blue Cadillac sedan that squatted on the far left side of the driveway like an overgrown juniper bush. "You need to find a woman, a better one this time, get married, start a family, and be more involved in the community. If you're not careful, you're going to end up like me—a grumpy old man, left all alone. Is that what you want?"

"I could do worse."

"Really?"

"I'm proud of you, Grandpa."

"Maybe you shouldn't be." He looked in the direction of the cemetery where so many of his family members were laid to rest, and his voice became distant. "The wind will sweep over my grave just like it sweeps over the rest. I'm not sure my life has made much of a difference, one way or another."

Ted rested his hand on his grandfather's bony shoulder. "Your life meant a lot to Grandma, Mom, and . . ." He had never said it before, but not because he didn't mean it. "And to me too."

The distance that had separated Ted and his grandfather over the last few years collapsed for a few silent seconds. The wind rattled the drought-damaged leaves and pushed dust across the county highway. Wild Bill Raines waited for whatever it was that was transpiring between them to pass. When it had, he picked through his thoughts and focused on what was most important. "Ted, happiness is not found in law books or knocking yourself out writing briefs. You have to find what is important to you beyond your work."

The idea of finding a hobby or a cause settled poorly. "Grandpa, I'm doing what I want to do."

"You may need to try harder. For starters, you need people in your life to make you happy."

"I'm not ready for another wife. Lisa wore me out. My dog, Argo, is a great companion. I deal with people all day long. I like my time alone in the evenings and on weekends."

"Ted, you're wrong. Clients aren't enough. You know that. I want you to realize the best life possible. You had better pull your head out of the sand and take a good hard look, before it's too late."

"I'm only thirty. I've got a few more years."

His grandfather's steely blue eyes seemed to pierce him. Grandpa Raines cranked the hand control on his geriatric go-cart and spun to the right. "If that's what suits you, fine, stay here in Crossing Trails with your nose buried in books. Work night and day. It's your life to squander."

"I don't think I'm squandering my life, Grandpa. I just don't want to take a vacation in your RV. That's all."

His grandfather spun the scooter and, without looking back, spoke over his shoulder. "Have it your way."

Ted took a few steps after his grandfather. "Okay, Grandpa. You win. I'll close the office, sell my house, and leave in the morning to find what's missing from my life. You take the criminal docket and I'll ask Argo, the Wonder Dog, to handle the divorce cases."

Grandpa Raines looked up to the cloudless blue sky that spread over the prairie like an endless sea. He realized he had pushed his grandson a bit too far. "You don't actually understand what this is about, do you, Ted?"

Ted just shook his head, stared at the aged RV, and opened up to the possibility. "Grandpa, even if I could go, do you really think the Chieftain would hold up for one more road trip?"

"Of course she will. Besides, where's your sense of adventure?"

Ted let out a long, slow breath and wondered if his grandfather was right. He allowed his attitude to shift even further.

"Maybe in September, when the heat has passed, Argo and I will take a trip to New Mexico. I've always wanted to go."

"She's all tuned up and ready. Put that two weeks on your calendar now; otherwise, it'll never happen." The electric scooter brought him a few feet closer to his house before he stopped and added over his shoulder, "Now you're on the right track—aiming for a good life and not just hoping you'll bump into it while strolling down Main Street. Good boy."

Ted walked to his car. "Thanks for the talk, Grandpa. I'll come by and see you tomorrow. Right after lunch."

"I'm not going anywhere." Grandpa Raines went inside, put on his red corduroy slippers, and settled into his recliner. Even though most things on it either confused or disgusted him, he never missed the evening news.

Around seven o'clock he fell asleep. He dreamed about a murder trial, one early in his long career, back in the 1960s. It was one of his first big homicide cases. The defendant, a woman, looked different from how he remembered. He argued passionately for self-defense. While the jury was deliberating, he woke up. It was late, already ten fifteen. Feeling tired, he went straight to bed.

The next afternoon, when Ted came by for his lunch-hour visit, he found his grandfather still in bed, resting peacefully in his pajamas and reading the *Wall Street Journal*. He told Ted he didn't feel well.

Late in the afternoon, when the fatigue still had not lifted, Ted took his grandfather to see the doctor.

Two days later, Wild Bill Raines passed away in his sleep,

proving that even a big heart can fail. He left his small ranch-style house, the blue 1982 Cadillac, the Winnebago Chieftain, and his Merrill Lynch brokerage account—with over four million dollars' worth of investments astutely made over the last sixty years—to his only grandchild, Ted Day.

On Friday afternoon, July 20, Ted stood with nearly half the town of Crossing Trails at the graveside funeral. They came over one by one with tears in their eyes, shook Ted's hand, and recounted their personal struggles. Each story ended the same: somehow, his grandfather helped them to find a way out. While he was appreciated by all, there were also a few behind-the-back whispers: "You know, there's a reason why they called him 'the Shark.' "

After they had told their stories and gone home, Ted leaned against an old tree and looked out over the freshly turned topsoil. He felt tears on his face. Now it was just him and Argo.

Soon Ted's back hurt from standing so long. He knew, too, that he needed to go to work. Calls were piling up. He walked to the old Cadillac, which he had been driving the last few days, and gripped the handle. As he pulled open the door, he paused and whispered, "Good-bye, Wild Bill. Your life mattered, and thank you for sharing it with me."

When he returned to the cemetery five months later, his gratitude had extended further. Much further.

2

Angel Two Sparrow

Near the Lakota Sioux Reservation, South Dakota

In early June, Angel Two Sparrow sat outside in the shade of the porch and played the old Gibson her mother had given her just before she died. Larsen sat down beside his young, tall daughter and did his best to sing along in his crackling, cigarette-roughened baritone. As usual, Angel was wearing her hippie clothes. Her long black hair was pulled behind her head and clumsily tied with a piece of hemp rope left over from some half-finished art project.

When they finished playing Stevie Wonder's "A Place in the Sun," she leaned her guitar against the trailer and said, "Let's talk, *Ate*?" Angel used the Lakota word for "father" at special moments like this when she was hoping to cajole Larsen.

To white ears, Larsen's speech seemed unadorned. Almost flat. "Yes, let's talk."

"I would like to take a trip."

"Where?" he asked.

"I'd like to take Bertha on the road to start my business. I'd be gone for a while. Maybe a year."

"Business?"

"I'm a spiritual consultant."

Larsen gave her a very troubled look. A stare, really. He appreciated that souls often need healing, but he doubted that his aunt's retrofitted bookmobile, nicknamed Bertha, was the proper vehicle for Angel's quest. "Why is this a good idea?"

"I had a vision."

Larsen knew that Angel and her mother both believed that visions, more than DNA, were what made them real Lakota. He also suspected that they played the vision card when they wanted to manipulate him into doing something that he was not inclined to do. "Did this vision also tell you how you would pay for this journey?"

"No vision on that one, but I do have a business plan."

"Explain, please." Suspecting that Angel would need plenty of space to provide a rational explanation for this harebrained request, Larsen leaned far away from his daughter and waited for her response.

Angel was prepared. "Here is my plan, Age. I'll take Bertha down to the shop and paint my logo on one side. On the other side I'll paint my business card. I can make Bertha look catchy. You'll see." Angel held her hands up, middle fingers and thumbs touching. "Angel Two Sparrow, Native American spiritual consultant." She returned her hands to her lap and continued, "Under that, I'll put my phone number and say, 'first ten minutes free.' When she was finished, she looked at her father and asked, "What do you think?"

"I am not sure you want to know what I think." Larsen

operated under the theory that the females of the Two Sparrow family had something far more serious than visions to deal with. He believed their genomes were burdened by some loco gene. In his Aunt Lilly the gene expressed itself in reclusive, antisocial, and more recently even violent behaviors. For his wife, Angel's mother, it was the alcoholism that had finally taken her life while Angel was still a teen. For Angel he was not yet sure, but he was suspicious of her restless need for adventure, obsessive soul-searching, and inability to remain employed. Angel seemed poorly equipped to walk in a concrete world where men and women show up at work on time.

"What is this logo thing you want to paint?" Larsen patiently inquired.

Angel rolled up her sleeve and proudly displayed the tattoo on her arm, which she had designed. It was a monkey swinging from a coconut tree. At the foot of the tree, a female swami meditated. "This one, *Age*." She rolled her sleeve back down and explained, "I'll put the Black Hills in the background." Her still-youthful brown eyes shone excitedly from her fresh, makeup-free face.

Out of principle, Larsen tried to avoid looking at Angel's tattoo. Lakota women should not have tattoos of monkeys in coconut trees. It was not a proper Indian tattoo. Angel's mother had had a tattoo of a thunder buffalo on her right breast. That was a proper tattoo. Before the crazy gene had changed their lives, he had enjoyed resting his head on his wife's chest while Angel suckled her. He could imagine the buffalo's energy passing in this way to his daughter's spirit. He was suspicious of the energy of monkeys in coconut trees.

Larsen sighed again. Perhaps the tattoo did not matter. He raised his eyebrows and probed further. "What is 'spiritual consultant' and 'road trip'?"

Angel thought it should have been obvious to him, but she explained anyway. "*Age*, most men's souls are as broken as the trucks in your shop." She swept her eyes in a panorama. "Everywhere, people need help. This is what I will do as a spiritual consultant." Without any pretense of sincerity, she added, "You could go with me. There is room in Bertha for you and No Barks."

Larsen did not ponder long before responding. "I'm not a pilgrim. I don't like to travel with dogs—particularly not your Aunt Lilly's wolf dog that growls at men. I have a job. Repairing old cars and trucks is how I pay our bills."

"I'll be back in a year or so. I promise."

"May I comment on your business plan?"

"Sure, *Age*."

"I offer a service. Repairing cars and trucks. It sounds like you are offering a service, too. Fixing souls. My service works because people know where to find me. I've been here for many years. I cannot operate a service out of an old bookmobile driving across America. People would not know where to find me."

Angel was not only nimble with her fingers but also quick on her feet. "My service will be like a tow truck. I will come to them."

Larsen was unconvinced. As much as he loved his daughter, he had no confidence in her ability to implement this plan. "Angel, when a car breaks down on the road, people know they must call a tow truck. When a man has a sick or broken soul, how will he know to call Angel Two Sparrow, Native American spiritual consultant?"

"I am still working on that part, but I think the friends in my study group will help me."

"Those coconuts?" Larsen asked, wondering whether the crazy gene was dominant or recessive.

Aunt Lilly had been very proud of Bertha—the bookmobile she had converted to her personal residence. When Angel was a young teenager, she spent a week with Aunt Lilly on the reservation living in the bookmobile. Lilly convinced her that it had magical qualities. It was not a hard argument to make, for every night Angel experienced vivid and unusual dreams. Aunt Lilly told her that Bertha was a dream catcher on wheels: a sacred place where the spirit world can enter our lives. Lilly assured Angel that someday the bookmobile would pass to her. It was the right and proper thing for an aunt to give her niece.

It was not, however, Aunt Lilly's passing that brought about the untimely transfer of Bertha the Bookmobile. It was the crazy gene. Larsen felt very guilty for not paying more attention. He should have known from his last visit two years ago that her condition was deteriorating. Larsen had driven a long way on the virtually abandoned road before he reached Lilly's secluded driveway—not much more than a path of flattened grass cleared of large boulders. She was sitting proudly in a lawn chair near Bertha, holstering twin .45 caliber pistols while chanting some old Lakota song about White Buffalo Woman. There were man-sized wrinkles in the old woman's face. Her brown eyes seemed unconcerned about focusing on anything in particular. She was wearing a strange vest of her own invention. She called it a harness. When Larsen asked her about it, she said, "My energy is low. I need the power of Mother Earth to revitalize my spirit."

Larsen looked down at his bandolier-sporting aunt. She smiled and it was apparent that she had eschewed the reservation dentist along with most everything else from the white world.

It was unclear what was going on with her harness. A ripped and stained orange fluorescent hunting vest seemed to anchor the apparatus. There was a can of Skoal chewing tobacco peeking out of the front pocket like some shy marsupial. Duct-taped to the front and sides of the vest were various bones, wires, shotgun shells, fishing lures, and hawk feathers. Out of the back of her collaged jacket she had used a bolt to attach a green garden hose that snaked across the yard until it disappeared under a large boulder. Larsen did not believe that the earth's energy could be so conveniently harnessed, but he respected that he did not know everything. "Have you tried coffee for your low energy, Aunt Lilly?"

When she shook her head no, he inquired further. "Is your diet lacking?"

"I don't like coffee. Never did. My diet is fine."

Larsen rested his hand on his aunt's shoulder. She held it

softly and said, "Mother Earth has much healing energy. She gives her energy freely to those that can accept it. We are welcome to take what we need from her."

When Larsen tried to pull his fingers away, she squeezed his hand. "Would you like to charge? It'll relieve your gas and perhaps you can also learn to be less uptight." She patted his hand. "You seem tense." She caught him with her steel-gray eyes. "The harness makes your heart chant."

Larsen had never "charged" before and, though he doubted its efficacy, he was not sure when he would have another opportunity. Besides, there was no one around to ridicule him for indulging his aunt's crazy gene. "Yes, Lilly, I would like to wear your harness and charge."

The old woman rose. "Good. I'll make us tea while you charge."

Larsen's uncle Harry, who had been divorced from Aunt Lilly for several years, had counseled Larsen against the visit. "She's packing heat, crazier than a rabid skunk, and twice as mean. Be careful of that she-wolf, No Barks. It does not like men."

When Lilly slipped off her harness and handed it to Larsen, he noticed bruises on her arm. When he asked her about the marks, she said, "Man trouble."

Later that afternoon, after he finished his visit with Lilly, he called his uncle, whom he barely knew, and they discussed whether it was safe for Lilly to live by herself, isolated in the remotest corner of the already remote, desolate, heartbreaking, and poverty-stricken reservation. Like most of the others in the rural part of the reservation, she had neither electricity nor adequate water. "I bring her food once a week," Uncle Harry said. "She won't spend her Social Security checks. She's crazy, but what can I do?"

Larsen hesitated but decided to confront his uncle. "She had bruises on her arm. Do you know where she got them?"

"She probably fell. She drinks. Too much."

When Aunt Lilly had called him three months ago, it had surprised and embarrassed him. To the best of his knowledge, his aunt had never owned a phone. He had ignored the poor woman for too long.

"Larsen," Aunt Lilly began, "you have not come to see me in a very long time and I'm afraid that I am going to have to move. I want to give you my land, Bertha the Bookmobile, my dog, No Barks, and my new address at the women's home in Pierre."

A gentle breeze blew open the gauze curtains, and Larsen wondered, as he peered out at the fields of wheat ripening under the summer sun, whether Aunt Lilly was thinking clearly. "Why do you have to move to Pierre, Aunt Lilly? Are you sick?"

"No. The rez police came from Pine Ridge and took me away."

Larsen Two Sparrow became worried. "Why?"

"I had a dream vision. My bear told me that your uncle Harry would come and try to take my home, my money, No Barks, and my land from me. So when I next saw him, I shot him. It was him or me."

Larsen wanted to believe that his aunt had slipped into some state of delusion, a natural by-product of the crazy gene, but still he asked, "Whom did you shoot, Lilly?"

Her voice grew louder, like she thought Larsen was growing deaf. "Your uncle Harry. I shot him dead."

"Are you sure?"

"He didn't move for two weeks. I'm sure."

"I see."

"Larsen," Aunt Lilly continued, "will you take care of Bertha and No Barks? They've been good to me. No Barks is part wolf, but so am I. So is that daughter of yours. What do you call her?"

"Angel."

"Yes, that's what you call her. You're a good human, Larsen. I want you to have these things. Now find a pencil."

She gave him the address for the South Dakota Women's Prison in Pierre, and then the line went as dead as Uncle Harry.

Now his only daughter was ready to leave in Lilly's bookmobile to start this rather dubious enterprise as a spiritual consultant journeying across America. In the old days, his ancestors had hunted buffalo and families had stayed together, kept warm by the fire, and told stories. Now it had come to this: fixing old trucks, murders, runaway daughters, and crazy genes.

He dug in his pockets until he found the keys. He hesitated. While Angel was old enough to make her own choices, he didn't want to enable the bad ones. Crazy gene or not, he was proud of his daughter. Her spirit was unique and she loved the world in ways that most would not understand.

Larsen took Angel's hand and pressed the keychain to her palm. "I love you very much. I know it has been hard since your mother died. Take Bertha and paint her however you like. Put mountains on the side. I'll put a toolbox together for you. Get car insurance and, when you're ready, you and No Barks go and see what you can find in America. Perhaps there is something there you can fix."

Angel hugged her father. "Thank you, *Age*. You're the best!"

After Larsen finished his lunch, he decided to write to Aunt Lilly at the correctional facility. He had talked to her twice since her incarceration. She was not able to make bond, so she would remain in Pierre until the trial, which was many months away. She did not like the court-appointed lawyer who tried so hard to convince her that dreams were not legal defenses. Larsen would tell Lilly about Angel's journey and see if there was anything he could do to help her.

3

Anticipating his vacation foray into nature and the twelve-hour drive to New Mexico, Ted packed flea powder for Argo and car-sick medicine for himself. Before getting on Highway 56 to head southwest, he pulled into the Four Corners Convenience Station, filled the gas tank, and checked the oil and tire pressure. While the tank slowly filled, he adjusted the position of a piece of yellow ruled paper that was taped to the dash. At the top of the page, it read:

What to do on vacation!

According to several of the guidebooks he had purchased, Santa Fe, New Mexico, and its environs offered many excellent, canine-friendly activities, including hiking and superb fly-fishing. Also carefully detailed, below his list of activities, were directions and the names of several recommended RV sites along his route.

List making and other precautions resulted in a late departure from Crossing Trails. Strong winds dropped out of an otherwise clear sky and pushed forcefully against the tall profile of the RV. The safe practice was to drive a little more slowly. By seven o'clock that evening, the sun was getting low in the sky and Ted was an hour behind schedule. Confusing Argo with someone who cared, Ted announced, "It's going to be dark soon. We need to find the next RV park."

The old terrier lifted his jaw an inch off the floor, yawned, and went back to sleep.

About fifteen minutes later the entrance to one of Ted's approved campgrounds, Perfect Prairie RV Park, unexpectedly and without the least warning, sprang up in front of Ted. As he closed in on the entrance, Ted considered passing it, turning around at the next opportunity, coming back, and making a proper turn from the opposite direction. That was not, however, the choice Ted made. Instead he pushed the brake pedal hard and began his turn. The setting sun's glare on his windshield made it hard for him to see far down the road.

At about the same time a camouflaged, flying tanklike structure came barreling toward him.

Panicked, Ted let out a "Yikes!" yanked the steering wheel even harder to the left, accelerated into the turn, and gambled that the strange vehicle would yield and the Chieftain wouldn't tip.

Angel was onto something big—driving seventy miles an hour in a decrepit bookmobile while doing meditations to the sound of Lakota drum music—when she realized that she too had missed her turn. Believing there is purpose behind all things, she just drove on. Adventure lay on the unknown road. This is how she found herself driving east in a very remote corner of New Mexico in Bertha the Bookmobile. No Barks was sleeping beside her on an old piece of buffalo hide that Aunt Lilly had used for a curtain to block out the glare from the western sun as it flared and disappeared behind the Black Hills.

Angel, concentrating on the reduction of her alpha waves, was a bit slow to react to the lumbering vehicle that turned in front of her. When she noticed the Winnebago at twelve o'clock high, she applied her brakes hard. Bertha was as nimble as a Sherman tank. At nearly twice the weight of the Chieftain and with momentum at the reins, Bertha emerged the clear victor in the collision that followed.

4

When Ted finally brought the Winnebago to a complete stop in the first space off the highway, he was relieved (he was alive!) but frightened (how had this happened to him, the most careful of drivers?). He looked down at Argo and asked, "Are you hurt?"

The Chieftain continued to rock up and down on its shocks like a young Marine doing push-ups. Suddenly something clanged to the ground. Ted unlocked the driver's-side door and climbed out of the cab, anticipating seeing dead bodies strewn about the campground like autumn leaves. Fortunately there were none, so he focused on the property damage.

There was a sizable dent in the right rear quarter panel. On the ground near the rear of the vehicle was the back half of the water tank, which had broken off from the chassis. It could have been worse, much worse. The sound of a poorly muffled engine caught Ted's attention. The unusual vehicle that had just rammed him was slowly approaching from the highway. Having already wounded the Chieftain, Ted suspected, the driver was now going in for the kill.

Angel pulled in behind the damaged RV and pondered the meaning of the personalized Kansas license plate, SHARK. This was a strange name for a land vehicle. Something her father had said came rushing back to her. She cringed as she heard his too-soft words in her head. She leaned forward, slapped the dash with her open palm, and said, "Buffalo dung." She could not believe it. "I forgot the insurance."

If anyone was hurt, there could be serious trouble. She climbed out the cab door and cautiously approached the Winnebago, holding her breath and hoping that her business plan as a spiritual consultant was not about to receive a serious revision.

She was expecting an elderly driver. Instead, a very frightened-looking young white man was circling about, dazed. He was neatly dressed and about her height. He was attractive in a frat-boy sort of way, with blue eyes and brown, neatly trimmed hair. He finally looked up at her. Though dazed, he asked, "What happened?"

Angel took one look at the dented right rear quarter panel of the Chieftain and summed it up for him. "I think we had an accident. Are you and your family okay?"

Ted looked back at the tall, dark-haired woman. "It's just me and my dog and we're fine. What I meant to say was what do we do now? Should we call the police? How about you? Are you hurt?"

Angel put her hand just above her hip bone. "My lower back is a tad whacked and your RV is a bit dented." Hoping to avoid the insurance quagmire, she tried to reach down and touch her toes but pulled back, wincing in exaggerated agony. "Maybe we should just call it an even swap—my bad back for your little dent?"

Ted scoffed, "It doesn't quite work that way when the accident was your fault."

"Mine?" Angel asked with her hands still on her hips.

"Yes, I believe it was your fault. Ted Day is my name."

"I think you turned in front of me. Angel Two Sparrow." She stuck out her hand.

In lieu of a proper greeting ritual, Ted dug in his wallet and offered Angel his insurance card. "Have your agent call my agent. There's no need for us to argue over it."

Angel casually rebuffed Ted's offer as she walked away. "Never mind all that insurance stuff. We'll sort it out tomorrow."

Ted shook his head and thought to himself, *Grandpa, this is exactly why I don't go on vacations.* Beyond the constriction in his chest, Ted noticed another thing: there was something very unusual about this woman. He needed another look to complete the thought.

He turned and watched Angel as she walked back to her strange vehicle and climbed in. One glance was enough. It was her clothing. While attractive, she wore a bizarre combination of things that had no business being put on the same body at the same time. It was much more in your face than wearing stripes with plaids. Black combat boots do not go with frilly lace, calf-high socks. Jean shorts are not to be patched with fluorescent yellow duct tape. He tried to remember the letters on the tiny wooden blocks strung on her necklace. It came to him: I-M-A-G-I-N-E. He found this word particularly irritating under the circumstances. When it came to driving and most everything else in life, *knowing* would always trump *imagining.* This Angel Two Sparrow (he wondered what kind of a name that was) needed to do less *imagining* and a lot more paying attention.

Having seen enough to close the book on Angel Two Sparrow, Ted looked back at his grandfather's RV. For so many years his grandfather had kept it in nearly perfect condition. Now, as the new owner, on day one of trip one, he'd had an accident. Upset, Ted had a childish impulse to curse the vacation gods.

Instead, he stomped back inside the Chieftain, slammed the door behind him, and, for Argo's benefit, put a fine point on it. "Barely out of Kansas and our vacation is ruined." Argo refused to participate in the rant. This was Ted's problem.

The more he thought about his dented RV and her IMAGINE necklace, the more frustrated he became. This much was clear: Angel was some New Age nutcase. As if this were a legal quandary that could be analyzed and resolved with sufficient analysis, Ted removed a pen and a yellow legal pad from a drawer on the left side of the sink. He listed his options, along with a candid assessment of each.

1. Sue her for every dime she's got. *Bad option. She clearly has nothing. Plus, the accident was probably my fault.*

2. Return to Crossing Trails and never try a vacation
   again. *Hold that one for now; come back later in case
   there are no better options.*
3. Fix the RV and try to go ahead with existing vacation plans. *Remember what Grandpa said about finding adventure on the road.*

Not particularly fond of any of his options, Ted stopped
pondering for a moment and instead thought about the necklace, picturing in his mind another word sculpted in the same
crude script. He printed K-N-O-W-I-N-G! across the top of his
legal pad.

He laid his pencil down and sighed. He would go with option three. There was no sense in fighting it; the accident had
been his fault. He'd be lucky if she didn't sue him for hundreds
of thousands of dollars for back surgery she didn't need. He
picked up the pencil as option number four came to him.

4. Sneak out in the middle of the night and never deal
   with Angel Two Sparrow again. *Hold that one too. It
   might be better than #3.*

Argo finally woke up and joined Ted at the small kitchen
table, suddenly very interested in the calamity called Ted's
vacation. The dog wagged his tail and seemed to be coming
back to life.

"Are you excited, old boy?"

Argo pawed at his leg.

"Isn't vacation great?" Ted got up from the table and dug through the kitchen drawer looking for a leash. "Hope you enjoyed it. In another five or ten years, we might try it again."

Once outside, Ted removed his lawn chair from the external storage space and set up camp beside the green plastic picnic table so generously provided by the owners of the RV park. By flipping a toggle switch just inside the door, Ted extended the motorized awning to protect him and Argo from the last glaring rays of the setting sun.

Ted and Argo practically had the entire campground to themselves. Bertha the Bookmobile was parked at the other end, more than sixty yards away, so Ted let Argo sniff around without his leash. The dog was very good about not wandering off.

Settled into his lawn chair, Ted closed his eyes and made himself comfortable in the raw outdoors. He glanced at the cover of one of the books he'd brought along, *Religion for Dummies*. Shortly after Grandpa Raines had died, Ted had been stumped by a form that asked about his grandfather's religious preferences. He didn't know about them, and he wasn't sure about his own, either. He laid the book on the ground. Later he might have the energy for salvation, but for now he just wanted to relax and consider his carefully crafted options for this ruined vacation.

He had not been resting for more than five minutes when the other paw fell. He was startled by the appearance of an enormous dog trotting uninvited toward his campsite. Argo was nowhere to be seen. As the beast came into better view, Ted stared at it in utter disbelief. When it was close enough for him to really get some sense of its size, Ted realized that it wasn't so much a dog as a wolf. A big-ass wolf.

He opened and shut his eyes twice, thinking the hulking gray and white apparition might disappear. Surely he must be experiencing a problem with his contact lens. A smudge, maybe, like the Virgin Mary appearing in an ordinary caffe mocha, or just a strange play of shadows. When it didn't disappear, Ted gripped the sides of the lawn chair, wondering how this could be possible. A wolf?

Within a few short hours, he'd had his first automobile accident and met a very strange woman, and now a wolf was stalking him. He wondered if management knew that they had an indigenous wolf population wandering about their campsite. The wolf was still closing in on him. Ted looked at the door of the Chieftain and shifted his weight to the edge of the lawn chair, ready to bolt for the door.

The wolf stopped about twenty yards away and stared at Ted. Her green eyes were haunting. As the wolf assessed the metabolic value of one human male, her ears perked. Suddenly, she turned to her right and all hell broke loose.

From the periphery of Ted's field of vision, Argo came running around the corner full speed, teeth bared and the yellow hair on his back bristling with courage. He approached the wolf with a menacing and very toothy growl.

While Argo distracted the beast, Ted moved up and out of the lawn chair and slunk closer to the door of the RV. He found a long-handled broom, a dustpan, and a mop in the narrow galley closet by the front door.

It wasn't much as weapons go, but it'd have to do. He

deftly grabbed the mop handle and walked back outside. The two dogs appeared to be circling each other, sizing up their adversaries. Screaming at the top of his lungs, Ted closed in on his prey.

The scary white man charging at her with a mop and the yellow dog circling about her were a formidable combination, so the wise she-wolf took off running with Argo chasing right behind her.

The dogs disappeared behind the Chieftain, and by the time they made their way back around all that aluminum, the deadly battle had deteriorated into a rowdy doggy version of "Sniff, you're it." Ted collapsed back into the lawn chair, relieved to be alive but still clutching his mop-lance . . . just in case.

Vacation is hell.

Before Ted could catch his breath, Angel, on her own evening stroll, appeared out of nowhere, sat down uninvited at his picnic table, stared at the knight errant, and asked, "Did you really just charge my wolf with your mop?"

Under ordinary circumstances, Ted would have been humiliated by the question. Surely real men did not attack wolves with mops. That's why they owned assault rifles, hollow-point bullets, and Apache helicopters. But there was something in Angel's lighthearted smile and dancing, sparkling brown eyes that suggested she was somehow rather pleased with the Man from La Mancha, Kansas, impressed by a man who would risk life and limb for an old yellow dog.

Ted looked at the long, wood-handled lance with its dangling Raggedy Ann hair and a grin crossed his face. "I don't know what I was thinking. I'll lay down my weapon. Is that your wolf?"

"No Barks is her name. She won't hurt you." She pointed to Ted's beer. "You have another ale in that tin castle of yours?"

5

Ted returned, beer in hand, and found Angel lolling in his lawn chair flipping through *Religion for Dummies*. This was a rather personal reading selection and he had no desire to share it with Angel. The sun was getting low, so Ted walked to the front door and flicked on the outside lights to the Chieftain. Ted returned and offered the beer to Angel.

She accepted the beer from Ted's outstretched hand. "Are you interested in religion?" When Ted failed to respond, she added, "If so, you should probably take this one back. You think you don't understand it, but I doubt that's your real problem."

Ted was still trying to get over an auto accident, a ruined vacation, and a wolf encounter, so he was a little slow to respond. He finally asked, "What do you mean?"

"Have you ever tried to hike up a mountain with a boat strapped to your back?" Angel asked, waving her hands in the air and grinning at the very notion.

"No," Ted answered, suspecting that this woman had been en route to a mental institution before she and her wolf ran into him.

"There you go. That's why you don't need the book."

Ted began to look about the campsite nervously, wondering if armed security was a feature of the Perfect Prairie RV Park. He forced himself to make eye contact with Angel and realized that, however unusual she might be, this young woman was very attractive. "I'm sorry, but I have no idea what you're talking about. Hiking with a boat on my back?"

Angel had changed into a loose-fitting flowered dress in muted and faded tea colors, but she had not abandoned her muddy black combat boots. Her long, dark hair was pulled back away from her pretty face, which was graced with a wide smile and slightly crooked but strong white teeth. Her olive skin showed a little blemish on her right cheek, just below her eye, that was either a small scar or a birthmark.

Ted got up from his lawn chair and sat down across from Angel at the picnic table, grinned nervously, and asked again, "I'm sorry. I don't get it. Why would anyone hike with a boat on their back?"

"Well, I'm not one to give advice, at least not for free, but it's like this: oftentimes religious doctrine is the boat that gets us across the lake. Very helpful, essential really, in the beginning stages of our spiritual development, but when we get to the shore and we're ready for the next stage, the boat can become a real pain in the ass if you're not willing to leave it behind."

Ms. Epiphany-in-Combat-Boots made a good point, and Ted was willing to concede the same. "You mean it's not so much a case of 'I don't get it' as it is a case of 'I may not need it.'"

"Well, I guess it depends if you have just left the shore or if you are already across the lake. My clients are at different places in their spiritual journeys. It waits to be seen where you're at."

"Clients?" Ted asked.

"Yes, I'm a spiritual consultant." Angel pointed to the giant painted business card on Bertha's side panel. "The phone number is there and everything. That is, if you want to hire me. I might be able to help you. Trust me, you're not going to get what you need out of that book."

Ted was unsure what to make of Angel; she differed so much from the women he'd known in Crossing Trails. "I've never heard of a spiritual consultant."

"There aren't many of us around and we don't advertise like we should. We don't have a Washington lobby or any tax breaks to offer. We fly under the radar of public consciousness."

"What does a spiritual consultant do?" Ted asked, leaning his elbows on the picnic table.

"I'm a guide. I help my clients move further along their spiritual path." She leaned a little closer to Ted and said, "Tell me your name again. I already forgot." She stuck out her right hand.

This time he accepted it. "Ted. Ted Day." Her hand was warm and soft and Ted hated to let it go.

"Angel Two Sparrow. Call me Angel."

"Yes, I remember."

She leaned back again and continued. "You see, Ted Day, most people are stuck, stagnant. They need help or they won't grow."

Angel had an accent that Ted could not place. The more he tried, the more he decided it was less an accent and more an affect. Angel's speech had an unusual cadence and phrasing. "I'm pretty agnostic, so I'm not sure my path is going anywhere."

"You're a lucky honcho. You've got a blessing."

"A blessing?" Ted asked, wondering where his dog and that wolf had gone.

"You're a spiritual consultant's dream client. You have no baggage, nothing that I have to unpack just to get you to square one. You could get right to work finding your unrealized self."

Ted scowled. "At the end of the day, I've realized enough for one day." Ted did wonder, however, if he had misjudged her. Sure, she seemed a little different. True, she had hit him with her tanklike vehicle and allowed her wolf dog to practically maul him, but perhaps spiritual consultants were all this way: different. She was also rather hypnotic, and Ted enjoyed listening to her speak, even if what she said made very little sense to him. Knowing it was a dangerous to ask a saleswoman about her wares, he smiled and did it anyway. "Do spiritual consultants charge a flat fee or by the hour for their work?"

"It depends on what you want. . . ," she stammered, "I mean, your goals."

"What if you make me worse and totally dent my spirit the same way you did my fender? Do I get my money back? Do you carry malpractice or, like car insurance, are you just not that interested in such details?"

Angel stared at him blankly. This white man was smarter than she'd thought.

Ted realized that not everyone appreciated his humor. "I was just kidding about the dent."

"Charming." Angel raised her voice confidently. "Being such a poor driver must make life difficult, so let me do what I can to help you. I'll start with a ten-minute free consultation."

"Really? I'm intrigued. What are we going to talk about?"

"Well, I'll tell you this much. I am carrying around some very valuable secrets and I'm just waiting for the right person to help. It could be you."

As if it were someone else's voice coming from his mouth, he heard himself say, "I'm curious. Do you have some degree or are you just a natural at this?"

Angel realized that she had left a few details out of her business plan and scrambled to come up with answers. "Yes to both. And it's one hundred bucks for the initial session. I'm not promising anything, but I might be able to help you." She dug in her purse, which appeared to be something handmade from an old army blanket, and pulled out a mechanical pencil and the back of a bill from the Paradise Diner, where she had stopped for a cup of coffee a few days earlier. She quickly scribbled a few digits and her name on the paper and said, "Here is my number, in case you want to hire me. I mean, after we get your RV fixed and my back worked on."

Ted dug in his wallet and gave her his own neatly engraved card. "My cell number is on it too."

Angel thanked Ted, put her fingers to her mouth, and let out a loud whistle that brought No Barks and Argo rushing toward them. She stood, turned, grimaced from the twist to her torso, and said, "Thanks for the beer. I'll see you in the morning."

Ted stood up. "My ten minutes is up already?"

"Gone."

Angel and Two Barks vanished into the now almost fully set sun. Ted spent the rest of his evening reading and working Sudoku puzzles on his phone. He liked to make the numbers add up, and he was good at it. Before he finally went to bed, a sound came from his phone alerting him to a text message. He tried to remember the last time he'd received a text message. He picked up the phone and read, "Goodnight from the other end of the campground. Sorry about the accident—even if it was your fault. A. Two Sparrow."

Ted texted her back, "Save it for the jury. Good night. Ted."

A few seconds later, his phone buzzed again. "Want to walk the dogs?"

6

Ted and Angel walked along the periphery of the Perfect Prairie campground. The moon, shaded by space and time alone, cast light through a cloudless, star-filled sky. Ted tilted his head back and gazed at the heavens. "Amazing, isn't it?"

Angel said, "It's good to notice."

They walked along with their dogs for another few moments, before Angel gently returned their attention to earthly matters. "What brings you to New Mexico?" she asked as No Barks brushed up against her.

Ted grumbled, "Vacation."

Hearing the irritation in his voice, Angel did not answer right away. Her hesitation suggested to Ted that she was waiting for him to elaborate on his cryptic response. He wasn't inclined to tell her that there were more black spaces than white spaces on his vacation checkerboard. Nor did he feel it was necessary to point out that the words "Angel Two Sparrow" were etched at the top of the black rectangular square where he was now stuck. As he often did when he was uncomfortable, Ted instead slipped into his lawyerly mode and just kept to the facts. "When my grandfather died, he left me the RV." He pointed in the direction of the Chieftain. "Just before he passed, I promised him I would take a road trip to New Mexico." Ted asked the same question back to Angel. "How about you?"

She answered, "I just missed a turn."

Ted wondered if Angel was skirting the issue. "Are you on a vacation?" he prodded.

"Not really." Angel wasn't sure what to say. Being on the road in Bertha the Bookmobile, she was beginning to realize, would not make sense to Ted. Or anyone else.

Wanting to have a conversation with Angel and not cross-examine her, Ted tried to gently get behind her mushy answer. "So if not vacation, why are you here?"

She put the unvarnished truth on the table for Ted. "My aunt is in jail for shooting her ex-husband. Dead. She had converted her bookmobile into her residence before she gave it to my father. It was wasting away in our driveway. So, like you, I decided to take a road trip."

This talk of murder put a sinister chill in the night air. Ted shuddered. "Your aunt murdered your uncle?"

Not withstanding Ted's effort, Angel did feel like she was on trial. "Yes, I'm afraid so."

"Is homicide a frequent issue for your family?"

Angel tried to have fun with it. "Not really. Before Uncle Harry, our last family massacre was at the Little Bighorn."

Ted clutched Angel's elbow, mocking his own fear. "Is it safe walking with you in the dark?"

Holding her hands up, she answered, "No hatchet."

Feeling more secure visiting with the niece of a murderer, Ted asked, "So what happened between your aunt and uncle? He must have really pissed her off." Again Angel was quiet, so Ted prodded, "Were they arguing over the remote? Whose turn it was to feed the cat?"

Angel was enjoying Ted's humor. While a tad insensitive, he was clever. A long sigh escaped her before she answered, "It may not make sense to you."

"Murder rarely does."

"True." Angel continued, "Aunt Lilly is a very powerful dreamer and has a close affinity with her spirit animal, a bear. Any dream with her spirit animal in it will be especially powerful." She directed a question back at Ted. "I'm guessing that you don't really remember your dreams and don't have a spirit animal?"

"Good guess."

"So, like I said, this might be hard for you to understand."

"Try me."

"Three nights in a row, Aunt Lilly's spirit bear came to her and spoke of Uncle Harry's evil intentions. On the third morning, after she woke from the dream, Uncle Harry showed up at her place. She was so scared that I think she just shot him. That's all we really know."

Ted could feel her sadness. "Are you saying that she shot him because of a *dream*?"

"Yes, and her lousy Legal Aid lawyer insists that the law doesn't believe in dreams."

"He may not be so lousy."

"He says she'll never get out."

"So here you are? Have spirit, will travel in your murderous aunt's bookmobile. Is that what you mean when you say you took a wrong turn?"

"Perhaps."

Ted tried to change the subject. "Tell me what you mean by a 'spiritual consultant.' I've never heard of that."

"No, I suppose not."

"You mean people see your sign and call you because they are confused about God or the purpose of life?"

Articulating her plan made its limitations glaring, but she did it anyway. "Many people are lost, so I help where I can. I have some friends doing similar things. I'm going to visit them while I'm on the road and get some tips. They're going to help me get my business going."

"How will they help you?" Ted asked.

"We're all interested in spiritual matters. I'm trying to make a living at it as a sort of traveling spiritual consultant. Most of the others are more academic; they write books and give presentations at retreats. People come to them; maybe that works better. Time will tell. For now, I'm excited to give this a try." Angel's respect for her friends shone through when she said, "They're very successful."

Ted made a little bumping motion into Angel. "Are you sure spiritual work and driving go together?"

Angel bumped Ted back with even more force and poked his larynx with her index finger. "People that cross the yellow line often have accidents. Just a hint."

"I'll try to remember that."

Angel stopped, tilted her head upward, and looked again at the stars. "A remembrance trip, in your grandfather's honor, is a good thing. This is something he wanted you to do?"

Angel's own self-disclosure, however strange, had been so graceful and vulnerably given that Ted let his lawyerly guard down. "He said I was in a rut and that I needed to get away from work and open up to the world. Sometimes Argo and I tend to isolate ourselves a bit too much."

"So you never leave the house, except as necessary?"

"Pretty much. That's why getting in the Chieftain and going on the road was a challenge for me. There are certain spaces I feel comfortable in, and an RV isn't one of them."

"He must have loved you very much to give you such brave advice."

"I think so. He was always talking to me about life's bigger picture. I'm a detail kind of guy. I put my nose down and do the work that's in front of me. I wasn't very good at listening to him. I just thought he was saying old-man stuff. Strange, but even though he's gone, I still hear him talking to me in my head, so now I'm trying to listen to him better."

Angel could feel Ted opening up and tried to get the door to swing a bit wider. "When he speaks to you, what does he say?"

"Mostly little things like . . ." Ted shifted his voice an octave lower and tried to sound like a determined old man. "Ted, you better get that brief on file or the judge is going to kick your ass!"

"So this voice prods you to do the right thing?"

Ted thought a moment. "Yes, that's right. We practiced law together for a few years, before he retired. Truth is I'm not half the lawyer he was, but I am good at managing the office, keeping things organized. We were a good team."

Capitalizing on an opportunity to move their conversation to a place that might benefit Ted, Angel observed, "We have many voices in our heads. Sometimes voices can be tough on us and we have to be tough right back; otherwise they can haunt us for our entire lives. We have to say, *Scram! Get out of my head.*"

Ted wondered, "But surely there are some voices we should listen to and some we should ignore?"

"Not exactly. For instance, I hear my father, Larsen, a lot. *Get a real job. Wear normal clothes. Be more realistic.* Now, I love him and respect him, and his voice is a good voice, but the trick isn't to sift through and find the right voice; the trick is to find our own true voice and ignore the rest."

Ted paused and touched Angel's arm. "Hey, stop a minute. Close your eyes." He pressed his hands over her eyes.

Angel smiled and asked, "What?"

"Listen very carefully and tell me what your own true voice says to you."

Angel allowed her mind to settle before answering, "Beware of careless white man driving west in RV."

Ted closed and covered his own eyes. "I hear, *Imagining is great, but not while you're driving.*"

Angel arched the small of her back. "Like your ancestors, do you plan on giving me beads and trinkets for the good health you have stolen from me?"

Ted heard his grandfather's voice in his head again. *I like this Angel a lot better than the little blonde girl. She's got spunk.* Ted leaned down and cautiously petted No Barks. "My grandfather would have approved of you, Angel Two Sparrow. He wasn't that much into my wife. He couldn't remember her name."

"You're married?" Angel asked, surprised.

"No, not now. She left me, traded up."

"Are you sad about this?"

Ted puckered his lips and faked a little sob. "Broken up." He quickly recovered. "We both woke up and realized that there was a stranger sleeping in our bed. She hated living in a small town in Kansas. She went home to Chicago for the weekend and never came back. She was good about it. Didn't really ask for much, just a chance to start over. She was right."

"What attracted you to her in the first place?" Angel asked.

"She would say it was one of three things."

"All anatomical?"

He threw up his hands. "How did you know?"

"Most men are obsessed by the holy trinity." Angel crossed her chest with her right hand and then let it trail down into her abdomen.

"There's more to the story."

"Let me guess: She was ready for children. You weren't."

"I was just starting my law practice; it was a timing thing."

"It's an old story."

They walked a bit farther in silence. Angel stopped and asked, in a teasing tone, "So what's it like for you being a divorced, one-dimensional, agoraphobic, workaholic lawyer trying to find love in a small Kansas town?"

Ted refused to take the bait. "Fantastic. Couldn't be better. Everyone wants my life."

She slapped playfully at his arm. "You're ahead of the pack, Ted Day. You have a good job and you don't have to wait for your aunt to murder your uncle to get your own set of wheels. Could be worse."

"I sent my résumé to the DOJ and the FBI. I'm sure they'll be getting back to me soon. Until then, I fill a need. The only lawyer in town."

"And I'm betting you manage to stay very busy at this job?"

"There you go sounding like my grandfather again. What's wrong with being busy?"

"Good things usually get in the way of great things."

"What do you think, Ms. Spiritual Consultant, I'm chasing the wrong rainbow?"

"Could be, but I'll need a down payment before I'll know for sure. Saving souls is hard work. I insist on being paid in advance."

"How hard can it be?"

"You could be a project."

"I was afraid of that."

"I'll tell you this much for free. Some people spend their life studying maps but never start the journey; other people blast off the starting line full speed ahead without first charting a course. Most of us could benefit from a better balance between planning and doing. You're a doer, Ted Day, but I'm not sure you have a clue where you are going. That's where I'd start, giving you a better plan."

Ted bent down and patted his dog on the head. "Maybe the animals have it easy. They don't have to plan; they're content to just live."

When they neared Ted's RV, Angel pointed to the dent, which was clearly visible, even in the moonlight. "You sure this wasn't already there? Looks like an old wound to me."

Spurred by moonlight and hormones, a generous impulse overtook Ted. "Look, Angel, forget about the accident. This trip is very likely the Chieftain's last dance around the campfire. I'm not really an RV kind of guy. Who cares about a little dent? I'll just get someone to reattach the water tank and I'll be good to go. No harm, no foul."

Relieved, Angel leaned toward Ted and kissed him gently on the cheek. "Good night, Ted Day, Champion of the Mop, Forgiver of Dents. Thanks for the walk." She started to walk away, then turned back and smiled at him. "Strange, but I think my back is feeling better too. By dawn it might be healed."

"I thought so." When Angel was a little more than twenty yards away, Ted called out, "Good night, Angel Two Sparrow, Healer of Men's Souls and Keeper of Wolves. Dream well!"

Before they went to sleep, Angel and No Barks spent twenty minutes meditating together. Angel took two deep breaths and muttered her mantra as she dug her hands deep into the scruff of fur around No Barks's silver-gray neck. She was pretty sure that No Barks was a natural at meditation. The dog seemed to enter the alpha state with little or no effort. The tension in her back was welling up; it started at the top of her spine and shot down her sciatic nerve. Maybe she actually had been hurt.

Angel had adopted the meditation techniques of a Burmese Buddhist monk she had met on one of her failed attempts at a junior year abroad, modified slightly by several insights she had gained from her kabbalah study group. Angel found that concentrating on various sensitive parts of her body while engaging in systematic breathing patterns reversed the polarity of her nervous system. Tonight, though, a rather disturbing illumination emanated from around her spinal column and cerebellum. In other words, she lit up. This aura—one of the objective and verifiable aspects of enlightenment—hung over her until just before midnight.

At midnight, Angel rang a small and very old Tibetan bell that had been given to her by a friend who had journeyed to Dharamsala in northern India. She waited for the tone to merge into the cosmos, subsumed but not lost, as a reminder of the unity of all things. When her mind was totally at peace, a tranquil sea without ripple or wave, relaxed, the answer came rather easily.

Angel was in need of a client. Ted was in need of a good spiritual consultant. Aunt Lilly did not like lawyers who did not believe in dreams. The pieces were all there, staring her in the face.

There were no accidents.

7

Instant oatmeal, cooked in the Chieftain's microwave oven, was Ted's choice for breakfast. It was a double portion served in one of the red plastic bowls that he'd bought at a sporting-goods store. When he finished washing up and putting away his dishes, Ted changed into his newly purchased hiking gear. It only made sense that he should get some use out of his purchases before he returned to Crossing Trails and got back to work. Already he missed the energy, neatness, and reliability of his law practice.

Releasing the latch, Ted opened the door and stepped outside with Argo. The sights and sounds of the wolf-infested outdoors and the soft, promising morning light beckoned him into the RV-park wilderness. After giving the dog a few minutes on his own, Ted joined Argo and they wandered toward Angel's bookmobile. There was still some unresolved business that needed his attention.

When Bertha came into better view, he had to stop and assess what he saw. Angel was sitting not at but on top of her standard-issue green plastic picnic table. Ted walked twenty yards closer and waved at her, but with her eyes closed, sitting in the lotus position, and deep in meditation, she seemed unaware of him.

Staring at Angel, Ted sensed a tranquility surrounding her. At first he wondered if there was some kind of glow emanating from the crown of her head, but then he realized it was just the light reflecting off the early-morning dew.

Not wanting to disturb her, Ted took a few steps closer and hesitated. He approached slowly, and when he was nearly into her designated space, Lot 16 West, Angel opened her eyes, smiled, and gave Ted another of her disturbingly benign smiles. She shifted from the lotus position into a more conventional pose, with her legs crossed and dangling over the edge of the picnic table. Holding up her hand, Angel waved and said, "Good morning, Ted. I was expecting you."

As her long legs swung to and fro, Ted noticed her considerable muscle tone and chuckled nervously before asking, "Really? Am I that predictable?"

Angel leaned back, turned around, and pointed to the huge business card painted on the side of Bertha. "If you're ready, we should start our work together. You made considerable progress last night. Don't you think?"

Assuming Angel was misunderstanding the reason for his visit, Ted tried to get her focused. "Could you drive me to the local auto shop so someone can fix my water tank? And we can check your back out too—that is, if it still hurts."

Angel stood up. "I have really good news for you, Ted."

"Is your back better?"

"It became quite clear to me. Last night, after our walk."

No matter how hard Ted tried, Angel simply was not going to join his side of the conversation. He finally gave up. "Okay, tell me your good news."

"I know this might sound strange, but hear me out. How many days of vacation do you have left?"

"Two weeks, give or take."

"Perfect. Not a lot of time, but it should be enough to complete a crash course. You're a quick study. Ted, I've decided to accept you as my student."

"What are you talking about?"

Angel had hoped this would be obvious, but she went ahead and connected the dots for him. "It's perfect, Ted. I can be your own personal spiritual consultant. You can help my aunt Lilly with this murder thing and we'll call it an even swap." When Ted did not respond, she continued, "By the way, Ted, I want you to know that as a Native American, I am not offended by the name of your RV. Still, I think Bertha will serve us better for our work. She's practically a school on wheels."

Ted still said nothing, so she nodded and continued. "A true win-win-win for all of us, isn't it? You need a consultant, Aunt Lilly needs a more resourceful lawyer, and I need a client." She finally looked him straight in the eye and tried her best to convince him of the genius of her idea. "I can introduce you to some of the most fascinating people you'll ever have a chance to meet. It will be the pilgrimage of a lifetime. You'll be telling all of your rich friends about me and your perfect vacation." She grew even more excited. As is so often the case, the pitch did more to convince the salesman than it did the customer. "What do you think? I'll make it worth your while."

The skin surrounding his eyes wrinkled upwards. "Not a bit of this makes sense to me." The idea of climbing into Bertha with Angel and her wolf dog pushed Ted far outside of his comfort zone.

Angel was a little surprised that the customer did not appreciate the value of her wares, but she tried to remain patient; after all, her father had been similarly perplexed. "It's simple, Ted. Can't you see that what you need is a pilgrimage, a journey to find your true religious roots, with me as your spiritual guide? That's what you want, right? That's why you were reading that book. That's why you're on vacation—to find out what's missing from your life and to honor your grandfather's last request. I can help you do that. It wasn't an accident that we"—Angel hesitated for the right words—"ran into each other. And if you could help my aunt Lilly out, you wouldn't even have to pay me. It would be a bargain for all of us. Maybe you could pay for some gas and food. I am a little short on cash at the moment. You could do that, right?"

"Angel, I don't think you understand what lawyers do. Your aunt Lilly is in South Dakota facing a murder charge. I'm a Kansas lawyer. I've never tried a homicide case. My specialty is more research and brief writing, divorces, little criminal matters. I couldn't represent her. I'm just looking for a simple vacation, not to go on some spiritual quest. It's kind of you to offer, but this is not what Argo and I had planned."

Angel felt as if someone had thrown cold water on her psyche. She realized she had done it again: great ideas, poor execution. She looked down. "I see."

Ted stammered, "Angel, I just think that you've misunderstood. Argo and I want to take a hike or two. Do some fishing. My ambitions are more limited than yours. I just go to my law office during the week. On the weekends maybe I watch a little football, basketball in the winter, and when the opportunity presents itself, I go on a date with a girl from town. I appreciate the holy trinity. That's it. I don't want anything more. I'm sorry, but I don't understand why everyone thinks that something is missing from my life."

Angel hadn't anticipated resistance from someone who needed her help. She tried to reassure him. "You needn't worry or be afraid about anything. I'm not going to ask you to wear a funny robe, chant, or burn incense. I'll help you in a way that makes sense for you. That's my job. I'm a spiritual consultant, remember?"

As the shock of her proposal for him to take a spirituality course—what he might call "Spirit Tech"—wore off, his skepticism returned. It occurred to him that maybe she had found out about his inheritance and this was an elaborate scheme to get his money. Maybe she was right. It was no *accident.* "Sorry, Angel."

"Would you like to try just a few days and see how it goes?"

Angel was a mixture of beauty and beast—she both frightened and excited Ted. "Not really. Pilgrimage-as-vacation doesn't interest me. I wouldn't even know where to start with your aunt Lilly. I think we would both be better off if we just got the Chieftain repaired and went our separate ways, before some other disaster hits me." Ted could see the disappointment on Angel's face, so he turned to avoid her gaze. "I'll make some calls and see who can help us out with the RV."

Pretty quickly, Ted's day got worse.

As he turned to walk away, Ted stumbled over Argo's leash, which had tangled itself around the base of a concrete grill, and fell straight to the ground in one grand, thunderous capitulation to his vacation demons. The ground was hard and dry and, for the first time in his life, Ted had the wind knocked out of him. The sudden lack of oxygen caused him to panic and he gasped for air.

As he struggled for breath, Angel moved quickly to his side and held his hand. Argo was licking his face. The wolf dog was poking her nose into his ribs. Angel's voice was soothing but sounded like a far-off echo. "Just relax for a second, Ted, and let me help you."

When enough oxygen had returned to his lungs, Ted sat up and felt his head. There was no blood. "I think I'll be okay. I must have tripped."

"Just the same, come inside out of the sun and rest for a few minutes before you start walking around." Ted allowed Angel to support him as they went inside the strange-looking vehicle she referred to as Bertha. The inside was not organized at all, just as Ted had imagined. Angel cleared a spot beside her sleeping bag. "Rest here for a minute."

Once Ted was prone, Angel placed a pillow under his head. "Do you feel better?"

Enjoying the attention, Ted let out a little pitiful groan

and said, "I think I'll be fine. You're right. I just need to rest a minute."

Angel gently massaged the fingers of Ted's right hand. He felt rather dreamy, so he was not sure how much time elapsed before he next heard her voice. "I want you to concentrate on one thing and one thing only." Starting at the root of his fingernail and working down to the knuckles and into the palm, she gently massaged his ring finger. "I want you to think about nothing but the sensation that arises when my fingers touch yours. Is the sensation soft or firm? Does it tickle or scratch? Is my touch cold and dry or warm and clammy? Imagine that your entire essence, everything that is Ted Day, is encapsulated and concentrated into this one space where our hands are coming into contact. There is a lot going on in this tubular corridor; try to imagine it: blood, muscle, bone, nerves, and skin. Billions of cells are interacting; try to focus all of your awareness on this seemingly small aspect of yourself. Try, if you can, to visualize and sense all of your life's energy focused in this one stamp-size speck in your infinite field of awareness. Think about nothing else, Ted, but your finger and how it feels."

As she spoke to him, in what Ted could only describe as a vaguely hypnotic tone, she continued to rub his right ring finger.

Ted had never been invited to pay such close attention to a single aspect of his physical being, and the effect was immediate—as if he had been released from a terrific burden, like a heavy backpack slipping off after a long day's hike. His leg twitched involuntarily, and Angel knew that he was almost asleep.

Once he was fully asleep, Angel tried to tidy Bertha. She then dug into her tool closet, pulled out her portable field welder, and went outside.

When Ted woke from his little midmorning nap, he felt simultaneously comfortable and somewhat shocked to be resting inside Angel's strange vehicle. He looked around, confused, and it took him a few seconds to put it all back together.

He had not only fallen asleep but also experienced a vivid, almost Technicolor dream. The voices had been crisp and clear—but now the dream was gone. Argo was resting quietly beside him as if nothing had happened, but something clearly had happened. And while it had obviously been a dream, it had had a very different feel to it. Before they slipped away, Ted put words to the images.

Ted was young and sitting on his grandfather's lap while the old man read to him from *The Lion, the Witch and Wardrobe*. In the dream, young Teddy became agitated and pleaded, "Stop, Grandpa. Stop reading."

"What's wrong?" Grandpa Raines asked.

"Don't let Lucy go through that door at the back of the wardrobe! She doesn't know what's on the other side."

Grandpa Raines, fully alive and in good humor, laughed, "Lucy wants to go through the door."

The images were so real that Ted wondered if instead of a dream it had actually been some ancient memory from his childhood that had broken loose from its moorings and floated to the surface of his consciousness.

Ted sat up and looked around for Angel. Not seeing her, he stretched and got up. "Come on Argo, let's go find Angel. I have no idea why I'm taking a nap in the middle of the morning."

Once outside, Ted looked around the campsite. When he didn't see Angel, he walked toward the Chieftain. When he got closer, he saw No Barks sitting at the rear of the vehicle next to a gray box that looked like a piece of well-worn carry-on luggage. Extending from beneath the RV was a pair of long brown legs capped with black combat boots. Ted heard a crackling noise that carried on for few moments and then stopped. He peered under the RV and asked, "What are you doing?"

"Don't worry. When it comes to welding, I'm an artist. Come look."

Ted scooted under the chassis and nestled in beside Angel. Lying on his back, he looked around. The sagging back half of the water tank had been reattached to the frame with the skill of a plastic surgeon. It was a beautiful weld. There were also two brand-new bolts securing the busted metal strap that kept the water tank in place. Two rusted and sheered bolts rested on the ground nearby. Ted rapped the tank with his knuckles. It seemed secure. "I'm impressed." He knew enough about welding to know that it was a lot harder than it looked. "I'm thinking you should add 'field welder' to your spiritual consultant sign."

Angel's neck was tired, so she inched over closer to Ted

and rested her head against him. She stared at the welds as if they were Rembrandts. "I do damn fine work, don't I? My father lets me create art by welding old auto parts together. That's how I got interested in welded sculpture."

"You have lots of talents."

"Most pay poorly or not at all."

Angel scooted out from under the chassis and brushed the dust and small pieces of gravel from her shorts. When Ted also emerged, she gave him a casual hug and said, "You're roadworthy. Good luck."

Ted, very grateful to have met Angel and feeling a little guilty for thinking that she was trying to con him, smiled. "It was really nice crashing into you."

"Come on, No Barks." Without another word, Angel Two Sparrow walked away.

Ted wondered why there weren't women like Angel in Crossing Trails. She was interesting. He sat down at the picnic table with Argo and waited until he heard Bertha's engine start and the gravel crunch as Angel pulled out onto the highway and headed west. He imagined her driving with her drum music blaring. He had the urge to yell out and tell her to wait. Maybe he'd made a mistake. A pilgrimage wasn't such a bad idea, but he also suspected that on some level it was an awful idea. Angel was just a pretty palm reader, a traveling tarot card reader. Not for him. He'd made the right decision. Stick to what was safe. However great Angel might be, she was on a very different path. Ted closed his eyes and suddenly recalled the second part of the strange dreaming episode.

The four of them—Angel, Ted, and the two dogs—were around a campfire in the woods, by a gurgling creek surrounded by mountains that were small by the standards of the Rockies. Still, the geological formations were primitive and beautiful—different from anything he had ever seen. Vivid red embers floated up into the sky like parachutes in reverse and dissipated into the black nothingness of the night. The moon was nearly full. They were dancing in the dark. Moon dancing.

Ted smiled to himself. Dogs don't tango on their two hind legs, and neither did Ted Day. It was a crazy dream. What did it mean? Tangoing with Angel and their dogs under the full moon in a strange forest was definitely not a *normal* dream for Ted Day. He wanted only normal dreams. Ted resolved that this one meant nothing. That's what it meant. Since when did dreams communicate to Ted or anyone else? Believing in dream communication was dangerous. It had landed Aunt Lilly in jail. He wondered if spiritual consultants knew anything about dreams.

Ted shook the dream off like water from a dog's back. He pulled out his phone and checked for messages. There were none. He saw Angel's text from the night before, and for some reason he found himself missing her. Willing to bet that Angel would know about dreams, and with every shred of self-confidence he could muster, he decided to call her, thank her again for welding his tank, and ask about the dream.

He waited for her to answer. On the third ring, she did.

"Hey?"

"Angel, Ted Day. I wanted to thank you again for welding the tank. You did a great job. Also, I wanted to say . . . I enjoyed our little time together." Ted paused, wondering if he sounded professional, and then asked, "By the way, what do you know about dreams?"

"I'm a Lakota. Dreams are very important for us. I know a lot. Just ask me," Angel responded, turning down her drum music.

"While I was on the floor of your bookmobile, I had two very strange dreams. They were dreams like I never had before."

"This does not surprise me. Bertha is a dream catcher. Significant dreaming events occur under her roof. Also, powerful dreamers—like myself and Aunt Lilly—can further widen these dream spaces. Would you like to tell me about your dreams?"

Ted sighed and tried his best to describe the dreams. She interrupted for details as she saw fit, and when Ted was finished, she asked, "Before I say anything, Ted, it's important that you tell me what you think these dreams were trying to tell you."

It suddenly became very clear to Ted exactly what his dreams meant. He did not need Angel to tell him. It was obvious. It was the same thing his grandfather had told him. The same thing his ex-wife had told him. He didn't want to hear it, but now even his dreams were telling him the same thing. His attraction to Angel was the final nudge Ted needed. He stammered, "I understand what the dreams meant. Angel, is that offer of yours still open? Argo and I could join you and No Barks. You could be my teacher." While not sure it was possible, he wanted the arrangement to be fair. "I'll do my best to help your aunt Lilly, but no promises. If that doesn't work, I can afford to pay you. I'll help with gas and food too. That's no problem."

Angel was excited to have her very first client, her first soul to heal. Still, she wanted to make sure Ted was sincere in his interest. "This work is not easy. Are you sure?"

"This is what my grandfather was trying to tell me. That's what you're trying to tell me. I think that's what my dreams were saying too. Maybe it's time for me to listen. I am willing to try it."

"I agree. The dreams are auspicious signs of your willingness to engage in the work we do. If you're ready, we can start."

"Someone is filling in for me for about two weeks. Is that long enough?"

"I've been working on this material for more than ten years. Two weeks is really just an outrageously short period of time, but if you're willing to work hard, you can make considerable progress."

Angel had been driving around in Bertha for a month hoping someone would call her. Now that she finally had a client, she realized that she needed to develop a curriculum, fast. She thought of Father Chuck, one of her favorites from her little spiritual group. He was always so organized. She hoped it would rub off on her. "Ted, meet me at five o'clock at the Benedictine monastery in Pecos, New Mexico. We'll talk more then." This would give her an hour or two to meet with Father Chuck before Ted arrived.

Ted hesitated. He wanted to tell her that he needed answers first—before he drove halfway across New Mexico. He also knew that if she was going to be the teacher, her pupil needed to trust her.

"Say that again? Where do you want me to meet you?" asked Ted, searching for the address in his GPS.

"The Benedictine monastery just outside of Pecos. My friend Chuck—he's a priest—he's on a retreat there. He's part of my group and I wanted to visit him anyway. I'll be waiting. And Ted . . ."

"Yes?"

"Nothing personal, but please drive carefully."

After he hung up, he battened down the hatches on the Chieftain and prepared to get back on the road. Why should Spirit Tech with Angel be different from any other academic study? There was no need to worry. Was there? He hesitated again. Was he choosing the course work because it was of interest or because the teacher had very nice legs? Perhaps, for now, it didn't matter. Some attraction was pulling at him.

Turning the key in the ignition, Ted brought to life the 420-cubic-inch engine and said aloud, "Grandpa, here we go! Just like you told me. Adventure on the open road!"

A few hours later he found Angel standing next to Bertha in the monastery parking lot. She was talking to a priest. It had been a hurried discussion. Father Chuck encouraged Angel to find a structure but to allow the instruction to unfurl in an intuitive way. They also discussed three possible obstructions that might impede Ted's progress: lack of intellectual ability, lack of desire, and fear of change. When she waved to Ted, the priest turned and walked away, apparently busy with his own matters. Angel waited for Ted to join her and wondered if the two of them were up to the task before them.

8

Ted sat on the meditation pillow—a brown corduroy cushion that felt like Velcro on wolf fur—and waited for further instructions. Getting comfortable in his new surroundings was a tall task. Bertha's interior was a rather strange hodgepodge of steel, animal skins, incense, candle sconces, calendars from the last century, bones from some archeological dig, old bookshelves, a metal librarian's desk—still anchored to the driver's side wall—blankets, pillows, clothing, tools, towels, and items that generally appeared to be broken, discarded, and evidently of no further value to the civilized world. Most of the bookshelves had been removed from the walls, but some of the mounting brackets remained. Also on the wall of the driver's side was one remaining set of floor-to-ceiling shelving. On the shelves were just under a hundred of Angel's favorite books. Between the driver's seat and the passenger seat was an open space where No Barks liked to perch.

Angel began her first lesson by pulling from the shelves and tossing in Ted's direction paperback copies of what she considered to be classic spiritual texts. He glanced quickly at the first three titles that rained down at his feet—Stephen

Batchelor's *Buddhism Without Beliefs*, Richard Rohr's *The Naked Now: Learning to See as the Mystics See*, and John Neihardt's *Black Elk Speaks*. Editorializing on her selections, Angel said, "These books may seem inconsistent, and yet, in their own way, each finds the same truths about why we are here on this planet and our life purpose." She finally stopped tossing books and concluded, "Reading may not be a substitute for doing, but it's a start."

Angel walked away from her bookshelf and began to shove some of her belongings into a pile toward the front of Bertha. "For now, you take the back and I'll take the front. We'll do some work here together at the monastery first. Later today we can drive up into the mountains. Father Chuck and I have an exercise in mind for you. You'll love it."

When Ted tried to inventory his surroundings, what struck him as most strange about Bertha was not what was there but what was missing: there was no bed, no proper kitchen, a very inadequate bathroom, no microwave, no dishwasher, no refrigerator, no sound system, no flat screen, no iPhone docking station, and only one electrical outlet. Ted sighed. If he'd paid for this school, a tuition refund would be in the works. This vehicle was ready for salvage.

Once Angel finished dealing texts to Ted like playing cards and reshuffling her belongings, she grabbed a pillow of her own and sat down close to Ted in the open area of Bertha, just behind the driver's seat. "Ready for your first class at Spirit Tech?" she asked.

"Let's start."

"Father Chuck and I believe that there are some preliminary lessons you should complete before you'll be able to do any serious work. Each of the three preliminary lessons—we call them realizations—will have two parts: instruction and practice. I could try to introduce all three realizations to you today, but it's a great deal of work and it'll take at least several hours. Are you up to this much work after a long drive?" Angel gazed at her student intently.

Ted looked around the bookmobile, still having major misgivings about Spirit Tech on Wheels. His dog, however, had no such problems. Argo, nestled in by No Barks, gently licked the wolf's ears. If Argo was comfortable with the wolf, Ted decided that he could get comfortable with a Lakota spiritual consultant teaching from a dilapidated bookmobile. "Let's push ahead."

After a few moments of stillness, Angel began. "Let's start where we left off earlier this morning. You passed out before I could finish the instructions for the first realization." She leaned closer to Ted and again took his hand in hers. "Do you remember what happened when I did this earlier today?"

Ted was starting to get nervous and hoped he would not lose consciousness again. He more asked than answered, "I fell asleep?"

She put her other hand on his wrist and gave him her condolences. "I'm afraid that it is more serious than that, Ted." She pulled both of her hands away from him and placed them back on her own lap. She sighed a little louder than she intended to and looked at No Barks as if seeking guidance from a wolf. When the wolf said nothing, she finally asked aloud, "How can I best say this?"

Ted wondered what humiliating things he might have done while in his trance. An embarrassing list of possibilities raced through his mind before he asked, "Was it that bad?"

"Like most people, Ted, the bulk of your available consciousness has been asleep on the Tarmac. It's time for you to take off—so you can be truly alive, alert, healthy, and whole."

There was something rather condescending in her tone that put Ted on the defensive. "I might be more awake than you think."

"To be clear, Ted, by 'awake,' I don't mean your eyes are open. I mean something quite different."

"Like *awaken* to the possibilities?" he asked.

"No. That's not it, either. For most of us, only a small fraction of our mind is actually conscious. So by 'asleep,' what I mean is that your unconscious mind is in control and your true self has not yet actualized. It's sitting quietly at the back of the auditorium with no voice." Angel's voice became more excited. "Now is the time to get it front and center, at the podium and in control. That'll be the essence of our work together. This can be very exciting for you."

Ted shrugged, not yet clear why waking up would be such a good thing, and wondered how Angel could sit so naturally and comfortably in that awkward cross-legged pose. If he sat like that, he would surely come crashing down like a poorly stacked pile of stones. "All right, then, sound the alarm and wake me up!"

"Some of the things I am about to say might not quite make logical sense at this point in your journey. Don't worry about that. You're a smart guy; it will sink in with time." She again took his wrist as if she were offering him her condolences. "Just listen for now. Do you mind doing that?"

Ted took another long look at her, and while he found the proposition of listening without trying to understand both strange and implausible, he tried to be agreeable. "Sure. I'll try."

"Good. We'll start at the beginning. We call it the first realization."

"*We?*" Ted asked.

"Yes, me, Father Chuck, and the rest of my friends. The study group I told you about."

"I remember."

"After we discuss the first two realizations, we'll drive up to the trailhead to the lake, and along the way I'll give you your first training exercise."

"I have to do exercises?"

"Yes. There is a difference between grasping that a bike can be ridden and actually climbing on it and taking a ride; it takes time and practice to train the brain."

The afternoon sun reflected off Angel's black hair so that it sparkled with thousands of points of light. Ted's hesitation about the curriculum did not apply to his tall, dark, and confident instructor. He flexed his muscles as if he were doing arm curls with thirty-pound weights and said, "I don't mind exercises."

"What if I told you that you could wake up and operate from your fully conscious or true self. Would that be of interest to you?"

"Sure, why not?"

"Good. Do you know how the word 'Buddha' translates?"

Ted had no clue. "Hindu slang for 'Buddy'?"

"Not really, Ted. It means the *awakened one*."

"So was the Buddha more awake than the rest of us?"

"A better way to help you understand the concept of waking up is to view consciousness as variable—existing on a hierarchy of awareness from a deep coma at one end of the spectrum to a fully awakened, enlightened being at the other end."

"I take it you see me on the wrong end of the spectrum? Pretty much a zombie?" Ted asked.

"Not just you but most of us. Me too. This first realization—we are not awake—is simple to understand. You must accept this realization or nothing else we do together will matter or make much sense. A spiritual quest is always about transformation, increasing awareness."

"I get the concept: some people walk through life in a seemingly more conscious way than other people. Still, I've got to ask a few questions before I'm all in."

"Fire away."

"Is what you are describing Maslow's concept of self-actualization?"

Angel stood up, walked to the shelf of the bookmobile, handed Ted a book from her mobile library, and sat back down.* "You're close, Ted. The absence of consciousness is the absence of a fully actualized life."

"So what's the difference between spiritual work and psychological work?"

"This is my take on it. Psychology focuses on working with what you've got: how to have the healthiest ego possible. Spiritual work asks you to step away from and transcend the ego entirely: to let go and become egoless. It's probably best seen as progression. You first need a healthy ego before you're strong enough to leave it behind."

"Okay, Angel, I'm with you on this first realization. How do I fill my life with more awareness? Should I double my caffeine, buy a saffron robe, or chant a mantra in a Himalayan cave?"

"I wish it were so easy! To answer your question, we'll need to turn to the second realization, but first let's walk the dogs and stretch our legs. I want to check out the bookstore too." She stood up. "A-plus on the first realization. One down and two to go. A spiritual vacation is not all bad, is it?"

Angel started to exit Bertha with No Barks before Ted

---

* Angel had come across this book in her Psychology 101 class at Haskell Indian Nations University. She thought that Maslow offered a very helpful insight into the way we progress through life developmentally; only to the extent the needs from the previous level have been satisfied can we move on, unfold, or become more actualized. Abraham Maslow, *Toward a Psychology of Being* (New York: John Wiley & Sons, 1962).

could answer. The posterior view of Angel was remarkable. Ted removed his yellow legal pad from the kitchen drawer of his mind and sketched Ted's First Total Undisputed Realization: Angel Two Sparrow was hot.

He nudged Argo. "Get up or they're going to leave us behind." He gave the dog's collar an affectionate tug. "Day one and you're already licking that she-wolf's ears. Very impressive. Do you think there's any hope for me and Professor Two Sparrow?"

9

Angel and Ted each took a turn holding the dogs while the other one wandered through the monastery bookstore. With a formidable pile of books already tossed his way, Ted limited his purchases to snacks, fruit, and two bottles of water while Angel waited on a bench and stretched her legs. Ted handed her one of the water bottles and a polished red apple. By way of an explanation, he proffered, "Hey, it's a tradition on the first day of school."

She ignored the apple and took a bag of unsalted peanuts from his other hand. "Thanks. These are perfect."

Even though the bench was small, barely large enough for two, Ted plopped down beside Angel and spat out a question that was bothering him. "I'm surprised by something."

"What?" Angel asked.

"You said that the focus of all good spiritual work was elevating consciousness or awareness. You didn't say a thing about God or heaven. Why not?"

Angel leaned over and nudged Ted with her shoulder. "Whoa, Ted! You're getting right to the heart of the matter."

Ted leaned away from her and said, "I only have two weeks. Remember?"

"We all have a God problem," Angel observed. "It's not day-one stuff."

"A God problem?" Ted asked.

"We want to believe in a personal, discrete God that exists like an object and sits around making the world right for us, but as we get older—more sophisticated—we realize that we are worshipping a god of our own creation, a superparent figure."

Ted had never shared his own frustrations on the subject, but he doubted he would meet another spiritual consultant anytime soon, so he sat his bottle of water on the ground, puffed his chest out slightly, and started one of his rare rants. "God is the most illogical and really extraordinarily unlikely concept imaginable. Something that can know everything, be everywhere, do everything, and yet can't communicate with us in an intelligible way—a way we can understand and even agree upon—is a gigantic farce. Why would God choose to act like some Phantom of the Opera that lurks in the shadows of our lives without letting himself be known to us? That makes no sense to me. In fact, this is precisely what pisses me off about religion. To get into the club, you have to believe in something stupid."

"I'd say you have a serious God problem," Angel said, smirking.

Ted tried to come down off his rant. "If there is God, then why wouldn't he just stand up, manifest, and be heard? How hard could that be for an omnipotent being? I'm pretty sure most of the major networks would give him airtime. He wouldn't even need to ask nicely."

"You're falling into the opposite end of the God problem.

You're assuming that any real god must play by our rules. Defining God like an object seems to always result in feeling abandoned and somehow unworthy. Like, *Everyone else seems to get God, so why can't I?*"

Ted tried to convey a primal feeling of rejection. "It's like inviting the most popular kid in school over to your house, and making all of the arrangements, and then he just never shows up."

"What I want you to understand is that our God problem is part and parcel of our self problem. Man has always created gods in the cauldron of his own mind. We have to be strong enough to admit that there are no unicorns, there are no Santa Clauses, and there are no gods like the ones we create in our heads. Gods can't be created, only experienced or realized." Angel smiled and rested her hand on Ted's wrist. "We all experience this frustration, but it's a necessary step along the way. Tomorrow you get to meet Father Chuck." Her voice turned more affectionate. "He's been such a blessing in my life, particularly on this topic."

"What is he like?"

"He's a Catholic priest. That's why he is here at the monastery. He has helped me to understand that we don't so much have a God problem as we have a 'knowing' problem. Trying to *know* God is like trying to use a microscope to find a duck. You're using the wrong aperture and the wrong tool. Frustration is inevitable until you find the right tool."

"Are you going to put the right tool in my school supplies?"

"Yes, but for now your goal is much simpler: waking up and expanding your awareness beyond mere *knowing*. In this expanded state, many things will become clearer for you. Who knows, God might be one of them."

"Angel, I'll be perfectly honest. A long time ago I decided that church just doesn't work. I agree with you that God can't be known, but I get there for a totally different reason. There is no such thing."

"A perfectly reasonable place to begin."

Ted stood up. "I'm sorry for jumping ahead, diverting you like this. For now, I'm satisfied with your first realization. Most of us are not fully awake. I don't see how anyone could argue with that." Ted bent down and retied the laces on his hiking boots. He stood back up and asked, "What's the second realization?"

After emptying the remaining peanuts into her hand, Angel drank deeply from her bottle of water, stood up, and began to walk slowly back to the parking lot with No Barks. "Give me a minute."

Ted and Argo kept close beside her. She walked slowly as she collected her thoughts on the second realization. Halfway back to Bertha, she found another bench and motioned to Ted to sit down beside her again. She concentrated, exhaled, and let her mind relax, almost going blank. Envisioning a shroud of loving acceptance wrapping around her and Ted, she began, "Ted, these realizations grow, one on top of another. This one will be slightly more difficult. I need you to be open and curious."

Ted locked his fingers and stretched his arms behind him. "For you, I'll do it. No knowing."

"To even begin comprehending the second realization, you'll have to give up something that you find very dear."

"Brats and beer? Krispy Kremes?" Ted asked.

Angel wondered if Ted was using humor to avoid doing this work but then decided there was nothing wrong with Ted trying to make the work fun. She took No Barks's paw in her own. The wolf dog enjoyed the touch and her tail wagged enthusiastically. "This second realization may seem strange on the first pass. It goes to the essential nature of self."

"If it's my essential nature, what do I have to give up?"

Angel stood up and tried her best to emulate a pitcher's windup. "Here you go, a softball right down the middle. If you miss it, don't fret. Just let the concepts sit in your mind without trying to grasp or know them. How you see God and how you see yourself is in large part a labeling problem."

Ted moved to the edge of the bench and pulled his arms back like he was holding a baseball bat. "Let her rip. Teddy DiMaggio is all ears."

"Hopefully, I can explain it in a way that makes sense." She sat down on the ground in front of the bench and pulled No Barks close to her. Her voice took on a professorial tone as she dug deeply for her lecture notes. "Really simplistically, the left side of your brain likes to formulate and define concepts and give them shorthand names or labels—each object and every encounter. Once you formulate the concept for an object and use it a few thousand times, it becomes fixed in your mind and the distinction between the actual pebble and the symbol or sign you hang on it becomes blurred.* This is the price you pay for rapid mental processing."

"Makes sense to me," Ted said. "That way, Romeo need not thoroughly investigate a pebble every time he wants to toss a stone at Juliet's window."

"That's right. There is no reason to slow down and dissect the attributes of a pebble every time you want to skip a stone, load a slingshot, or flirt with Juliet. This allows our mind to function at light speed. The left brain's software uses words as convenient placeholders to process our environment. Most concepts in our universe—God, rocks, Ted, Argo—are eventually given a name. By naming these concepts, we make them fixed and inflexible."

Ted asked, "What is the right side of the brain doing while the left side is so busy labeling?"

"New encounters are processed in the right brain. Once we believe we have grasped a concept, it becomes familiar and it's moved from the right brain, where things are still open to exploration, to the left brain, where *known* things are stored. This is why children are more right brain–focused. They have not yet had time to fully label and inventory their universe with words."

"Are you going to tell me that there is a price we pay for our brain's labeling system?"

---

* For a thorough and intriguing discussion of how our brains process information, see Daniel J. Siegel, *The Mindful Brain: Reflection and Attunement in the Cultivation of Well-being* (New York: Norton, 2007).

"You guessed it. In the spiritual dimension, you'll have to train the left side of the brain to lighten up a bit. This will free you to uncover some interesting treasure that has been locked away for a very long time."

Ted was not sure he liked the implications. "Surely in most ways our logical, conscious mind works quite well. It got me through law school. It pays the bills."

"It's not that there is anything wrong with your logical-thinking brain, Ted. It's just that you have a brilliant parallel mental operating system that is underutilized. Your left-brained worldview has co-opted your higher or more entire self and tricked you into believing that the left brain of Ted is the entirety of Ted, that nothing else really matters or is even real. You are not your left brain, Ted. You are much more than that. It's our job to get the entire, true Ted back in the game of your life."

"You make it sound like I'm possessed."

"Neurologists can teach us that we do not have a unified brain. It would be more accurate to say we have a brain system with many parts that sometimes come into conflict with each other. This brings us back to this fundamental confusion over exactly what we are referring to when we refer to ourselves—when we say 'me,' or 'Ted.'"

"You're saying I'm the sum of my parts and not just one part—the labeling left brain."

"Yes, that's right. It's not just our larger brain that separates us from the other primates. It's also our considered reliance on the left hemisphere of that brain."

"Can we consciously choose which hemisphere to use?"

"Like muscle function, brain function is a use-it-or-lose-it paradigm."

"There may be a problem with what you're saying, Angel. Without that left brain, could we even have this conversation? It seems like Juliet was more than willing to let Romeo drive her to the prom, but now that she has arrived and shown off her pretty new prom dress, she wants to dance with Mr. Right."

"You're reacting exactly the way I did the first time I heard this. We'll come back to this concept several more times. For now, please just be open for a moment to the possibility that you have far more processing capacity than you realize. That should be exciting, right?"

Ted leaned back on the bench and rested his hands on Argo's back. "If you're correct and my left brain is a brazen usurper and a trespasser, am I being violated or betrayed by my own operating system? How does that make sense?"

"When you use the word 'me' to describe yourself or the word 'God' to describe the divinity and mystery in the universe, you have reduced yourself or all of life's beauty to a discrete and separate object that can be labeled and identified by the left brain. In many ways, using proper nouns is a very accurate, convenient, and helpful way of thinking about ourselves or the divine—just like it is with rocks."

Ted pointed to himself and said, "Using my *Ted* label makes it easier for my brain to have this philosophical conversation with you."

"However convenient and conventional it might be, thinking of ourselves or God as a discrete and separate object is actually a distortion, or at least a dilution of reality. My ancestors' language better suggested the connectedness of all things: brother bear, mother earth, father sun, sister wind, and so on. A better way to truly understand *Ted* would be as a very complicated system of interconnected and interdependent biological and emotional parts engaged in a process called life. A more accurate way to think about *God* might be as a verb and not as a noun—as a force, like love.* As a result, we shouldn't worship God as object so much as try to experience God-ing."

"Isn't that what I really mean when I say 'Ted' or 'God'?"

"What I am suggesting is that the way we use words reinforces seeing ourselves and the world around us as objects and not as complex systems. This is not only misleading, but it is at the heart of the psychological, spiritual, and religious problems that perplex us. It's a barrier to the natural evolution of consciousness—to waking up Ted! It's something you're going to have to move beyond. It is the essence of the second realization: we are in error to the extent that we see ourselves as discrete and separate objects."

---

* Angel found that her Buddhist study group gave her great insight into the true nature of self. She found her kabbalah group to also be of help in coming to a more mature and clear understanding of the mystery of God. She found these two texts to be most helpful: Rabbi David A. Cooper, *God Is a Verb: Kabbalah and the Practice of Mystical Judaism* (New York: Penguin Putnam, 1997), and Jay Michaelson, *Everything Is God: The Radical Path of Nondual Judaism* (Boston: Shambhala, 2009).

"So you're saying that we really don't know ourselves?"

"It's not just me. This is why every spiritual teacher, from the Buddha to Jesus, relied so heavily on aphorism and metaphor. Remember, they use metaphor to get around our labeling problem."

Ted shrugged, indicating that what she was saying was at least plausible. He pulled Argo closer to him. "What do you think, Argo? Should we wake up and figure out what it really means to be Ted or Argo?" He held the dog's left paw in the air. "He says, 'We're ready.'"

"Good. Let's go deeper into this second realization with an example."

"You're very sneaky, Angel. I know what you're up to now. Another hemispherical sleight of hand!"

"Just go with it." Ted didn't argue, so Angel began. "Imagine that your ring finger, the one I was touching earlier today—let's label him Mr. Digit—has some left-brain logical-thinking skills, the basic five senses, and language."

"My fingers have been known to talk."

"So if this finger had these things going for it, it would adopt an operating system or a worldview that saw itself as a separate entity. In some ways, he would be right—each finger is unique and separate. Mr. Digit would pretty quickly start engaging in whatever survival strategies were necessary to be a finger and probably find some drama about the irritating adjoining digits: the rude Mr. Middle Finger, the fat thumb, etc. What do you think Mr. Digit's body might say to that slumbering, unaware, confused little Mr. Digit?"

Ted got the point. "Get over yourself, Mr. Digit. You're really part of my hand, which is part of my arm, which is part of my torso; the whole person is the real deal, Mr. Digit; you're just a part."

"That's right, and Mr. Digit would have to disidentify from his inherent sense of being a glamorous little stump of a self and all the dramas that accompany that worldview of the noble, ring-bearing finger. I'm rather sure that he would also be certain that he was created in God's image, which is pretty much saying that he should consider himself the center of the universe. I assure you that he would not comprehend anything you told him about his role as part of your hand; Mr. Digit would not get it for even one moment. It is the nature of all living organisms to be blind to the bigger picture, unable to see the levels or systems that exist beyond their small, little, however marvelous, unique, and separate selves."

"You're saying that a finger may know about fingernails and perhaps even other fingers but doesn't see the whole hand. Hands know hands but don't know arms, and so forth."

"For now, you've got it. If you want to go deeper, I've got a book for you."*

Ted interrupted. "If Mr. Digit wasn't a selfish little stump, he might just find himself on the wrong end of that hammer.

---

* Ken Wilber, Jack Engler, and Daniel P. Brown, *Transformations of Consciousness: Conventional and Contemplative Perspectives on Development* (New York: Random House, 1986).

If the parts don't take care of themselves, then there can be no whole, right?"

"The parts are important, but to evolve spiritually, we must also recognize that we are vibrant pieces of the whole and not just the champions of our own universe."

"I'm still with you. This is better than law school."

"Good. So here is what's next: Our left-brained consciousness, our ego, is very much invested in believing we are the entire enchilada, the apex of creation, and not just a lump in the messy sauce of life. It can't see or even conceive of anything upstream. The left side of the brain scoffs at nirvana. It's simply unable to process the whole; it only sees parts. Your left brain might be threatened by the prospect of being dethroned as your central and dominating operating system. You might hit considerable resistance. If it helps you to get the point as we move forward, I could call you Ted Digit."

Ted frowned and said, "I don't think that's necessary, but let me ask you something. Can this shift of perspective away from my Mr. Digit's left-brained operating system happen? How can I help labeling myself in terms of my very personal, discrete Tedness?" He leaned back on the bench, with his hand still resting on Argo, and continued. "You said it's the nature of all things to be somehow blinded to how they fit into the bigger picture. I think it was Albert Einstein who warned us that you cannot solve a problem with the same consciousness that created the problem in the first place."

Angel leaned back on her hands and smiled to acknowledge the point. "We have to learn to rewrite the software; otherwise, we'll continually generate the same answers, and that is why most people are spiritually stuck."

This concept seemed daunting to Ted. "It can't be that easy rewiring our brain's circuitry. Are we at risk of losing some good things if we try?"

"It's a journey of becoming more aware of what is upstream, more global, and bigger than us and less identified with what is below us, downstream, or the drama beside us. You see, our brains have neuroplasticity:* the ability to generate new synapses. It is within the brain's capacity to rewrite and improve its 'software.' As we get older, we tend to value certainty of the left brain over the curiosity of the right brain. In the face of this, we have to train ourselves to let go of knowing and take a more open stance to life. Some call it wonderment. Otherwise, it's easy to educate ourselves away from being right-brained students of life to becoming left-brained experts or technocrats. We load up with facts and knowledge but don't access much wisdom about life."

Ted concurred only in part. "Clients pay me to be an expert and not a student."

Angel nodded. "Perhaps we can allow ourselves to be experts in our trades, but students of life."

---

* Angel had studied many books on the subject of neuroplasticity, but when all she needed was a reasonably accessible refresher, she just opened a browser and went to http://en.wikipedia.org/wiki/Neuroplasticity.

"I don't mind being a student, but I prefer to do it on a full stomach. I'm getting hungry."

"So am I, but one more thing. Most of us intuitively grasp that there is more to the world than 'me,' but we struggle to put a word on all that rests above and beyond us. That's why Father Chuck calls most religious teachings 'signposts.' At best, they only point us in the right direction."

"That makes sense to me."

"Good, then you're ready for the third realization! Let's grab a snack; the brain needs a lot of glucose to function. Would you like to take No Barks and Argo for a walk around the monastery's lake?"

"A short break would suit both the left and the right sides of my brain."

Much to Ted's delight, Angel jumped up from the ground and reached for his hand. She held it softly for a moment and then gave it a yank. "Let's go. There is no time for sitting around at Spirit Tech."

"Is there a limit on just how enlightened I can get one day?"

Angel laughed. "Love your enthusiasm."

10

Student, teacher, and canines wandered along the edge of the small monastery lake chatting and enjoying the sun on their faces. The wind rippled the surface of the water and stirred up the scents of juniper, cedar, and pine from the desert and nearby mountains. They walked shoulder to shoulder. Angel reached out from time to time and clutched Ted's elbow, particularly when she wanted to make a convincing point. He had bruised this same elbow in his fateful accident, so the contact was both painful and exhilarating.

They stopped and Ted threw a small stone into the water. Facing the lake, Ted said, "It's been a long time since I've been in the mountains. Grandpa Raines chided me for never getting out of Crossing Trails. All this beauty was just twelve hours away and I never bothered to see it."

"So how did you end up in Kansas?"

"When I was a boy, I spent summers with my grandparents in Crossing Trails. They were the two constants in my life. When I got out of law school, the economy was tanking and jobs were limited. My grandfather asked me to come out and take over his law practice, so I did. Not long after that, Lisa went back to Chicago to be with the handsomest man in our law school class. It worked out well for both of them. They're already partners in big corporate firms making boatloads of money."

"And how did it work out for you?" Angel asked.

"I'm fixing tickets and drawing up estate plans in Crossing Trails. Need I say more?"

"But you do some criminal work?"

"Sure. Why?"

"Aunt Lilly."

Ted felt a little guilty for monopolizing Angel's spiritual talents and wanted to show her that he had a few of his own. "Tell me more about Aunt Lilly."

"Poor Aunt Lilly is a bit nuts."

"I'm sorry."

"I'm not sure Legal Aid has the resources to get her out of this mess. She could use a good, caring lawyer like Ted Day."

"Truthfully, Angel, I don't know about that. I'd like to help her, but like I said this morning, South Dakota is a whole different jurisdiction. This dream defense of hers bothers me too."

"Didn't you tell me that you experienced a vivid dream while sleeping in Bertha?"

"Yes."

"Didn't that dream tell you something important?"

"I suppose so, Angel, but this is different. You can't go shooting people, regardless of a powerful dream."

"So, like that, you've already decided that she's guilty?"

"The process—not the lawyers—decides who is inno-cent or guilty. The lawyers just make sure the process is fairly applied."

"I see. Would you be comfortable making sure the process is fairly applied to my aunt Lilly?"

Ted doubted there was much he could do to help her aunt, but Angel was insistent, so he said, "I'll make some calls and see if there is anything I can do."

Angel again grabbed Ted's sore elbow. "Our family would appreciate it."

Angel found a nice grassy place not far from the shoreline. "We can sit here and get back to work, if you're ready?"

"Bring it on! I'm ready for more, but first I'm stuck on something."

"What?" Angel asked.

Without wanting to whine, Ted thought it important that he be honest. "Spirit Tech is a bit depressing!"

Angel should have anticipated Ted's remark, but given that he was her first real student, she was caught off guard. "Really?" she asked.

"First you tell me I'm asleep. Second you tell me I don't even know who I am. These aren't self-esteem-building exercises."

"I'm glad you mentioned this, and I want you to know I've taken your observation very seriously. It's not my intention to depress you, but you're right."

"That's good news?"

"Did I tell you what Father Chuck and the rest of my spiri-tual compatriots call ourselves, our little group?"

Ted thought a moment. "No, I don't recall you telling me."

"It wouldn't have made sense to you then, but now it will. For two different reasons, we call ourselves *coconuts*. One, we're poking fun. Most of the world probably thinks we're nuts. But second, on a deeper level, getting to the milky essence of life isn't that easy, but it's the whole point. You have to crack the hairy, hard outer shell of the self. A coconut is a metaphor for the spiritual journey."

Ted couldn't help himself. "That's it—in a nutshell?"

Angel playfully slapped at Ted's arm. "For our group, cracking the shell, or transformation, is the most important human task. And you're absolutely right; it's not necessarily easy or fun. At times it is downright difficult, but the good news is that you can learn good techniques for shell cracking."

"Is that where traveling spiritual consultants come in?" Ted cowered, covering his head, as if expecting a blow.

"Not just me. Father Chuck argues that transformation— shell cracking—is the true essence of Jesus's teaching. My Sufi friends, and Mashid Marabi in particular, describe the paths that transform consciousness as 'the Work.'* The eldest of our group, Steve Singleton, would point out that Buddhism is a

---

* Angel's friend Mashid was very involved with the Diamond Group, a spiritual school founded by A. H. Almaas. They too describe the spiritual journey as the Work. See A. H. Almaas, *Diamond Heart*, books 1 through 4 (Berkeley, CA: Diamond Books). G. I. Gurdjieff, an early-twentieth-century spiritual teacher, also used the term "the Work" to describe the process by which we wake ourselves up.

path of transformation that starts with the First Noble Truth. All of life is suffering. We all have shells to crack."

"No pain, no gain?" Ted asked.

Angel rolled her eyes at Ted and continued. "I suppose so. 'The Work' is a general term for the pain we take on, the spiritual lessons we must learn, in order to gain, or wake up, and enjoy the good stuff that rests beneath the shell."

"Thank you. That makes me feel a little better about spirit school, but it begs yet another question. Do you have enough energy for one more?" Angel did not answer, so Ted checked his watch and prodded, "What—are you in the teachers' union?"

"One more, then let's break."

"How do we do this *Work*—crack open the shell?"

"When you look closely, the best workbooks are very similar."

Surprised by her answer, Ted asked, "So a Christian workbook might not look different from a Muslim or a Buddhist workbook?"

"Yes, and there are other workbooks that aren't religious. At least not in the traditional sense."

"Like?"

"I'll describe a common spiritual approach to cracking the shell of ego. What Mr. Digit needs to thrive, to really sink his roots into deep, fertile soil, is another convenient left-brain construct. We call it *time*."

Having to keep daily time sheets and charging by the hour for his work, Ted had an unusual slant on time. He saw it as having considerable intrinsic value. "Time is how we order our lives. Without time, life wouldn't be precious. Knowing that I only have fourteen days at Spirit Tech provides us with a structure to do this work."

"Yet when we dig deeper into time, we find something very interesting." Angel leaned back and the wind swept a thick strand of her long black hair off her shoulder and onto her face. Ted reached over and returned the unruly strand to its proper place, where it would not distract his professor. Angel smiled and continued, "To get here, Eckhart Tolle and other spiritual teachers make an important distinction between psychological time and clock time."*

Ted was not going to give up easily. He took the errant strand of hair and tossed it back in her face. "Surely thinking about the past and the future are worthwhile endeavors— glancing back at where we've been and thinking ahead about where we want to go? We all have to do that."

"Yes, that would be a very good endeavor in theory, but it's just not what we do. Your mind processes time more like a daytime TV game show."

"Are you going to ask me if I'm smarter than some third grader?"

"Trust me, you're not." Angel picked a bit of grass off No Barks's back and flicked it onto Ted before continuing. "The game show called *Ted's Deal* is just like the real show; you get to choose between three doors."

---

* Eckhart Tolle, *The Power of Now: A Guide to Spiritual Enlightenment* (Novato, CA: New World Library, 1999).

Ted straightened up, confident he would win the trip to Disneyland. "Sounds fun. Let's play."

"Close your eyes and imagine the stage. Visualize three garage-size doors ready to be peeled open by the attractive hostess, Vanna Digit."

"Tall, dark, long black hair, right?"

Angel stared at her boots. "Probably, but with a slightly different wardrobe." She continued, "Door number one is always left open. It's the given. Look up at those mountains on the horizon, Ted, and take in everything that's around you right now. Door number one is your life as it exists precisely at this moment—warts, hiccups, and all."

"Thank you, Vanna."

"Now close your eyes again and think about something that really pisses you off that your ex-wife did or said."

"That's a long list."

"I'm sure it is, so just pick one thing. That scene is waiting to be played out behind door number two like a looped tape that never ends."

Ted whined, " 'There is nothing to do in Crossing Trails!' "

"Sounds good. Now for door number three, think about something you want or desire."

"With or without clothing?"

"Your option."

Ted let a wicked little grin cross his face. "Okay, that one's easy. I've got all three spaces populated in my mind, so now what?"

"This can be a bit of a cruel game. When the doors open

up, what you'll see are just great big cardboard cutouts, pictures on the stage. Nothing real. So you have three choices: living this life behind door number one, imagining a soap opera called *Ted's Pissed Off* behind door number two, and salivating over an image that is not real of something you wish existed, projected behind door number three."

"Okay, you made your point. To win *Ted's Deal*, I've got to park my head inside door number one. That's the only space where things are real."

"That's right." Angel allowed Ted to get comfortable with the concept and then continued, "The consciousness of the true self is present in the real and the now and is never present in some imagined reality. Mr. Digit, however, thrives behind doors two and three."

"Angel, you're making it sound like I have some choice in the way my mind works. I'm not sure I can rub the stripes off that tiger. How can I possibly make door number one my exclusive haunt?" Ted asked, shifting his weight, checking his watch, and wondering if it was about time for an early dinner and whether anyone would complain about where he'd parked the Chieftain.

"None of this is particularly easy to grasp by discussion alone. For now, let me say that allowing our minds to operate like a game show is not the way to lead a fulfilling life."

Ted cringed. "So do you mean that I'm squandering my life?" After thinking a bit more about it, he asked, "Have I?"

"Everyone has an ego, so of course we spend way too much time behind doors two and three. Don't judge yourself harshly.

Instead, just find a way to stay more present. Remember the first realization: most of the world is stuck in a dream world, playing out the drama of the mind but not really alive to reality and the potential magnificence of human life."

"But not you?"

"Even me. Remember, Ted, awakening is a matter of degree. It's a journey. I'm a project too, a work in progress."

Ted held up his right middle finger. "Maybe Mr. Digit is right about one thing. One part of us is saying something rather rude to another part of us."

Angel smiled. "Has anyone ever told you that you are clever?"

"Frequently, but I still don't see how I can get rid of my personality. Even if I could, it seems like a drastic solution."

"We can't be rid of the entire ego-mind structure, and certainly not all at once. Our goal is not to chop the finger off the hand."

"So we're talking just a little ego tune-up?"

"A bit more than that, Ted. But that's the third realization, and you're not quite ready for that. Maybe tonight or tomorrow morning before you leave."

"Leave?" Ted asked, more than slightly concerned.

"We're going to get you to wake up. I can't wait to meet the real Ted Day!"

"Is this version that bad?" Ted asked. "If so, maybe you should just give me the third realization now. Besides, I hate to wander around with two-thirds of an equation in my head. It gives me a migraine."

"You're doing fantastic, and you do seem to be getting it at the logical, left-brain level, but before you can go much further, you need to move beyond left-brain concepts and labels. We have an exercise or two to help you with that. Does this sound like it's worth the effort?"

"Yes, but I'm not sure I can eat dinner on an unrealized stomach, and I'm starting to get really hungry." He crossed his arms and did his best imitation of a swaying swami. "Meaning passes not through the stomach that growls."

"I recognize that passage: I believe it came straight out of the Man Bible." Angel reached into her bag and handed Ted an apple. "Eat this."

Ted gladly accepted the fruit. "So what's this exercise you have in mind for me?"

"You'll see. Let's walk back to Bertha. We can drive up to the trailhead before it gets dark."

"The trailhead?" Ted asked.

"Patience . . ."

11

Ted sat on a cushion behind the driver's seat, closed his eyes, and, without even trying to understand what Angel meant by not thinking, started the exercise. While Ted was scanning the universe of his mind for some signal that was not Ted talk, Angel drove the old bookmobile through the parking lot at what Ted considered an entirely reckless pace. He opened his eyes and yelled, "Are you sure you don't want me to drive?"

"Nope, we're great."

"Did you tell me why we're going to this lake? If so, I missed it."

"Just close your eyes, Ted, and sense into all that is not Ted. See if you can discover what is resting behind that chatter. Leave the rest to me."

As Angel navigated the twenty-five-mile road leading to the trailhead in a remote corner of the Pecos Wilderness, she turned from time to time and gave Ted further instructions. Appreciating that approximately 95 percent of Ted's waking mental activity was mindless chatter, she barraged him with little helpful hints. "Your mind will wander off; just gently return to the task of staying present, observing. Watch your breath if it helps. In and out."

Ted became irritated at his inability to focus and tried to find something or someone to blame. "You're chattering as much as my mind. I got it. Door number one. Stay present."

"Are you able to quiet the discursive mind?"

"Yes, somewhat," Ted lied. He wished he was beside Angel in the passenger seat.

Over the hum of Bertha's engine, Angel hollered, "You can't do this wrong. Just allow your mind to relax, to take a vacation from its normal assessing of Ted's needs, wants, fears, and cravings."

Ted knew that Angel was trying to show him something she thought was important, so out of respect for her more than dedication to finding his own higher self, he tried to dig beneath his thoughts, but before he got far he realized that there was some sort of bolt on Bertha's floor that was rather unfortunately positioned under his right butt cheek. He scooted a few inches closer to Angel. Glancing at her, Ted noticed how gorgeous she looked driving the old, armored beast up the narrow, winding road.

The forest air was pleasant enough, but Ted wondered again what was next on their journey and why they were going to this lake in the first place. His mind quickly wandered further off task.

It dawned on him that spiritual consultants should be licensed. Was Angel's license in good standing? He should have researched her on Yelp or something. He tried to push away his suspicion of her scamming him and to remain open to whatever was beyond his thoughts—which was a rather boring thing to do and, at the same time, irritatingly difficult. No sooner had this intention formed than another thought occurred to him. Where would he sleep tonight? How would he bathe privately? He wondered what Angel wore to bed. A few seductive images came to his mind.

Angel correctly assumed Ted's mind had strayed far afield. "You'll find it is very natural for your mind to wander back to Ted thinking. If it's helpful, you can repeat a word, like 'open,' to keep your concentration focused."

"Shouldn't I be reciting something? The rosary or a mantra?" Ted asked, concerned that he was missing a vital piece of the instructions.

"No, don't try to make this religious. We're just watching and noticing our mind, seeing how it works or fails to work. That's all for now." After another few minutes Angel asked, "How did you experience this exercise?"

Ted opened his eyes and looked around. He was initially struck by the intense, deep green of the trees. They had gained considerable altitude. He stretched, smiled, and said, "Very frustrating. I'm no Buddha. My mind was absolutely unwilling to focus on what I asked it to do. But still, just for a flash, I found some brief moments of silence behind the chatter."

"How would you describe it?" Angel asked.

"It was peaceful. Seemed nostalgic. The rest of the time, I've got to admit, it was difficult. Nearly impossible to shut down the internal dialogue."

"Very good. Now go back to the first and second realizations and think about them in the context of what you just experienced." Moving his cushion closer to her, Ted looked perplexed, so she elaborated. "What did you learn about your thoughts?"

"It seems that my mind has a mind of its own."

With her hand resting on No Barks's head, Angel turned around briefly in her seat, laughed, and said, "Excellent. You just experienced the first two realizations for yourself. We are not awake to a great deal of consciousness, and we are overly identified with our minds."

"Actually, it's a scary conclusion. If I'm not my mind, then what am I?"

"Those are great questions for you to think about, Ted." Angel slowed Bertha, so that she was crawling up the mountain road at less than twenty miles an hour. "That's enough for now. Just rest and enjoy the rest of the ride. Later I'll try to explain the importance of what you just accomplished."

Ted climbed into the passenger seat, fastened his seat belt, and decided to just enjoy the rest of the ride.

12

Angel parked Bertha at a small campground near the trail-head for Stewart Lake. After pushing the emergency brake to the floor, she turned off the ignition. She craned her neck to get a good look out the windshield. "Isn't it beautiful? I'll wait here. Tomorrow morning you and Argo are going on a field trip, another exercise to help you metabolize the realizations. Nature is a remarkable teacher—much wiser than me. You need to learn how to spend time with her."

"Alone in the mountains?" Ted asked, not trying to hide his disapproval. Open spaces had always spooked him. Even as a kid he'd liked to build forts in his room. As an adult he preferred a roof over his head.

Angel ignored Ted's apprehension. "You and Argo are going to hike to the top of that mountain. The higher self speaks from places of silence. You tried to find it in your mind and, like most of us, you failed. So now you're going to get some help." She pointed at a distant peak barely visible through the windshield and continued, "It's just five or six miles that way."

"You mean straight up?" Ted asked.

"At about eleven thousand five hundred feet you'll find Stewart Lake, where you and Argo can spend the night, meditate, and get better connected to the silence where this truth I am describing resides."

"Really? Please tell me there's a nice little lodge up there." Angel shook her head.

"A Holiday Inn?"

"Sacred space is much better than a Holiday Inn. Up there you can listen and experience what is beyond your thinking mind. When you are ready, come back down the mountain and we'll talk about your field trip. You'll have a whole new outlook."

Ted's internal processors were humming and spinning, but nothing was registering except a rather panicked feeling of abandonment. If meditation was a strange, almost uncomfortable experience, then this was simply inconceivable. "What do you mean a field trip? Two days?"

"Don't worry, Ted. You'll do fine. I'll put a pack together. The trailhead is just over there. I've done it twice before. It's difficult. That's the point. You'll find that in some inexplicable way the experience changes you."

Ted found this disturbing. "Argo and I have never backpacked before. What about food, water, and supplies?"

Angel smiled and put her finger across her lips. "Shhh. Ted, don't worry. I have everything you need. You and Argo are going to have a good time. A great time. Trust me. It's part of the waking-up process. We Lakota say that the best place to find the creator is in creation. Tonight we'll talk some more about the third realization. Tomorrow morning you walk in creation. It's a great exercise in finding your true self, even better than meditation."

"Better than meditation?" Ted asked with more than a hint of sarcasm. "Where is this Father Chuck you said I was going to meet?"

Angel again pressed her finger to her lips. "At Spirit Tech, things unfold at their own pace."

"What if it rains?"

"Can you sense how, at just this moment, you're responding entirely out of your fear-based ego? Try to let go of planning, worrying, controlling, and just relax—trust that on this journey what comes next is what is supposed to come next. Trust that you can allow someone or something in the universe besides yourself to be in control."

"You?" Ted asked.

"Yes, in the beginning, me. Eventually you'll learn to trust a different part of yourself."

Ted knew students have little say in their course work, but he didn't recall a solitary mountain hike being part of the syllabus. His attraction to Angel was pushing him in unwelcome ways, and he felt some disappointment in her for putting him in this position.

Ted got out of the passenger seat, stretched, and looked at Angel. She was still smiling and sitting in the driver's seat, self-assured and confident. It occurred to him that if she joined him, this hike might be tolerable. It was the going it alone that bothered him. "Okay, I trust you. Argo and I will hike to the top of that Kilimanjaro, sit around with nature, and spend the night in the middle of nowhere with the wolves and the rattlesnakes. I suppose this is the kind of thing that people do on vacation."

"It's your vacation." Angel pointed to one of several piles. "Grab the two lawn chairs from under the blankets and meet me outside."

Ted knew that he was agreeing, at least in part, to impress Angel. But he also felt she was touching on something important that he would never do on his own. He grabbed the two lawn chairs and then spoke to his dog. "Let's go, Argo. It's not nice to keep Mother Nature waiting."

13

Angel plopped two cans, their "dinner," onto the small folding camp table. "Help yourself." The canned food was for emergencies, but she had been so caught up in her work with Ted that she had forgotten to buy groceries. Tomorrow, while Ted hiked, she would drive back to Pecos for supplies.

Angel dived into the can of enchiladas with a plastic fork. "Bon appétit." Ted seemed uncertain about the etiquette for sharing food out of a can. Angel assumed he'd never done it.

A month ago she would have taken one look at Ted and said he was not her type of man. Being Ted's teacher was a good opportunity for the Buddhist practice of equanimity—resisting the urge to judge all experiences as either good or bad. Now she realized that she was enjoying her time with him. Perhaps it was sharing all the teachings that were so important to her. Perhaps, too, it was something else. Ted had a softer take on masculinity that she found attractive. She had never considered herself lonely, but perhaps she was wrong. Whether a sunset over the mountains or just a walk around the monastery lake, good companionship, she reflected, enhanced every experience.

With the enchiladas consumed, Angel moved on to a can of Del Monte fruit cocktail. While she worked the handheld can opener, Ted asked her a question that had been bothering him. "How does religion fit into these realizations you've been describing? Are waking up and salvation the same thing? Wouldn't it be easier to just join a church and ditch all this spiritual work? There are churches on every corner and only one Angel Two Sparrow, Native American spiritual consultant, traveling around in a bookmobile. Maybe waking up is just too much work for the average Joe."

"Or the average Ted?" Angel asked.

Although he hadn't intended it, he realized that his words might have come off a bit harsh. "Of course, I always thought church was a waste of time, and Spirit Tech is great, but that's just me."

Angel set the can of fruit down on the table for Ted to share. She answered in a detached way. "An individual who succeeds in the spiritual journey is fully awakened. The Buddha, Jesus, and Muhammad are examples. Their followers understandably wanted to package and label their lives and teachings for consumption by a wider audience. This is religion."

"So what is the difference between a spiritual consultant like you and your garden-variety preacher?"

Angel looked longingly at the mountains before returning to Ted's question. "When I was growing up on the reservation in South Dakota, we were poor in ways you would not understand. We were often hungry. Our clothes were little more than rags. My brother and I would take turns drinking this sweet juice at the bottom of the fruit can. It was a treat, dessert, for us." She set the can down. "Now I get all the juice I want from the bottom of the can. This bounty makes me somehow rich. My brother and my mother, they are both gone, dead. My father, Larsen, is now far away in South Dakota. I wouldn't mind being hungry again if it meant I could share this juice with my brother and mother. Being alone and having it all to myself is not so good, not like I dreamed it would be when I was a child." She handed the can to Ted. "Drink some."

The juice at the bottom of a can of fruit cocktail did not sound like a treat to Ted, but he knew this offering meant something to Angel. He took a few sips of the heavy syrup. As he did, he pictured Angel as a small girl living in some run-down shack, sharing high-fructose corn syrup from the bottom of a can. It was difficult to imagine such poverty. He felt an echoing sensation around his heart. It seemed to vibrate, thick and low. It was dull and sad, neither quick nor joyful. It was as if Angel's sudden melancholy were resonating within him. He was owning some part of her sadness.

Before he could fully experience the sensation in his chest, Angel returned to Ted's question. "You see, Ted, I want to share the spiritual juice with others. Sharing makes everything better in life, don't you think? It's no good having it all to myself. That's not how it is supposed to be."

What she said rang true for Ted. He realized that his lack of sharing—after the divorce, after his grandfather's death—had left a hole. The hole hurt. "I agree."

"There is more to sharing than we realize. Do you remember when you asked how you could become more awake?"

"Yes, you said it was not easy."

"I should have said it's nearly impossible to do on your own. We're human—we're wired to empathize. It's another part of your awareness that waits to be more fully realized. We'll meditate again later, and this time I'll do it with you. You'll find it easier. Much easier. It turns out that, to some extent, through something neurologists call mirror neurons, you can graft onto my consciousness and use it like training wheels until you find this more awakened state on your own. This is why the world needs some variety of spiritual consulting. It's very problematic trying to wake up on your own."

Angel stood up and gazed at the mountains as the sun lost altitude in the evening sky. "I don't want to spend such a beautiful evening sitting here talking and analyzing any further. Let's walk among the mountains. You'll be able to see how your brain can resonate not only with other humans but also with nature herself. Try to listen and hear with something more than your logical-thinking left brain. Everything in nature talks, some things even sing, but very few humans listen. If you are interested, I can help you to hear this music."

Ted had no trouble laughing at himself. "You mean quit knowing so damned much?"

"That would help."

Ted stood up. "I don't think trees and rocks talk, but . . ." He shrugged as if to say, *Who really knows?* "I'll do my best to stay open on the subject."

"A good place to be."

Argo began to wag his tail and get fired up, spinning excitedly. "Argo loves to go for walks. The strange thing is, he seems to be able to sense that I'm going on the walk well before I actually grab the leash. As soon as I form the intention, he seems to know it."

"Argo, thank you for demonstrating my point. Dogs *know* very little, but they get along marvelously, sensing and intuiting their way through life."

Ted snapped a leash on his brave, furry yellow dog.

Hugging the old terrier, Angel whispered in his ear, "You can hear nature's music, can't you?"

When she leaned over, a strap from her black halter-top slipped off her shoulder. Ted gently put it back.

14

The two humans and the two dogs set off on an evening stroll up the steep mountainside. The sun was beginning to set, and its horizontal rays illuminated the wildflowers that were spread across the meadow, adding sprinkles of red, blue, and green to the rocky landscape.

Ted's question about the nexus between religion and spirituality was difficult. Angel had tried on churches, synagogues, temples, and mosques as if they were shoes, but she had not been able to find her glass slipper. Angel also knew that her upbringing and education had profoundly affected her attitude. She saw herself as a welcome guest at many destinations but at home in no place in particular or at all places in general.

Angel grabbed Ted's elbow to make sure she had his attention. When he stopped, she sat down on a large rock and motioned for him to sit beside her. A wisp of spiderweb was stuck in his hair. Angel reached over to remove it and said, "You asked a good question at dinner. The relationship between religion and spirituality is confusing. My mother used to say that religion was for rich folks that wanted to avoid going to hell, and spirituality was for poor Indians that had already lived there and wanted out."

"You mother sounds interesting."

"My father used to tell me and my brother that our mother was like a rainbow. She had many colors. It was his way of asking us to forgive her dark hues. He knew that little girls should not grow up waiting for their mothers to sleep off hangovers." Angel's voice cracked slightly and she paused. "She was absent from my life in that way. So when she died, nothing really changed. The absence just persists."

Angel did not cry, but it was clear to Ted that she was going into a sensitive area. Before, the chronic problem with alcohol on America's reservations had seemed very abstract. Now, with Angel sitting beside him nearly in tears, it felt immediate. "I'm sorry."

Angel regained her composure. "I will say there was no shame in my mother. She believed that the only way to climb up to heaven was to fall down on earth. In many ways I owe her a great deal for that insight."

Ted turned his head sideways, slightly surprised. "How is that?"

"Even with all of her drug and alcohol problems, she had a certain spiritual wisdom. My brother and I played on the floor and listened to the sobbing confessions of broken and healing souls at AA meetings. One day I heard my mother say to the group that she was glad she was a drunk and an addict." Angel knew Ted would find her statement hard to understand. "She believed that we are all broken and it's only when our brokenness reaches a certain desperate point—the AA people call it hitting bottom—that we can accept our fundamental brokenness and do something about it."

"With all due respect to your mother, I don't want to think I have to crash and burn before I can wake up. Is this the third realization: only broken souls can ascend?"

"I think what she was saying was that addiction is a most acute version of the first realization. To varying degrees we are all unawake, but for my mother and others the drowsiness descends to a drunken stupor."

Without warning, Angel got up and slowly began walking up the trail. She wanted to leave this discussion of her mother behind. It was too painful.

Ted fixed his gaze on her, admiring the grace with which she moved. Then he got to his feet and followed her.

Knowing that their lungs had not yet acclimated to nine thousand feet of altitude, Angel went slowly and tried to gather her thoughts, hoping to find the best way to communicate the third and final realization to her student. She and Ted were now to the marrow of their first day of work together. Whether he kept at it for another week or even a day might turn on this next lesson. She wanted to do it not just well but perfectly. She found a large log by the path and again sat to rest.

Angel's confidence was faltering. She wasn't sure that she was doing any of this right and felt ridiculous for thinking she could show anyone else a way, a path, that she could barely find herself. It was not her message that she was trying to pass to Ted. She was just a medium, a go-between, a spiritual Gutenberg trying to get the word out with the only printing press she had—her heart, her soul, and her mind. All she could do was try. She would have to follow the old adage: fake it until you make it. That would have to be enough for now.

Angel broke the silence. "Ted, if you're ready, I'll introduce the third realization. After that, I'm going to let Father Chuck take over."

"Guest lecturers at Spirit Tech?"

"Father Chuck is first on my list of teachers; he's been a great teacher to me. You'll be better off getting the lessons directly from him. I don't want anything to be lost in the translation."

Ted was surprised at Angel's apparent lack of confidence in her own skill. For his part, he felt differently about his guide. "I'm very pleased to meet some of your friends, but Angel, you're the best spiritual consultant I've ever met."

"I'm the only one."

"True." Ted knew that there was nothing in the world logical about driving around in a bookmobile doing whatever it was that Angel was trying to do. However naive, he also found her extraordinarily charming. "You're just the first one that had the guts to try it. Most of the rest of the world is peddling pots and pans; you're trying to sell something of true value. What could be wrong with that?"

Ted's acceptance was like a cool, steady rain falling on wilted flowers. It was exactly what Angel needed to hear. "Thank you for understanding."

Energized, she began the last teaching of the day. "I have stumbled across a way of thinking about the third realization and how religion ties into all of this. Hopefully, I can get it right."

"Give it a shot."

"For our purposes, let's assume there are five major religions in this, what we might call the modern era. Two are culturally based and three are creed based. To be a Christian, Muslim, or Buddhist, you simply adopt a belief system. Let's restrict my discussion to the three creed-based religions and throw in a little Native American spirituality on our pilgrimage together. Is that okay?"

"Four religions are more than enough for me," Ted said. He smiled and added, "Besides, I don't want to deal with a turban or a yarmulke."

"As I suggested earlier, our work together builds one realization on top of another."

"Sounds like math," Ted observed.

"When you get this next realization, Ted, you're going to have a revelation. It's a big one. Much of what seems crazy to you about religion, politics, and life will start to make better sense."

"I'll listen carefully." Ted's eyes lit up with enthusiasm; he wanted to know more. "Go ahead. Tell me this important third realization."

Angel closed her eyes and began. "A gun sight has both a vertical and a horizontal axis. Without both axes, the sight is flawed."

"Got it," Ted confirmed without argument.

"Likewise, we need to define and identify a vertical and a horizontal axis for this work we are doing together to wake up. Religions or spiritual schools of thought can be seen as the vertical lines on my scope. We'll look at Christianity, Islam, Buddhism, and Native American spirituality. Obviously, there are more schools or religions and an incredible number of splinter groups within each religion, but for now let's keep it simple. Along these vertical lines are horizontal notches that one might call levels or grades, which we travel along as we mature and become more awake or aware. Some say there are six; others say nine, or more. Let's keep it easy and just focus on six. This is the spiritual side of the equation."

"How is that?" Ted asked.

"Do you remember this morning when we spoke of awakening as a process existing on a spectrum?"

"Yes," Ted answered, "I remember."

"It turns out that we can measure with a reasonable degree of certainty the awareness that each of us has obtained along that spectrum. There are patterns. It's still a bit crude, and I suppose not everyone is in total agreement on this, but a consensus is definitely emerging. The levels define the spectrum from less awake or aware to wide awake or fully realized. At the lower levels the personality has not yet matured or opened up to its fullest potential—it is still pretty much asleep—while at the highest levels we find souls that are more actualized or awakened."

"So why is it helpful to know the spiritual level?"

"No matter where you are on the spiritual spectrum, with a little help you can gain more awareness, or move up the levels. Essentially, we all have the potential for spiritual genius or full awakening. Any decent geographer knows that you have to realize where you are before you can chart a path to where you want to go."

"So what does this gun-sight analogy have to do with picking a religion or knowing the difference between religion and spirituality?"

"Let me explain by asking you a question. If your parents were picking a school for you, wouldn't they want to make sure that they both picked the right institution and placed you in the correct grade with a skilled teacher?"

"Sure," Ted answered, shrugging.

"It's the same for us. We must find the best institution or school, but we also have to put you in the appropriate grade. You see, Ted, there is first-grade Catholicism and sixth-grade Catholicism. Same with the rest of the religions. If I show you sixth-grade Catholicism and first-grade Islam, what will happen?"

Ted got it. "I would naturally assume that Catholicism was more sophisticated."

"It would be like conducting a spelling bee between first graders at P.S. Mecca Elementary and sixth graders at St. Mary's and then, from the number of correct answers alone, asking you to pick the better school."

"I see the problem."

"If I introduced you to Mrs. Smith's sixth-grade classroom

before you were ready, when you were still trying to learn the alphabet, what would you think about her curriculum?"

"I might assume that Mrs. Smith was teaching gibberish." Ted had a sudden realization. "We do that all the time, don't we?"

"All the time and on many different levels. And Ted, do you know who makes the most fun of the first graders?"

Recognizing a rhetorical question when he heard one, Ted said, "Tell me."

Angel's voice rose as she swatted at a fly stubbornly resting on her nose. "The second graders! And now you should be able to recognize one of the biggest problems in the world today and the reason why we find it so hard to talk to each other about religion and politics. But just in case you don't, I'll tell you. We assume that our differences are at the vertical level—which religions or even denominations within religions we choose to follow—but in fact our real differences, and the root of much of the tension in the world, rest in the horizontal levels that mark our spiritual progress in awakening, or the progress we've made in ridding ourselves of the harmful aspects of our ego-bound Mr. Digit personalities."

Ted thought a moment, then said, "I think I understand what you're saying, but why does it cause a problem that your awareness is at a different level than mine?"

"The fact that we are evolving at different rates is not the problem."

"Then what is?"

"The problem is that most of the world has stopped evolving at all. Most of the world's population is developmentally stuck at the lower levels of awareness, and no one is out there showing them the way up the ladder."

"And you're saying that they can't really do it on their own?"

"Most people, and unfortunately almost all of the world's religious and political parties, fail to recognize that our life goal should be spiritual progress along the vertical axis and not arguing over our differences in dogmas and beliefs along the horizontal axis. As a result, the world is chock-full of first and second graders arguing with each other about their religious and political differences. The world is mired in petty conflict and destructive violence to the point of destroying itself. The human spiritual psyche of most of the world has been devolving into a one-dimensional, flat place, with our self-centered human ego as the head cheerleader screaming its worn-out chant: *us versus them.* That is why so many people are bailing on religion, frustrated with politics, and hoping for a new world order, something different."

Ted thought a moment, then said, "It's entirely too early to know for sure, but I think this third realization is a big one. I can see how getting this one point could really make a difference in our lives."

"That's good, Ted. Realizing is indeed a paradigm shift. It is more than a mere knowing or comprehension. That's what we need you to experience."

"Well, don't stop. I'm intrigued. Please continue."

"When you dig beneath all of the destruction, poverty, greed, and ignorance, you'll see this is where the disease originates—lack of spiritual development is another way of saying we live in a selfish world, and it's our challenge to be less selfish. First-grade Catholicism may seem trite, but let me tell you, sixth-grade Catholicism can knock you on your psychic rump faster than a shot of whiskey with a pint of Guinness for a chaser. It's the same with the other religions. It's a scary journey for these first and second graders of the world to find the upper-grade classrooms. The longer they linger, the harder it is to move them upward. No one is there to take their little hands and lead them down the hall. There are no directional arrows painted on the walls to allow them to find the way on their own."

"So why aren't there more spiritual consultants traveling around. Why is the world resistant to this message? Do you have to get behind the wheel of Bertha and run into them, like you did with me?"

"There is a strong host of impediments to our graduating to the upper levels. We might call this collection of forces evil. It would be easy to describe that evil as simply our natural survival instincts and a culture mired in selfish thinking, but that answer lets people like me, and maybe someday you, off the hook. We need a new, unified spiritual path along the vertical axis that arises independently of our religious affiliations on the horizontal path. We need to create a better map that is generally accessible to the world. Some of us have gotten together and are trying to share this message, but it's harder to communicate than we imagined."

Ted returned to his earlier question. "Why isn't religion doing this for us?"

Angel sighed, wishing it could be so. "Many of the world's

religious institutions not only fail to show you the path to Mrs. Smith's sixth-grade classroom but, I'm afraid, often discourage the journey too. Can you tell me why?"

Ted anxiously waved his hand in the air, accidentally striking the tree he was leaning against and dislodging bits of bark that rained down on them. Angel smiled, flicked the pieces of bark from her brow, and said, "Go ahead, Mr. Day. Tell me."

Certain he had this one nailed, Ted blurted out the answer: "They are in the business of selling us the boats we need to leave behind once we have reached the shore."

"All right. You got it. At the higher levels or grades, the values and beliefs pushed by many organized religious communities to their mainstream first and second graders become irrelevant, even impediments to growth. It is in this context that the Dalai Lama says that religion—the horizontal axis—is not so important. He means it is awakening—the vertical axis—that is important." Angel thought a moment before continuing. "It was also in this arena that Jesus was brilliant. We've lost sight of the fact that Jesus was a religious revolutionary. He was trying desperately to push his community of followers from their first- and second-grade thinking about mores, God, and laws into a more radical and higher place. Like the Buddha, Jesus was the sixth-grade teacher of a millennium. This is how religion so often fails us. It stuck Jesus on a horizontal plane and turned him into a religion instead of a savior."

"Did Jesus fail us?"

"How does the saying go?" Angel remembered the answer to her own question. "Christianity hasn't failed us; we just haven't tried it yet! The historical tragedy of Jesus's life is that his legacy has become mired in first-grade, thinking, and that's hardly his fault."

Ted looked confused, so she continued. "Let me put it another way. To convince the first and second graders who primarily populated the world two thousand years ago, and unfortunately still populate so much of our world today, that Jesus was the real deal, his followers just made him out to be the biggest, toughest, fastest first grader out there, and many continue to bang that drum. All religions do this, though."

"You mean virgin births, jihads, walking on water, rising from the dead, demons, and all the stuff that seems to dominate so much of religious thinking?"

"Religion needs to do more for us: help us move up the ladder of awareness—getting beyond the first-, second-, and even third-grade levels."

"Still," Ted said, "it seems like humanity has evolved a long way in two thousand years. So isn't the trend away from these lower levels?"

"It is hard for many to let go of the prepackaged reality that religion offers. Focusing on true spiritual growth is a rather scary venture."

"Letting go of knowing?"

"We'll talk about it later, but God as magic is one of the hallmarks of the first level. At the upper levels the goal is to experience the divine in this life, in the here and now, and not get bogged down in the terminology of the human biographers of Jesus, Muhammad, the Buddha, or anyone else. While this information was helpful, crucial really, in the early stages of our development, it is not the end point of the journey."

Ted scratched Argo's ears and continued, "I'm not sure I'm following every single thing you're saying, but I must say it's interesting, and it could very well explain a lot of the craziness in the world."

"It's getting dark. Let's stop for now."

As Ted and Angel walked back to the campsite on the narrow path, it was inevitable that they bumped up against each other now and then. It felt good. Ted wondered why the idea of taking a spiritual journey with a beautiful Lakota princess had never occurred to him before. His only regret was that the ghost of Wild Bill Raines wasn't tagging along behind them in his sky blue '82 Cadillac.

By the time the moon was high in the night sky, Angel, Ted, No Barks, and Argo were ready for sleep. They were arranged on the floor of Bertha like piano keys. To Angel it didn't seem particularly odd to have a nonrelative and nonintimate snoring away in close proximity. She'd grown up with neighbors from down the road who crashed on her floor or collapsed on the sofa for some dubious reason (usually not enough money or too much to drink). The last time Ted had had a similar experience was naptime in kindergarten.

Argo, lying next to his wild cousin, gently put his paw on No Barks's neck. The wolf dog gave a little shudder, sighed, and closed her eyes. When Angel rolled over, her blanket fell off. Her long, strong legs shone in the moonlight. She looked so extraordinarily beautiful that Ted wondered if she was even real. To avoid torturing himself, he rolled over and tried to fall asleep.

Before long his dream returned. The fire was now barely burning beside the same small, clear river. The campsite was empty and the sun was about to rise in the very early morning hours. Angel moved in and out of a stream with two does and a spotted fawn. She was alert and gracefully naked. She cautiously sniffed the air for danger, then carefully picked up her feet like they were delicate hooves. She nudged the fawn toward the bank. Her head tilted and her long, black hair blew sideways. In the distance there was the sound of human voices. Angel led her small herd into the thicket of brush on the other side of the creek, where they disappeared from view.

15

Ted shifted his pack slightly to the left. "Am I forgetting any-thing?"

Angel gripped and tightened the straps that crossed over Ted's chest and handed him a walking stick. "You need much less than you think. There is nothing in the pack you couldn't do without for two days."

"Water?" Ted asked.

"You're hiking to a lake. Lots of water in lakes." Angel checked her watch. It was nine fifteen. She didn't want Ted to feel rushed to get to the top before dark. "It's time to go."

Ted was still no Jeremiah Johnson, mountain man, but his attitude about the hike was improving. While not eager, he was feeling some sense of adventure. He looked down at his dog and commanded, "Let's go, Argo. Bears and mountain lions have to eat too. Someone has to keep the great circle of life spinning."

Angel grinned. "Try to relax and have fun. That's part of the point!"

"Nice knowing you," Ted called out as he departed the campsite and started toward the trail.

"Back at you!"

The mountaintop looked far away as Ted slowly distanced himself from the safe and secure campsite. He registered at the kiosk and took note of the moderate fire warning posted on the chalkboard—contained campfires were permitted. There were pages of signatures from other hikers who had both checked in to the trail and checked back out several days later. This put slightly more confidence in Ted's step as he began his ascent.

Within five minutes he had left the little meadow at the bottom of the trail and entered the forest. He promised himself never to complain about riding in Bertha the Bookmobile again. At least Bertha provided a roof over his head. He didn't see how anyone could possibly make it to the summit, where Lake Stewart was nestled, before sunset. He tried to recall Angel's advice: "The only way to the top, Ted, is one step at a time. Before you know it, you'll look back and realize you're there."

Like most novice hikers, Ted was anxious, and this caused him to start out too quickly. Besides, he wanted to appear intrepid as he walked away from Angel. At this confident but too-brisk pace, he passed along the first of a seemingly unending series of switchbacks. Before he had gone even a hundred yards, his breathing became surprisingly strained. Taking a break from trying to avoid the many sharp rocks that lined the path, Ted stopped a moment to catch a long, cool, fresh breath of mountain air. It was his first taste of real adventure in many years, and on some level he was proud of himself for taking this step out into the wild.

Ted removed his baseball cap and wiped the sweat from his brow, then grabbed one of the two water bottles that were strapped to his belt for easy access. After taking a drink, he poured a small amount into a collapsible water bowl he had brought for Argo. The dog was resting under a pine tree and glanced at the water with total disinterest. "Argo, at this rate we're going to go through our water much too quickly. We'd better slow down, or maybe just stop here and camp. What do you think? I won't tell if you won't!"

Argo sauntered over to Ted and circled him a few times, sniffing at the ground. Like a lone drop of rain mysteriously falling from a nearly cloudless sky, another thought plopped into Ted's mind: gratitude. He was a little chagrined that his grandfather had had to practically boot him out of Crossing Trails and that it had taken a Lakota spiritual consultant to nudge him up this trail. He wondered where that resistance came from. Was he too conservative? Frightened? He wasn't sure, but now that he was here, he was overcome with gratitude to his grandfather and Angel for the push. Without the least effort, the forest had managed to captivate Ted with her beauty.

Returning to the trail, Ted chugged along for another half hour at a more moderate pace. When he came to a sign that signaled his entry into the Santa Fe National Forest, he stopped again and checked the notes that he had put on his smartphone earlier that morning. Sure enough, his entry into the forest was at the one-mile mark of his trek. He checked his watch—it was eleven o'clock. It had taken about forty-five minutes to complete the first mile. He was tired but able to continue.

It was less than six miles total to the top. If they continued at this pace, and if he didn't collapse from exhaustion, Ted calculated that they would make it to Stewart Lake by 4:00 p.m. But why be in a big hurry to put even more distance between himself and civilization? "Argo, good news. We're going too fast. Even if we slow down a bit, we'll make it to the top long before sunset."

Ted looked down at the portion of the trail he had just hiked and was surprised by the amount of elevation he had gained in the last forty-five minutes. Angel, No Barks, Bertha, and the campsite had all disappeared from view. Something else occurred to him. He and Argo had walked for nearly an hour and not seen one other human being. Nor had he heard a car, a plane, a cell phone, or any other hint of human existence. It was surprisingly quiet—certainly not the forest scene from a movie, with brooks babbling in the background. The mountain felt like a void paradoxically full of presence.

Walking farther up the mountain trail in this silence, Ted began to feel naked, but not in an embarrassed or even a vulnerable way. It was more a sense of being uncluttered, floating free and unencumbered by his accustomed sense of identity. His reliable and fundamental Tedness had dissipated like the early-morning fog. Whoever this man was, walking up the mountain in the intermittent sunlight, didn't seem like Ted Day—educated male lawyer, thirty-year-old, dog owner, Crossing Trails resident, white man, son of a doctor, Republican, or anything else that might have previously defined him. He was just here, at this spot on the path, and moving ahead. Uncluttered. That bare nakedness did not diminish him. In fact, unencumbered by all the costumes and adornments that defined his life, Ted was alive and untethered.

With each step something different was arising. He was more aware of what was around him. By slowing his pace, inhaling deeply, and taking more brief rest stops on fallen logs and conveniently strewn boulders—by not pushing himself to the point where his breathing was strained—Ted was able to divert some of his energy to the simple task of paying attention to his forest surroundings, and the hike was becoming fully enjoyable.

A little before noon, Ted realized that he was hungry. He shed his pack and dived into the first meal that Angel had packed for them. Peanut butter and jelly had never tasted so good. Argo sniffed his dog chow but was uninterested. When the sandwich was gone, Ted reclined, rested his head on his backpack, and glanced up at the peaks on the horizon, enjoying the panorama. Interacting with the mountains, with a foot on the path, was a different experience. Angel was right about that.

Feeling drowsy, Ted knew he'd better get back to hiking or he'd be sleeping. On his feet and with his straps adjusted, he checked his notes; he was anxious to see what was around the next bend. They should be approaching an enormous hillside grove of aspen that spread over an entire mile of mountainside. It was at approximately the two-mile mark. "Let's go, Argo. I think something interesting is up ahead." They trekked onward and upward for another fifteen minutes until the terrain shifted its appearance, the pines giving way to aspen. Angel hadn't mentioned that between the trees were densely packed ferns and bushes with small red berries that Ted could not identify. In this silent and verdant forest, with a certain amount of reverence, he felt as if he had stumbled into the crucible of life herself.

Two hundred yards into the aspen grove, a sudden crash broke the peace of the forest, catching Ted completely off guard. Something very large was moving very quickly not far from where he stood. He flinched reflexively and jumped off the path, diving for cover. When he regained his composure, Ted looked toward the noise. It was just a flash of buckskin, really, but still he could make it out: thirty or forty yards below, a large elk was moving away from him. Argo looked at the beast, unsure whether to give chase or turn tail and run. The dog looked to Ted for guidance. Ted grabbed Argo's collar to hold him back. "He's a little big for us. Let's let this one go!"

There was something rather exhilarating about sharing the outdoors with a thousand-pound elk. Ted took a few quick breaths and let it really sink in that they were participating in such a wild space. He laughed and realized, with a significant sense of relief, that he had not been hurt. Having survived his first trekking calamity, Ted figured he had been initiated into the wilderness, and his confidence grew. Somehow the elk sighting had been a gift from the forest. He stood up, brushed off his shorts, and turned to Argo. "Come on, Argo, up we go. It's just an elk. We're already halfway up the path now."

At the top of the aspen grove the trail started to flatten and turn west, and it was easy going for the next few hundred yards. Still, Ted kept his pace slow and deliberate. Coming around a bend, he stopped and took another long drink from his first water bottle. After he had emptied it, he started on the second. He poured a little into Argo's bowl, and this time the dog lapped it up appreciatively. When Argo lifted his head, half the water in the bowl seemed to be dripping off the thick fur around his chin. "Argo," Ted said, "you're a sloppy drinker."

Ted's heart rate was almost normal when he heard another crash. This time it was much closer—not more than fifteen feet away—and above him rather than below. Worse yet, whatever the source of the noise, it was moving directly toward him.

Argo's reaction was much faster than Ted's. The dog panicked and bolted back down the trail with his tail between his legs. Ted simply froze. Instinctively, his hands went up in front of his chest to fend off any attack. From behind the trees a small—about 250-pound—black bear scooted out of the berry bushes and ran across the trail directly in front of him. The bear seemed as panicked as Argo and fled down the hillside, making a reckless descent as if fleeing for its life. It moved with such speed that it quickly disappeared into the underbrush below. It seemed, in the flash he saw of it, to have shades of gray or white above its left shoulder. Dazed,

Ted could hardly piece together what had happened. He concluded that the bear had been resting beside the trail, perhaps even sleeping, when he and Argo had stumbled across it. They'd scared the hell out of the poor creature.

Ted could not help laughing for pure joy. He had confronted a bear, and it appeared that he had survived to tell about it. He called out to Argo to rejoin him. When the dog returned, he remained agitated, uncertain whether the danger had passed. Argo kept weaving back and forth through Ted's legs, trying to find a safe and comfortable bear-free haven. Ted knelt down and tried to calm his traumatized dog. He held Argo tightly. "Don't worry, Argo. He won't hurt you. He's gone now."

Ted stood, took in a few deep breaths, and then let them back out again. He couldn't help smiling. The forest was quiet once again. He was in the middle of the Pecos Wilderness. There were bears, there were elk, he was hiking, and all the things he allowed himself to be anxious about in life—from unfiled legal briefs to house repairs—seemed insignificant. Almost laughable.

As Ted scanned the hillside for movement, it occurred to him that lots of hikers must meet bears on the trail and have similar, entirely safe encounters. How many of Ted's other fears were unfounded? How many bears and other dark creatures were merely frauds of his consciousness? After thinking more about it, he realized that the bear was a lesson on reactivity. His reaction—his worrying and anxiety over the bear—was causing him far more discomfort, unease, and problems than the bear itself. The whole lesson seemed vaguely familiar. It seemed to be yet another demonstration, like the meditation exercise the previous evening, that his mind was not always his best friend. In some ways, he was not his mind but something beyond it or behind it. Angel seemed to think that an insight into the essential nature of the self might just lie in this forest.

Ted was trying to allow this realization to fully sink in when, fifty yards ahead and lumbering right toward him, came a second black bear. To a seasoned hiker it was entirely predictable, but to Ted seeing a second bear seemed as implausible as lightning striking the same place twice. This one was larger, around 350 pounds, and wore a red tracking collar around its neck. The bear paused for a second, rose onto its hind legs, and sniffed the air. Its dark brown eyes locked onto Ted, each creature sizing up the other. Ted simply stood still and looked back at the bear. He felt no fear on his own part, nor aggression on the bear's. What he felt was more matter-of-fact. The bear was in the woods. Ted was in the woods. That was it.

Letting another hearty belly laugh rise, Ted felt a profound masculinity. It wasn't a violent or primal masculinity; he had not shot and killed the bear. This different kind of strength came from knowing that he could coexist with a bear and the bear could coexist with him. They both belonged on the earth and could respect each other's right to be on the trail without wanting to destroy each other. The bear went downhill, and Ted and Argo kept trudging uphill, putting one foot in front of the other.

Ted spent the next few hours slowly gaining elevation. Just before five o'clock he reached an intersection and turned onto a second trail that went back to the west. According to Angel's directions, he was almost there. Ted turned left and crossed a wooden bridge by a small tarn, or pond, at the edge of an enormous meadow full of elk tracks. He was only about a quarter of a mile from the lake. There was a sign prohibiting camping near the lake, so Ted decided to pitch his tent near the tarn. His pack dropped to the ground and he walked along the edge of the water.

Fallen cedars and pines had stained the water iodine red and tall lemon-colored grasses grew around the edge. Ted noticed an area beneath the canopy of the trees where stones had been collected and used to form a fire ring. He made a note of it and continued up the trail.

Fifteen minutes later Ted reached Stewart Lake. Though ten times larger than the tarn, with less than a mile of shoreline it was not a large lake, roughly triangular and with clear, unstained water. It deserved to be photographed and put on the cover of a hiking guide, he thought. It beckoned you to find it.

Ted sat on a rock, amazed to see small fish flirting with deeper waters. He realized that he had not seen anyone on the trail the entire day. He set his backpack on the ground and tried to sift through an unusual swirl of thoughts. On the surface was a dull exhaustion—it had been a long and difficult hike—but after he peeled away the fatigue, there was more. At first he thought it was loneliness, but with Argo nearby, he realized he could be just as lonely sitting by himself in the living room of his small house in Crossing Trails. Somehow this was different.

Walking away from a barrage of societal conveniences that surround us—everything from credit cards, appliances, and utilities to fast food, hospitals, and dry cleaners—had left him bare and unprotected. All of these conveniences, and hundreds more just like them, were the twigs that formed society's protective nest. What he felt was not loneliness but isolation: he'd managed to leave the nest. As Ted pondered the seemingly endless list of things he had left behind at the base of the trail, he realized that however intimidating, it was also liberating to be on the other side of the wall that society weaves for our protection.

This isolation made him alert, observant, and independent. As he tried to make sense of it all, he got even closer to the heart of it. What he was experiencing was not simply an emotional response; it was a subtraction from his identity or sense of self. Ted realized that all the fibers of the societal nest also define us—as much as or more than we define ourselves. Outside the bounds of the social contract, he had lost the mostly useless labels and measuring sticks he used to define himself. Ted thought back to Angel at the campsite and realized he was experiencing nothing less than her second realization. *We are not what we think we are.* Who are we when all the labels are peeled away and we stand naked, stripped of our identity, in the forest?

Just as Ted had begun to come to grips with his isolation,

he was startled by the sight of a lone fly fisherman on the other side of the lake, casting slowly and deliberately. Unsure of the proper etiquette for greeting the only other human in the middle of the wilderness, Ted just waved, and the tall man gave a friendly wave back.

Ted felt a grin spread across his face. He'd made it. He felt proud of himself for completing the hike to the summit, but more than that, for the first time in a long time he was experiencing the joy and peace that come from not being the least bit self-conscious about anything. It occurred to him that here, isolated as he was, he was released not only from his former sense of identity but also from worries about conforming or in any way reacting to the myriad complex rules of interaction that form the human social contract. Outside the nest he could fart, spit, yawn, snore, pick his nose, or just lie lazily on the banks of the lake with impunity, indifferent to all the rules that not only prop us up but also wear us down. The chatter in his mind that Angel was trying to get him to observe in her meditation exercises had naturally subsided in the absence of all the ought-to's and ought-not's. He was just there—no comment or observation was necessary; no thought mattered.

Something Angel had said to him suddenly registered. He squeezed his eyes shut and watched as amoebalike figures danced across the dark screen of his eyelids. He could hear Angel's words. *The most natural place to experience the creator is in creation.* If this stillness, this peace, was, as Angel suggested, a manifestation of the creator, then this creator was a still, silent, and subtle master. Sitting on the bank of creation, watching the sun slowly descend in the early-evening sky with his dog resting beside him, gave Ted a strange sense of his own insignificance—as if he were adrift, alone in deep space or floating on a raft in an endless blue sea. This sensation, however unusual, did not diminish or depress him. On the contrary, as the sense of his own importance faded, the surrounding peace and silence of the mountains seemed to seep into and fill these empty spaces with something of substance.

About ten minutes into the practice, he began to identify with the ripples drifting over the lake. Ted felt as if he were the ripples. Or at least there was no real separation between him and the ripples. What he thought was separateness was illusion. The thought was frightening. However false or illusory his sense of self might be, he did not want to let go of it. Feeling threatened, he opened his eyes, came back to his tried-and-true reality. Ted stood, collected his pack and his dog, and headed back down the trail to his campsite.

With the contents of his pack carefully unloaded and assembled on the ground for easy access, Ted pitched his tent and then built a small campfire in the pit lined with charred stones. Opening a can of soup was difficult. Once he could twist the lid back, he rested it near the coals to warm. Argo staked out a position guarding the front door of the tent.

The evening sun collided with the distant western mountaintops, causing an explosion of purple and crimson streaks across the sky. Ted saw that the fly fisherman from the other side of the lake—or perhaps it was the world—was headed up the trail toward him, covering ground rapidly. Argo jumped up, startled, and began to bark. The fisherman was carrying a string of freshly cleaned trout in one hand and a stout walking stick in the other. When he was within fifteen feet of Ted's fire, he held up the string of trout and asked, "Ted, are you hungry?"

16

Charles Richardson was one of the youngest priests in one of New Mexico's oldest Catholic dioceses. Father Chuck knew Angel from her brief academic sojourn at the Yale School of Divinity. Since her early departure from Yale, they'd kept in touch, and he remained a trusted member of Angel's spiritual cadre—another coconut. Father Chuck's prematurely graying hair and imposing physical stature gave him a military appearance that was inconsistent with his docile nature. He was tall but all legs, so hiking up the mountain had been a breeze. The southern route he'd taken up to Stewart Lake was at least half a mile longer than the northern end of the trail loop that Ted had trekked. Father Chuck had left an hour later than Ted but had still arrived at the lake around the same time. He was way too excited about his fishing to stop and introduce himself. There would be time for that later.

When Angel had challenged him to interrupt his little retreat at the Pecos monastery to assist in Ted's transformation, he had been reluctant. Angel had pleaded, "But Chuck, you know as well as I do that the best way to help him understand the vertical levels is to also develop horizontal awareness. What better person to speak to him about Christianity than a priest? That's you!"

"Angel, there's one problem," Father Chuck had responded. "Personal journeys are sometimes, well, personal. Does he want my help?"

"He's asked about you several times. You have such a solid understanding of Jesus. You'll do much better than I ever could." He didn't answer, so she applied a bit more pressure. "Chuck, is it not your job to transform souls?"

Being heavily under the influence of a love of fly-fishing, he conceded, "Perhaps."

"Then just get up here to Stewart Lake and teach Ted a little about fly-fishing and Jesus. How hard can that be?"

Reasonably skilled at shunning most earthly pleasures, Chuck considered fly-fishing a godly gift. He paused, then asked, "What time do you want me there?"

"Tomorrow, by early evening. And Chuck, if he has questions . . ."

"Don't worry, Angel."

Ted stared at the strangely clad, bearded man holding a string of fish. It was puzzling. His presence hinted at something, but Ted wasn't sure what it might be. The fisherman's calm countenance and accepting smile were disarming. Not knowing what else to do, Ted stuck out his hand and stammered, "Ted Day."

"Oh, I'm sorry." Chuck hung the line of fish on a tree branch, removed his backpack, and said, "I'm Angel's friend,

Father Chuck." When Ted stared at him blankly, Father Chuck went on, "She did tell you about me, right?"

Ted breathed a sigh of relief. The strange mountain man was not a stranger after all. "Well, she did mention that we were going to meet at some point. I'm just surprised that it was up here."

Father Chuck sat down on a boulder next to their campsite. "It's a good place to learn how to fly-fish. She asked me to take a few hours tomorrow morning and give you a little introduction to the sport. Are you up to it?"

"I'd like to learn. I have a book, but I've never tried it."

"Well, that's why I'm here. To introduce you. Tonight we can talk about your journey with Angel . . . if you'd like."

Ted grinned. However lacking in driving skills, Angel was turning out to be a superior spiritual consultant and vacation guide. "So Angel arranged for you to teach me about fly-fishing," he mused.

"It's not that hard. I can show you." Father Chuck dug in his pack and started to pull out his cooking gear. "The great thing is . . . it's not really teaching; it's just showing . . . . All the while, we get to fish and talk about things that really matter in the world. Not a bad deal for either of us, hey?" Father Chuck removed from his pack and tossed Ted his old rod and reel. "Check it out. In the meantime I better get these cooking and my tent unpacked."

Ted and Father Chuck ate their fill of trout. Argo waited patiently as Ted carefully separated a few tasty morsels from the bones and added them to his dog chow. With Argo fed,

Ted found his little flashlight, made his way to the shore of the tarn, tossed the fish bones out of Argo's reach, and cleaned up their plastic dishes.

With the sun now set, the temperature had plummeted and the fire felt good. Father Chuck unfolded a small tarp, slipped on some blue jeans, and pulled a deck of cards from his pack. He asked Ted, "Do you like gin rummy?"

"Sure." In fact, Ted thought he was a pretty good gin rummy player. Maybe, he thought to himself, on this subject he could be the teacher.

Father Chuck spread the tarp close to the fire where the dancing flames cast the strongest light. "Good. Let's play cards and you can tell me about your work with Angel and your hike up the mountain. Did you see anything interesting?" the priest asked, settling down on the tarp and shuffling the cards. He motioned to Ted. "Sit down, Ted, and relax."

"I saw two bears," Ted said proudly as he got situated on the ground with Argo beside him.

"Really? That's a bit unusual. How did your dog handle it?"

"The first one freaked him out a bit; fortunately, he didn't seem to notice the second one. It was probably upwind. The hike wore us out." Ted hesitated and then finished, "It was harder than I thought."

"It's one of my favorite hikes, but it isn't easy." Chuck picked up a king of diamonds from the discard pile. "Angel said you might want to ask me some questions. Did she mean you needed gin rummy tips?"

"No, I don't think that's what she meant, but if I need a

few pointers, I'll let you know." Ted drew his own card and, pleased with his pick, kept it and discarded another from his hand. "My questions are more along spiritual lines—she designated you as the official spokesperson for Christianity."

The young priest saw no reason to debate the point, but he hardly felt qualified to be the spokesperson for the nearly one third of the planet's population who considered themselves to be Christians. "Fire away and I'll do my best." Father Chuck flipped the king of spades onto the discard pile.

Knowing now that Chuck was not likely making a spades run, Ted quickly discarded his queen of spades. "I appreciate your help. To be honest, though, the whole church scene . . . It just, well . . . It hasn't really worked for me. I've tried a few different denominations, but they keep saying—'preaching' I guess is the better word—things that seem implausible at best and downright misleading or even untruthful at worst. Angel told me maybe it's not so much a case of 'I don't get it' as a case of 'I don't need it.' What do you think, Chuck? Is she right?"

Father Chuck pondered a moment longer than Ted thought necessary, leaving him unsure if the priest's intent focus was on the question or his cards. Instead of drawing, he picked up Ted's queen from the discard pile and replaced it with his own nine of clubs. "All right, Ted, I'll do the best I can to answer your questions. Actually, I don't totally agree. Let me rework a Buddhist parable for you, modernize it to suit our place in time."

"If you can play gin rummy and preach at the same time, give it a go."

"Here is how I see it." Father Chuck peered over the top of his cards. "The Buddha had this much right: we're all on the rocky and barren shore and want to get to the verdant, distant side of the lake." He glanced down at his hand a moment before continuing. "Unlike ancient India, we now have many, many different boats to choose from. For a reasonable fee there are boat companies that promise to take us across the lake in their own vessels, to do the work so we don't have to do it ourselves. We must only sit and put our trust in them. Their captains make optimistic promises about smooth sailing. Their marketing literature is slick. We stand on the shore today in a carnival atmosphere, with giant tents, neon signs, tweets, and Facebook pages. The boat promotion has been so successful that most travelers seem content to pay for the privilege of climbing in the boats and pretending to sail. If you're able to get past the fanfare and look out over the lake, it's pretty rare to see boats actually sailing."

"If you're saying that religion emphasizes the boat and neglects the journey, where did things go wrong?"

Father Chuck arranged the cards in his hand by suit before returning to Ted's question. "Let's start with Jesus. He is part truth, part legend, part myth, and part metaphor. The traditional focus of Christianity is on his divinity. He was the best boat captain that ever lived. For many of us, however, it's his humanity that inspires us. You, me, all of us mortals— have the potential to achieve a fuller and better life. Jesus was trying to show us how to row our own boats across the lake. Most of us just aren't there yet. In fact, we're a long way off and employing the wrong methods. If Jesus were standing beside us on the shore of the barren side of the lake, he wouldn't be promoting the Jesus boat or questioning the seaworthiness of the Muhammad boat. His only concern would be getting us to other side. He called the other shore the Kingdom."

"Are you questioning Christ's divinity?"

Father Chuck leaned over and dug his hands into Argo's warm fur. The terrier let out a little yawn. "This sure is a good dog," he remarked, then returned his attention to Ted. "Well, some people would certainly answer your question differently than I did. I don't deny Christ's divinity; I just don't deny yours, either. Not just saints and saviors make it to the Kingdom."

Ted laid down a two of hearts and declared, "Gin!"

"Rats. I was just a king away."

Ted shuffled the deck and dealt another hand. "What do you mean by Jesus's humanity?"

"Good question—that is what I like to talk about."

Father Chuck scooted closer to the fire pit so he could better see his cards. "Over the last century or so Jesus scholars have come to realize that this man was up to something incredible. Has Angel told you about her third realization?"

"I've got a general idea—in our lifetimes we have the potential to progress through multiples levels of awareness."

"When we go back to the earliest versions of the Jesus story, when we try harder to get the translations right, toss out what was probably added by the early church fathers, and focus on what was there from the beginning, one thing jumps out. Jesus wanted us off that shore, moving to the other side."

"You're saying Jesus recognized the third realization?"

"Of course, he wouldn't have used those words, but his teachings focus on this need to journey and grow."

Hoping Chuck would lay down a king, Ted added, "Angel said that Jesus had the ability to resonate with spiritual first graders through sixth graders and move us all farther across the spiritual lake."

"Angel and I both believe that the ego is mud gathering on the window of our divinity. The spiritual journey is engaging in a process to clear away the grime that blinds us so we can see the way. Jesus recognized that what primarily stands between us and God is our thinking, knowing, small self. This is why his life remains relevant and still inspires me today."

Ted reflected for a moment and had a troubling thought. "Chuck, if Jesus was all about helping us mature spiritually, why are you the first person to tell me this? Why is so much of Christianity focused on his divinity and not his humanity?"

"To sell boat tickets, religion has historically not always played fair. Sometimes it creates an unhealthy codependency. Let me give you one example that occurs in numerous places. Let's take the word 'repent.' We hear Christians use that word a lot to explain what they believe to be a fundamental aspect of their faith. What does that word mean to you, Ted?"

Ted was pretty sure on this one. "As best I can tell, I think it means that we're basically sinners and we need to believe in Jesus. Otherwise we rot in hell."

"Sadly, that does seem to be the message. We're all sinners, broken souls, and we'd better purchase a ticket on the Jesus boat or the Muhammad boat or the Buddha boat. Otherwise we're out of luck."

"Sounds familiar," Ted concurred.

"If by 'sinners' they meant that we are all stuck on the shore of our ego minds, living out our lives at the lower levels of awareness, they would get no argument from me."

"You're saying sin might just be a clumsy way of describing the first realization—we're all asleep on the shore needing to wake up and journey across the lake."

"Yes. This is why I chose the word 'repent' to make the point about religion's too-frequent sleight of hand. The Greek word from which the English word 'repent' was translated is *metanoia*. The literal translation is to reach 'beyond the mind' or 'into the larger mind.'* Do you think 'repent' is a very good translation for *metanoia*?" Father Chuck asked.

"Awful, I'd say. 'Transformation' would be much better." Ted had quickly gotten the point and had to admit he was a little surprised. It was profound and so far outside of what he'd expected that he felt the need to repeat it. "You're saying that Jesus was trying to encourage us to evolve our conscious-

---

* For an excellent and more in-depth discussion of the divergence between Jesus's message and the current state of Christianity, see Cynthia Bourgeault, *The Wisdom Jesus: Transforming Heart and Mind—A New Perspective on Christ and His Message* (Boston: Shambhala, 2008).

ness, to row our own boat, while religion has too often been delivering an entirely different message: that we should seek refuge in their boat."

Father Chuck shrugged. "That's it and why I am so excited to be a priest. I want to help people like you get back to rowing and quit fixating on the boat. *The Jesus boat was built with virgin timbers. The Buddha boat travels a straight course.* None of this matters. Jesus was offering a simple but extremely powerful spiritual equation for rowing. It makes E equals MC squared seem rather puny. As a priest, this is what I want to share."

"I'd love to hear the formula."

"Are you familiar with the mathematical arrow signs for 'less than' and 'more than'?" Chuck shaped his index finger and thumb into the sign for "less than": < .

Ted shrugged quizzically and said, "Sure."

Using the arrow sign, Father Chuck provided the bedrock formula that he believed Jesus offered for all of our spiritual growth. He took a branch from the fire and drew the formula in the soft earth using thick, strong strokes:

$$< \text{self} = > \text{God}$$

Then he translated the symbols aloud. "Less self equals more God."

Ted pondered the equation for a moment, smiled, held up his fingers in a sideways V shape, like a peace sign taking a nap, and said with enthusiasm, "I like your formula. Math always came naturally to me."

Father Chuck continued, "Jesus carried this equation to its logical conclusion. When he lost all sense of self, he became truly the son of God, or even God, a distinction in terminology that has been troubling the church from its very beginning."

Ted took the stick and drew the following formula by the campfire:

$$\sim \text{self} = {}^{\wedge}\text{God}$$

Chuck studied it for a moment and grinned. "Aristotle would have been proud. No self equals the most possible God."

After pondering the statistical probability of drawing the nine of hearts, Ted asked Father Chuck, "I get the math, the logic, but how do we get less self and more God into our lives?"

"The Christian mystics, like all mystics, believe that God exists within all things and is part of us, inseparable, and that through meditation or prayer we (the self) need only get out of the way—so to speak—to access God, to become Christ-like or maybe even God-like. The mystics abandon the dualistic way of seeing God as separate and up and out there somewhere."* Chuck pointed to the night sky crammed with stars. Then he pointed to his heart and head and concluded, "Instead, they look in here."

---

* Father Chuck could hardly put down a book by Richard Rohr, a Franciscan friar and Catholic priest who also lived in New Mexico. Rohr writes brilliantly on this subject: *The Naked Now: Learning to See as the Mystics See* (New York: Crossroad, 2008).

What Chuck said triggered a palpable sense of relief in Ted. The tension in his shoulders subsided. For the first time, he was not excluded from religion, left on the outside looking in. Instinctively, he had resisted buying into a destructive and misguided message about his own sinful nature. Seeing God as not "out there" but part of him and all things made him worthy and integrated, not unworthy or cast out. It gave him a sense of hope. Maybe Ted and religion were not oil and water.

Ted leaned back and with all the concentration he could muster said, "All right, I get it. Our psyches or our souls are like glass laboratory beakers. If you fill the glass up with water, or self, then there is no space left for air, or God. True spiritual growth is an emptying process."

"You've got it, Ted Day! We must work on fostering and allowing the God within us, our higher self, to expand. Our journey is not to find Jesus's divinity but our own."

Ted laid down another card and again declared, "Gin."

Father Chuck was not used to losing at this rate, but still he deftly shuffled the cards. He was enjoying Angel's student. Ted was a quick study.

"So how do I shed the self?" Ted asked.

"You get in a boat that's actually going to leave the shore, cast off, and learn how to row. We call it the Work. Angel and some of our other friends will help you. You and I have a far simpler task."

Deciding to go a new direction with the cards, Ted rearranged his hand before asking, "What's that, Chuck?"

"We're going to sit beneath the stars, play cards by the fire, get a great night's sleep in the mountain air, get up with the morning sun, and then, my friend, to top it all off, we're going trout fishing in paradise. You see, Ted, sometimes good rowing is just good living."

"It's that easy?" Ted asked.

"Does a rose have to work hard to bloom?"

"Not likely."

"Should we care if it tilts to the left or tilts to the right?"

"No concern of mine."

"What do you expect from a rosebud?"

Ted thought about it and answered, "To bloom?"

"To realize its potential. That's the crux of learning how to row, doing the Work. That's why Angel wanted you to climb the mountain. From where you and I are sitting, doing life right may start to look different."

Ted liked the message. "Thanks."

Father Chuck drew the ace he needed, laid down his cards, and for the first time that night said, "Gin."

17

Father Chuck gathered about twelve feet of the leader from the reel in his left hand while he raised the rod to a vertical position with his right. When the rod was at the apex of its arc, he brought it forward. He repeated the motion several times, whipping the line back and forth, until he had the entire leader fully engaged in the cast, then took his thumb off the leader and let it whip the nearly invisible microfilament line, carrying the small fly through the air to flutter and land on the surface of Stewart Lake. It took several attempts, but Ted performed a similar motion and to his delight experienced a similar result.

Argo sat and watched patiently. Twenty minutes in, the process took an interesting turn. Ted moved from practicing fly-fishing to fly-fishing. He caught his first fish.

While Father Chuck gave Ted a crash course on fly-fishing and further discussed Christianity, Angel drove down the mountain several miles to a small camp store and purchased a few groceries. She put away her groceries and drove a bit further down the mountain to a secluded place on the river, where she parked Bertha the Bookmobile, washed some of her clothes, and bathed in an icy-cold pool of water from the Pecos River while No Barks stood watch. With her hair shampooed, Angel felt invigorated. She was resting for a moment on a boulder with her feet dangling into the cold water when a slight movement fifty yards upstream caught her eye. She sat perfectly still and watched as two does and a fawn moved into the water. She closed her eyes and imagined herself moving with them. When she opened her eyes, they had disappeared.

Angel dried off and pulled on a warm sweatshirt, found her cell phone, and called her father. He had left two messages and she knew he would worry if she did not call him back.

When Larsen answered, Angel said, "*Age*, it's Angel."

"I was worried. Where are you?"

"I'm on the Pecos. It's very beautiful and it makes me think of our time together fishing on the Cheyenne. I've been out of coverage for a few days or I would have called sooner."

Larson had steeled himself against many losses in his life, but no matter how hard he tried, he worried too much. Angel's loving presence on the phone, instead of the lingering pain of her absence, brought small tears of joy to the rims of his eyes. He said, "It does me good to hear your voice."

"*Age*, I wish you were here with me. I have good news."

"Tell me."

"I have my first client. He's a lawyer from Crossing Trails, Kansas." She then carefully found a way to suggest to her father that there was not yet any intimacy between them. "He has the white man's disease, but there is hope for him."

Larsen preferred to avoid the subject of white men. "How is Bertha the Bookmobile and your Aunt Lilly's dog, No Barks? Do they like this pilgrimage?"

"They are both fine. Did you know that Bertha only has eighty-five thousand miles on her? She's practically new."

"Yes, but I want to talk to you about something else," Larsen answered. "I went to Pierre to visit your Aunt Lilly at the girl jail."

"How is she?" Angel asked.

"I think she is good. They take good care of her. She has a doctor. I spoke with him. It may be that your Aunt Lilly is crazy, and maybe not so crazy. She spoke of missing No Barks. She thinks that I need a dog too. She also said something about Bertha that I want to share with you."

"Yes?" Angel asked.

"On the floor, near the back, there is a bolt that sticks up slightly above the floor."

"Yes, I've sat on it accidentally, and it is not comfortable."

"Get a wrench and remove the bolt. When you do so, a piece of the floor will lift out. Under the floor, Aunt Lilly told me that she kept things she did not want to share with your uncle Harry. She said that he tried to take things from her. There may be nothing in this space but wolf shit. I do not know for sure, but perhaps you should look into it. If there are weapons in it—unless you need them to protect you from the broken white man you are trying to help—you might want to throw them away."

It made sense to Angel that her aunt would have had a secure place for important things. She had been reluctant to explore the dark recesses of Bertha and had not been interested in unlocking the small librarian's desk. Besides, there was no key. Even though her aunt had gifted Bertha to her father, snooping still seemed like an invasion of Aunt Lilly's privacy. Larsen had generally cleaned up the interior and Angel—not being a picky housekeeper—left the rest alone. "Do you think Aunt Lilly will mind if I open it?"

"I don't think she would have told me about this space if she did not want you to look into it."

Larsen did not want to meddle in his daughter's life, but he felt it prudent to ask one more thing. "Tell me more about this man from Kansas."

"*Age*, you need not worry. Ted is a smart and kind man. He has promised to help us look into Aunt Lilly's case. To help if he can. He has a dog too. No Barks even likes Ted."

"No Barks does not like men."

"Well, he likes Ted."

Larsen thought a moment and decided that this was a good sign, which gave him a sense of relief. "Angel, I'm proud of you. Many men have daughters, but only mine wants to heal men's souls." He felt the tears gather again. He wished his daughter would return, but he also knew that she had important work to do. "I will say a prayer for you to *Wakan Tanka* so that you walk along the right and red road."

"*Age*, don't worry. We may be heading home soon to help Aunt Lilly."

"Good, I look forward to seeing you and this Ted." Larsen hung up. To say good-bye would have been to acknowledge the end of a conversation that he prayed would continue for many years to come. He returned his attention to an old rusted Camry with over three hundred thousand miles on it, contemplating whether the transmission could be rebuilt for the $127 that Martha Walks Lightly had offered him from the jar she kept near her refrigerator. It was enough.

Larsen believed that whatever task *Wakan Tanka* assigned him was a good task. How much he was paid was an entirely separate issue. He raised the car on the lift and began to remove, one at a time, the bolts that secured the transmission to the engine block. Maybe Aunt Lilly was right. Perhaps, with his wife and children all absent, he needed a dog. There was a horrific dog problem on the reservation. Perhaps he could take in one of the hungry strays that wandered about abandoned. One dog, one car transmission, one soul, one planet: Larsen knew that in some ways it was all the same thing.

Even blistered and sore, coming down the mountain was easy for the two hikers. Six hours up was only three hours down. They met Angel in time for a late lunch of trout, two of which Ted could claim as his own. No Barks worked the edges of the Pecos River as it twisted and turned near their campsite.

Argo did not join her but instead rested in Bertha, exhausted from the hike.

Angel said very little while the two men ate, talked, and recounted their exploits. After wiping his mouth with a paper towel, Father Chuck said, "If I don't get going, I'm going to be late for vespers."

Chuck stood up and pulled his car key from his pocket. Angel leaned over and placed a warm kiss on his cheek. "Thank you, Chuck."

Ted felt very grateful for Father Chuck's willingness to share his knowledge of religion and fly-fishing. Suddenly wishing he were one of those men who gave hugs, Ted said, "I've never met anyone quite like you, Father Chuck. You've inspired me." He made the sideways peace sign and said, "Metanoia."

Chuck smiled and realized that, like Angel, he found doing the Work with someone like Ted gratifying; it was what had called him to the priesthood in the first place. He glanced at Angel and said, "May a rich life rest ahead for you both. God bless."

Ted wondered why he hadn't met more people like Father Chuck in his life. The priest returned to his rusted car, pulled the creaky door shut, and drove away. As Ted watched the dust settle on the gravel road that led back down the mountain, he concluded that Father Chuck had helped to usher in a miracle of sorts—three excellent vacation days in a row.

18

Sitting cross-legged in the driver's seat of Bertha, Angel quietly meditated. Ted did his best to get comfortable on the hard, metal floor, nestled between the two dogs. With very limited success, he was trying to read the Koran by flashlight.

The key to Angel's mediation practice was not to cease all mental activity, a virtual impossibility, but simply to give no energy to the chatter of the critical mind—the knowing, right-and-wrong, labeling, time-bound activity of the left hemisphere—and to unfetter and engage the open light of the right-hemispherical awareness. Tonight this was proving difficult. Her mind wandered and she found herself making plans.

Tomorrow they would get up, drive down the mountain, and continue their discussion of the third realization and the six levels of spiritual growth. They would talk while traveling through Pecos and Santa Fe and then on to Taos to meet Mashid.

Angel felt a little surge of anxiety. Much as she respected her, she was not always comfortable around Mashid. She had been able to do what Angel had not: find a way to wed spiritual teaching with real-world economic survival. Mashid was not a vagabond traversing America in a worn-out bookmobile trusting that she would find clients. Mashid was grounded. She had a following, an audience, and a career—people bought her books and attended her retreats.

The hard critic within leveled accusations of Angel's unworthiness. She breathed deeply and invited the critic to roost elsewhere. She whispered, *Leave. No one asked you for your opinion*, and tried to return stillness to her mind.

Ted turned off the flashlight, pulled Argo closer, closed his eyes, and ran his fingers through his dog's scruffy fur. Argo had a bottomless reservoir of affection for Ted.

As tired as he was, Ted suspected that he would have a difficult time falling asleep on the hard floor of the bookmobile. He again found himself situated on that pesky bolt that protruded from the floor, and he shifted away from it. Ted's mind was electric and energized. Angel and Chuck had introduced to him more new thoughts and experiences in the last twenty-four hours than he had experienced in the previous thirty years. He felt like a young boy marveling at the number of packages beneath the Christmas tree—each with a carefully written label: *To: Ted, From: Angel and Chuck.*

Fly-fishing, new friendships, profound teachings, bears, and backpacking: it was all almost overwhelming. Even more remarkable, it had happened while on vacation.

Even hours later, with the lights long off and the night half over, though exhausted, he was simply too stimulated to sleep. Staring at the long, curved shape beneath the covers,

Ted wondered what kind of woman dwelled in the marrow of Angel Two Sparrow. She was intriguing, but was she kind, loyal, and supportive? Would she be a good life companion, a nurturing mother? Was she the kind of woman who could survive in Crossing Trails, Kansas? Or, like the last one, would she grow bored and yearn for her own Thor?

It might be unsafe to let Angel into his life, smarter to draw a boundary: student and teacher. Soon enough, like all vacations, this one would end and he would return to Crossing Trails. Infatuation and one-sided admiration were a dangerous foundation for a relationship.

Good partnerships are built with equals. Helping Aunt Lilly was the only thing Angel was asking of him. It was the logical place for him to shine in her eyes and find some balance in their relationship.

Though it was late, Ted could not hear the measured breathing of sleep and wondered if Angel was still awake. Perhaps he should try to mention Lilly now. But listening more intently, he realized that Angel was making little puffing sounds. She was asleep. It could wait.

That wolf, No Barks, was nestled in beside her—a position he would prefer to occupy himself. He wanted to maneuver his way around the wolf and get slightly closer to Angel, hoping that somehow in the night she might *accidentally* wake up in his arms. He didn't want to make it obvious, but if fate had that in store for him, he would help it along. With each repositioning, he simply found himself closer to No Barks. He reached out and placed his hand on her paw. The wolf gently turned and licked his hand. Ted took her paw and rubbed it gently. He felt surprisingly content lying on the floor of an old bookmobile with insomnia.

Soon Ted's breathing synchronized with the wolf's and he fell into a thick, deep sleep and began to dream. The stark colors were absent, but the shapes and forms were better defined and the perspective seemed more accurate than in his normal dreaming state, as if the lens of his dream had moved from close-up to wide angle. No Barks and Argo were sitting on top of a grave—guardians on a lonely vigil. It was dark. Life and death were coming and going with peaceful indifference, like the movement of clock hands. Then something upsetting happened in the dream and Ted woke in a fright, startling both dogs. Argo scooted closer to Ted so they could comfort each other. Lying there on the floor, Ted felt an extraordinary sadness. He shuddered as a cold chill came over him.

It was not the action of the dream that had frightened him. There was no bogeyman chasing him across a dark cemetery. The terrifying moment had been a sensation, premature but plausible. He had experienced just for an instant the feeling that comes right before death—when there is no turning back, no second chances; when one knows this will be the last breath drawn. It was Ted Day in the deeply dug grave. And the feeling in the dream had been that his life was over.

The wolf had also situated herself closer to Ted. He wanted to thank the two dogs for their graveside vigil. He reached over and draped his arm on No Barks's shoulder and tried to fall back asleep, wondering what the dream might mean.

For breakfast Angel and Ted ate some of the granola bars and fruit she had purchased the day before. Ted casually mentioned a preference for pancakes, bacon, orange juice, and coffee. "Ted," Angel responded, "Bertha is no diner, but I know a great place in Santa Fe. Eat the fruit now, clog your arteries later."

Once they had broken camp and were heading down the mountain toward Pecos, Ted tried to call his office to check for messages—not that he expected any of importance. Each time, the service was poor and he was not able to complete the call.

When they got within a few miles of Pecos, two bars magically appeared on his cell phone and a little bell indicated that messages were waiting to be retrieved. Ted apologetically justified returning the calls. "Even Mr. Digit has to eat and pay his rent."

After Ted set the phone down, Angel asked, "Any new cases?"

"A crowded school bus full of darling kindergartners was hit by a carload of drunk neurosurgeons on vacation from New York City. Should be a ten-million-dollar fee. Another normal day in Crossing Trails."

"You are kidding, right?"

"Yes, I was kidding. Not much going on."

"So you can enjoy your vacation?"

"I can and will."

"With this little slowdown, maybe you'll have time to check into Aunt Lilly's case."

Ted nodded slightly but said nothing. He was still feeling a bit gloomy from a poor night's sleep and a disturbing dream.

Angel glanced at him and asked, "Is there a problem?"

"I will do what I can for Lilly, but you need to know that the criminal justice system is a bit like a freight train."

"How so?"

"No matter how much you spit at it, you rarely change its course."

"So don't spit at it. Change tracks. Can't you do that?"

"It's unlikely. Your aunt shot him. Self-defense is going to be difficult when there is no evidence that he was threatening her at the time of the shooting."

"What if he threatened her in the past and this made her afraid of him?" Angel asked.

"I thought about that too. I don't know. That would make more sense if he was inside Bertha, but from what you've told me, the police found his body thirty yards away. She had a lot of options, like just shutting and locking the door or firing a warning shot. Self-defense justifies lethal force only as a last resort."

Aunt Lilly's situation seemed desperate and Angel had no idea how to help her. "Will you come with me to South Dakota and visit Aunt Lilly? Hear her side? Maybe there's something there we're all missing. It's only a day's drive out of our way. It would mean a lot to me and my dad, and to Aunt Lilly too."

Ted wanted to hold up his end of the bargain and repay in some small way the kindness that Angel had shown him. "Of course we can do that."

Angel reached out and brushed her fingers across Ted's hand before giving it a gentle squeeze. "Thank you, Ted. I know my aunt Lilly is different, but I never thought of her as being violent or anything but a kind spirit. If she were evil, Bertha would not be such a fine dream catcher."

There were a hundred reasons why he might not be able to help Aunt Lilly, but Angel was right about one thing: there was no risk in simply listening to the woman's story. Ted leaned down from the passenger seat and pulled Argo closer to him. He felt a surge of something positive flow from his furry friend and into his very being. It was a sense of content-ment in the now and a lapsing of concern over the tomorrows of his life. "Truth is, Angel, I'd be very pleased to help your aunt Lilly. I'm looking forward to it. Head to South Dakota as soon as you're ready."

"Good, Ted. You just relax while I drive. We'll start north, but we have a few stops to make along the way."

Ted closed his eyes and worked on several of the breathing and sensing exercises that Angel had demonstrated to him, but he found his mind returning to Aunt Lilly. Angel had mentioned that Uncle Harry might have been abusive to her aunt in the past. Ted would have to do some research, but perhaps Angel was right; this might have justified a height-ened sense of concern on her part. It was a long shot, but maybe he could put another spin on Lilly's dream the night before the shooting. Perhaps everyone was missing the point. Lilly's dream was not evidence of a future, unrealized threat but evidence of her state of mind at the time. She had been anxious, perhaps even terrified of the man, and that had been the impetus for the dream. Had she been terrorized to the point of having nightmares? The question hinged on whether Uncle Harry had put her in this state of mind, or whether she was simply delusional.

After Ted finished his last bite of bacon and eggs at the Santa Fe diner, he was prepared to concede Angel's argument that The Pantry served the best breakfast in the Southwest. He paid the bill with his credit card and strolled about inspecting the art and photographs on the walls before they got back on the road. Their next destination was Taos to meet Mashid.

Once they were situated in Bertha's front seats, with their old lap belts secured, Angel headed east on Cerrillos Road. After they reached the mountains, she asked Ted, "Are you ready to get to work? Before you meet Mashid, I want to get you started on the grades or levels of awareness."

Ted watched the Rio Grande rush down the mountainside bringing life to the arid land. He wondered what kinds of people had populated the area over the last few millennia.

When Ted returned his gaze to her, Angel continued. "The first three levels of spiritual development have a common theme. These worshipers are looking to religion for comfort and to protect them from the frightening and painful aspects of our human existence—primarily our anxiety over loneliness and death. So levels one through three are about assuaging our fears. The next three levels of development are generally more concerned with experiencing life fully, finding the divinity within, moving away from fear and toward love, and fully respecting the truth in our lives—even when it's painful or uncomfortable."

"Makes sense. I'm ready now."

"Good. Let's start with the first grade."

"There were a few problems with the first grade on the last go-round in Moline, where I grew up. I wore thick glasses and was teased unmercifully."

"The first-grade worshiper is dependent, not yet separated and individuated from her parent-God figure. For people at this level, God is primarily a creature of their own imagination. Their god is the God that atheists say does not exist."

"It sounds like you're describing religious development as being part and parcel of garden-variety human development. The first grader sounds very childlike."

"Bingo. Most people do mature and develop beyond the first grade, but for reasons we will later discuss, some people get developmentally stuck at this level. First graders see God as a parent figure and in very human terms. God is simply a smarter, faster version of themselves. God shares their beliefs, feelings, and prejudices. It's a buddy God founded in a personal and intimate relationship of 'You validate me and I'll validate you.' Anything different from me is not God-like, including different races, religions, or even sexual orientations."

"Not very tolerant."

"Not at all. Crusades, inquisitions, jihads, and witch burnings are all justified in God's name. The first-grade worshippers simply project their own fears onto something they call God. First-grader religion is magical. You want a new car, a nose job, or a treadmill? Just pray and God will deliver. Misbehave and you're a pillar of salt."

"The evening news would suggest that most of the world is stuck in this place."

"Bad behavior gets the most coverage. Most of us move beyond first-grade thinking quite naturally by the time we reach adolescence. We quit praying to God to give us what we want, if for no other reason than we eventually figure out that it doesn't work. At the upper grades, God is a force of love indiscriminately available to all of us and is no longer the personal shopper for the worthy alone. This is what Jesus may have meant in Matthew when he said that God allows the rain to fall and the sun to shine the same way on both the good and the evil."

"Why do you say 'most' but not 'all' worshipers move beyond the first grade?" Ted asked.

"To move up to the next level, the second grade, you need appropriate modeling; otherwise there won't be progress. Certain kinds of learning simply have to be modeled. Spiritual development falls into this category. No one could begin to explain the hundreds of complex movements that go into walking. You have to see it to get it. Likewise, to move us along the transformative path to the upper levels we need spiritual consultants—if not our parents, then others."

Ted considered the concept a bit further and said, "I never bought the cozy notion that some magical power was going to meet my needs, so I won't have to work at letting go of this first-grade worldview."

"Ted, there's nothing first-grade about your thinking. Nonetheless, let me make sure you understand first-grade thinking before we move on to the second-grade worldview. First graders are generally unable to grasp symbolic thinking; they tend toward literalism and fundamentalism. The first-grade deities behave like we do, although they're typically slightly better looking. Hence we have jealous, angry, and even horny gods. The first-grader controls the deity with very childlike manipulations. *If I whine (pray), I'll get what I want, including the grand prize.*"

"The grand prize?" Ted asked.

"Something called *me* must exist; for after all, something called *God* created *me.*"

Ted swallowed some of his bottled water and said, "It seems like this is going back to the second realization: we tend to be unsophisticated in how we define ourselves and God."

"Exactly, and that very imprecision is another hallmark of first-grade thinking. You get it, so let me introduce the next grade to you."

Ted sat up, somewhat proud that he was graduating to second grade, and asked, "Do I get a diploma?"

"Not yet."

"A graduation dance?"

Angel rested her hand on Ted's forearm. "I'm afraid not." She pulled her hand away and continued down the road, keeping an eye out for fuel. "If the first grader is mired in magical thinking, the second grader is defined by mythical thinking. Strong 'others' will come to her rescue. The first grader will cover her own eyes and think that if she can't see you, you can't see her. She is simply too self-centered to believe that anything could exist independent of her."

"I'm seeing some of my clients in a whole new light."

"The second grader, however, evolves and comes to understand that she is not at the center of the universe, not omnipotent, not in total control of all other beings, and certainly not God. She is not capable of moving mountains with her thoughts like a Jedi knight. She has individuated to the point where she can differentiate herself from others and grasp the limitations of that equation. Her crying, whining, or praying is not likely to change the universe. She can no longer deny that this just doesn't work. But the notion is still so compelling that she does not quite want to let go of it. A slight evolution in thinking occurs, and the first strand of the ego's coiled rope begins to unravel. It's like this, Ted. Maybe she can retain that control over her life she so desperately seeks in a roundabout way."

"Sneaky, those second graders."

"As she differentiates more fully, perhaps these newfound 'others' in her universe could do the magic for her?"

As Angel reached an intersection where she needed to turn, Ted continued the thought. "It's logical. The child soon learns that her crying per se does not magically cause food to appear, but the effect of the crying on her mother results in a meal. She needs a strong intervening force to meet her needs.

"Hence, the hallmark of the second grader is the fixation on intervening powerful surrogates that have the magical powers that she now painfully recognizes she does not possess. So with the second grader we get angels, Santa Claus, fairies, elves, saints, Easter bunnies, dragons, leprechauns, saviors, and messiahs, to name just a few. The second-grade worldview is incrementally wiser and more evolved."

"What prompts her to let go?" Ted asked.

"There is always a natural tension between the ego's desire to keep us unchanged and our higher self's desire to become more closely aligned with the universe, God, or our true essence—the world beyond Mr. Digit. It's always a difficult transition, but this one is actually much easier than the levels that follow, for one very important reason: society, our parents, and our peers demand it of us. You see, Ted, our society and our religions, in general, encourage us to let go of the magical first grade and move on to the mythical second grade. What makes the subsequent transitions more difficult is that we lose that support and, in fact, the opposite occurs: we encounter resistance from the very people and institutions that should be encouraging our spiritual growth. For after all, why would the mythic helpers want to be out of a job? Some of

God's agents prefer virgins tossed in the volcano; others will settle for a healthy tithe."

"I'm opting for the tithe. So is that where we find mainstream Christianity and Islam—at the first two grade levels?" Ted asked.

"Most religions have a tough grip on this second-grade worldview. We find these notions very comforting, and therefore it is hard to let go of them or even tolerate other people's movement to higher levels. The gravitational pull of the moon is nothing compared to the cultural pull of second-grader religion. Great wars are fought over designating the proper agency of God. In Islam, for example, the Shiite and the Sunni are still fighting over the proper successor to Muhammad; the winner is no less than God's agent. The early Christians fought many a bloody battle trying to define Jesus. People are willing to die to prove that they are not calling the wrong number in the sky."

"It would be nice to have a savior or a leprechaun or someone I could dial up in difficult times. It always seemed to me that no matter how many different numbers I might call, no one picked up the phone."

"Like all herd animals, fear causes humans to react quickly and impulsively and to conform to group behaviors—even when they might be illogical. If the rest of the pack runs off the cliffs for grins, then you had better pack a parachute, 'cause you're going over." Angel checked the gas gauge again. "You never had anyone modeling the second-grade mythic worldview, so it's not surprising to me that you would not spend much time in this classroom. We need to stop for gas soon."

"Are we running low?" Ted asked.

Angel looked down at her map. "Yes, we'd better get off here and fill up."

Angel cranked the old cracked, white vinyl steering wheel to the right and coasted off the exit ramp. When Bertha came to a complete stop, Ted watched Angel open the driver's-side door and get out. He was going to pump the gas for her but hesitated, instead taking in the afternoon sun, which cast an amber light over the desert.

A fog was lifting or a layer of consciousness had been peeled back. His awareness of the world and how he fit into it was subtly shifting. Although Ted could not recognize the importance of these shifts, being here with Angel, No Barks, and Argo in Bertha the Bookmobile he no longer felt strange or uncomfortable; it was nothing less than exhilarating. Ted exited, took a few hurried steps, and caught up with Angel as she stood over the gas cap. He put his hand on her shoulder. She stopped and turned toward him.

"Thanks for being my spiritual consultant—choosing me to be your student. I'm lucky you crashed into me. . . ."

A slightly embarrassed but pleased look crept across Angel's face. She squeezed his hand slightly. "I'm glad you swerved in front of me too."

19

Bertha wound her way up through the mountain passes. They flanked the Rio Grande as it coursed through the southernmost part of the Rocky Mountains—sometimes gently but more often in a fervent roar.

At the end of a self-imposed moratorium on conversation, Angel reminded Ted that among her people, the Lakota, silent spaces are valued. "There are ways to connect with everything around us without using words." She asked him to simply allow his mind to rest in the scenic beauty and to focus on his surroundings in the same way that he might try to listen to the notes of a symphony.

This particular exercise was well suited for Ted. As far as he was concerned, men and dogs are on good terms because they can be together without feeling the need to continually share words. Considering Angel's advice, he tried to expand this mode of being that he enjoyed with Argo outward and toward her and his surroundings in general.

Once Angel had a sense that Ted was settled and calm, she offered him an opportunity to expand on the exercise. "Your ears and eyes and the sensations they register in your mind are not the only way to process life. Try to register sensations that arise in your body and see them as separate and distinct from the thoughts that arise randomly in your mind. These are equally valuable communications. Try to notice the subtle sensations in your abdomen—there is much more than just digestion going on in the gut. Try also to feel into your heart spaces. Do you sense warmth—perhaps a reverberation? See if you can feel into the other discrete spaces within you where sensations might be arising. Take an inventory of the areas where sensations arise. Perhaps you can feel the right lobe of your lung, a slight pain in your left kidney, or a sense of peacefulness that seems to originate around your diaphragm. Try to feel into these spaces and be more cognizant of the biological and emotional processes that are occurring within you and around you. Sense too, if you can, your entire body—shift your focus and awareness away from these neglected spaces and then back to your body as a whole. Is your body trying to tell you anything?"

Ted found this exercise much easier than meditation. In fact, it gave him a sense of reclaiming something pleasant that had been lost—like an adult discovering a favorite childhood toy crammed in the back of the attic. He had become disconnected from a vital part of Teddy Day. When it came to bodily sensations, if it didn't hurt or feel good, it was ignored.

Angel moved on to the final part of the exercise. "Ted, you can learn to listen not only to your body's most vociferous signals but also to more subtle sensations. To gain this skill, I want you now to visualize your body as a vessel and a

warm, gentle fluid filling the empty spaces of your body, starting at the tip of your right toe and gently spreading to the
adjoining toes and into your right foot and up and into your
ankle. Sense this fluid pooling in your entire right foot, and
hold that sensation for a moment." After allowing Ted time
to let the sensations register, she continued, "Now allow the
fluid to continue to move away from your right foot and up
and into your right calf. Let it pool there for a few moments."
Angel spent the next ten minutes helping Ted to experience
the sensations within his body, directed carefully from his
toes to his cranium. When she was finished, she said, "Ted?"
When he opened his eyes and she thought she had his attention, she continued, "How do you feel right now? What is the
feeling that this exercise is evoking for you? I want you to try
to answer this question more from your body and less from
your mind."

Angel's timing was good. Ted had just asked himself the
same question. There was, therefore, no hesitation. "Angel, for
the first time in a very long time, I feel at home with myself."

"That's right, Ted, comfortable, at home. I'm very happy
for you."

The outskirts of Taos were littered with clumsy little strip
malls and fast-food restaurants, but they quickly gave way to
the far more charming historical city center. Angel found a
good parking spot for Bertha in one of the public lots not far
from the Taos Plaza. They walked the dogs in a nearby park

and grabbed a cup of coffee and a thick cookie generously studded with nuts and chocolate. When Argo and No Barks completed their sniffing and territory marking, the four of them wandered about, shopping in Taos.

Angel excused herself to call Mashid and let her know they'd arrived. She was just leaving Denver and would not be back until late that night, she said, but they were not to worry. The key to her front door was in a pot by the mailbox, so they could let themselves in. She warned that because her Earthship home was off the power grid and short on lights, it was hard to find at night, and she provided detailed directions.

Angel had done a little research on the Taos Earthships and was intrigued by the concept of homes that were crafted primarily from recycled trash and functioned off the grid with their own power and heating sources. As they window-shopped, Angel described what she knew about Mashid's home.

As the sun set over the desert, the four of them crossed the Rio Grande and watched in amazement as they came upon the compound of strange dwellings that stood on the desert floor. Ted felt like he had stumbled into a community of hobbits. The Earthships did not appear to actually be from earth.

Bertha's headlights illuminated the strange but magically playful structures. Following Mashid's instructions, they turned right on the second gravel road and then into the driveway of the darkened home on the left. They used flashlights to find the key. Once the lights were turned on, they could see that the interior was more traditional.

The kitchen space was combined with a south-facing

greenhouse filled with vegetables. The nutrient-rich gray water from the kitchen sink drained into the plant beds. Fish swam in a small concrete pond at the center of the greenhouse space. Angel found a note on the kitchen table. After reading it, she summarized for Ted. "Mashid says the bedrooms are at the end of the hall. You can have the green guest bedroom and I can have her room across the hall. She'll take the sofa when she comes home." She set the note down. "The code for her router is here if you need it."

"Sounds perfect." Ted was looking forward to a traditional bed and shower and some time on his laptop. He went back to Bertha, grabbed his pack and Argo's dog bed, and begged off for an early night. He wanted to thumb through some of the books that Angel had given him to read. But more important, he wanted to do some legal research for Aunt Lilly.

Once online, Ted searched legal databases to frame the central legal issue. He needed to know whether self-defense was based on an objective or subjective state of mind. Was it enough that Aunt Lilly *thought* Uncle Harry was going to hurt her, or did the fear have to be justified under some more objective "reasonable man" standard?

He was surprised to find that there was less law on the subject than he might have imagined. In a way, this was good. It gave defense counsel more room to argue. Open and ambiguous issues make prosecutors nervous and more inclined to offer a plea bargain. After an hour or so of research, he decided he would need a full copy of the police report, and, as Angel had suggested, he needed to interview Aunt Lilly so he could get a better understanding of the facts.

Ted got up from the small desk where he had been working, sat down on the bed, and beckoned Argo to jump up and rest beside him. He rubbed the old dog's face and asked, "What are we doing, Argo? We're in an Earthship in the middle of the desert and traveling across America with a spiritual consultant. Would Grandpa be proud of us? I'm as happy as that day I brought you home from the animal shelter. Kind of strange, isn't it?"

Ted leaned over to the bedside table and pulled the Bible from the stack of texts that Angel had suggested he read. He thought of questions that he wished he'd had the time to ask Father Chuck. Ted could almost be jealous of those who claimed to be saved and to have a personal relationship with Jesus. No one was telling him to run for president, start a church, work in a ghetto, or firebomb an abortion clinic. He wondered why Jesus or God never spoke to him. The lack of dialogue made him wonder if he was just unworthy. Maybe it was his own fault for not trying to speak to Jesus. Even if he wanted to find God or Jesus, the distinction between the two was lost on him. Where and how was he to seek such a relationship? Was the Bible just a composite of very old and very tall tales or a doorway into something profound?

Ted flipped through the pages, and a sense of awe unfurled as he read the book of James. As he read the Gospel of Mark, he was overcome by a sensation he couldn't identify. Was it physical or psychological? He closed the Good Book and laid it on his chest. He tried to put his finger on the feeling in his chest cavity. He sensed a connection with humanity.

Loneliness—to which he'd grown accustomed and which often seemed to haunt him—was absent.

Even if what Jesus said had already been said by others before him, he said it in such a convincing and beautiful way that the text left Ted feeling inspired. There was a sense of the man, Jesus, behind these words. Was he experiencing real faith, or was it something else? Was this what allowed Christianity to put so much confidence in the power of believing? Ted recalled the lesson he had learned from Father Chuck, and it occurred to him that maybe all of these questions only made sense when God was objectified and treated as something separate from himself. Perhaps these were the struggles one needed to have to move past the primary grades of spirituality that Angel had started to show him. Perhaps, he concluded as he returned the Bible to the bedside table, the answers to these questions would become clearer with time.

Ted closed his eyes, not yet sleepy enough to turn off the lights, and rested quietly for a few moments before more corporeal questions and quandaries arose.

Ted could hear Angel rustling across the hall. He had to admit he enjoyed sleeping on the floor of the bookmobile—if for no other reason than it seemed to throw him into some nominal intimacy with Angel. Ted imagined her moving about in her room, with No Barks lying on the floor patiently watching over her. He wondered if he should manufacture some excuse to knock on the door and talk with her. Perhaps just to say good night. Ted lamented that his relationship with the wolf dog was progressing faster than his relationship with the tall, dark woman. He knew how bad an idea it was to even entertain such thoughts, but he couldn't help wondering if he was becoming infatuated with Angel. Could any man spend three days with this woman—beautiful, courageous, wise—and not be smitten? After his own divorce and after handling divorces for so many clients, Ted had serious misgiving about marriage. Now here he was questioning whether it was healthy to go through life as a single man.

Ted turned off the light, shut his eyes, and tried to resist fantasies that would only set him up for disappointment. It had been a long time since he had been this close to a woman he respected and desired. He needed to savor every minute of their brief two weeks together and then get back to a healthier, saner life in Crossing Trails without her. Angel and No Barks would soon only be fading memories.

Giving up on sleep, Ted got up from the bed and sat down at the small desk, again opening his laptop. He went into his zone, drowning out uncomfortable thoughts. He went where he was good, brilliant, really. His grandfather had said Ted was the best researcher and brief writer he'd ever known.

As the night hours passed, Ted raced through cases one after another, trying out theories and piecing together the elements of Aunt Lilly's self-defense argument. He found cases from courts as far apart as Maui and Chelsea. By 2:00 a.m., Ted knew what was behind, beneath, and beside this defense. He had a very good sense of when it worked and when it failed. Without something more from Aunt Lilly, he knew, it would fail. As he suspected, the defense was firmly grounded in a reasonable-man standard. Reasonable men did not wake up from dreams and shoot people.

Ted made a complete list of his questions, the things he needed to know, and the arguments he might be able to make, with citations and cases to support them, then closed the laptop and slipped out of the lawyer zone.

20

There was a knock on the door. "Are you alive in there?"

"Barely."

"Hurry up. I want you to meet Mashid."

Ted dressed quickly. He and Argo joined Angel and No Barks at the kitchen table and the four of them waited for Mashid to emerge from the guest bathroom. Angel had showered and changed into a skirt and light blue T-shirt with a darker blue dolphin leaping over her shoulder. Her crossed legs swung back and forth as she ate a piece of toast. Ted tried to move his thoughts to their studies. "I've been thinking more about your aunt. I have some theories, but I need more information."

"That's good. We'll be in South Dakota in a few days. You can dive in then, but today let's work on the levels."

Suddenly, Angel stood, walked across the kitchen, and embraced a dark-skinned woman in a hijab and blue jeans. Ted was taken aback. This woman was strikingly beautiful. What was a woman like this doing in the desert of the American Southwest? Ted realized his jaw was hanging open and tried to close his mouth and regain his composure.

Like most of the other coconuts, Angel had known Mashid for years. Just as Father Chuck was committed to showing the true path of the Jesus ministry, Mashid worked to bring an upper-level perspective or awareness to adherents of the world's fastest-growing religion—Islam. Angel gave her friend a strong, warm hug. "How wonderful to see you again. You look radiant." Angel then pulled away and made her introduction. "Ted, I would like you to meet my friend Mashid."

Mashid held out her hand and Ted nervously accepted it. To his surprise, she playfully pulled him closer. Ted felt a glow of warmth and acceptance emanating from the young woman. In a rare moment, Ted trusted his intuition and stepped closer to give her a heartfelt embrace. He stepped back and said, "Angel has said many wonderful things about you. I love your house! It's a real pleasure to meet you."

Mashid chuckled, turned to her old friend, and said, "Angel, your first student. How exciting!"

Angel did not want to belabor the point that her traveling practice had not been a smash hit, so she kept the focus on Ted. "And he's a good one, too." Angel took them both by the hand and led them back to the kitchen table. "Let's sit and talk. We're so grateful to you for sharing your morning with us."

Ted let out three deep breaths and relaxed into a small pressed-back chair with a cane seat. He felt strangely comfortable around Angel and Mashid. A few weeks ago he would have been put off by their unconventional clothes and out-there lifestyle. But now being a student at Spirit Tech seemed *normal.* In some ways it wasn't that hard. He just listened, asked questions, and let the curriculum unfold.

"Mashid, what took you to Denver?" Angel asked.

"I was at the airport. I just got back from doing a spot on BBC One in London. Tomorrow morning I'm off to Dallas to speak at a Sufi retreat. I'm doing the Enneagram."*

Ted had never met a television personality and was impressed. "What did you do in London?" he eagerly asked.

"I was a guest on a talk show. It was about being a lesbian and a Muslim, but more than that, I spoke about tolerance and the true nature of our life's quest."

Angel hummed knowingly and Mashid continued, "Tolerance and Islam are too often estranged these days. It is part of the Islamic crisis that we were discussing on the show. My faith is being torn apart by extremists, and I maintain that it is younger Western Muslims, like myself, who must lead the charge to defend the faith from first- and second-grade fundamentalism that detracts from Islam's true message. What Father Chuck is trying to do for Christianity I want to do for Islam."

---

* Most of the coconuts found the Enneagram to be a helpful tool, particularly the Sufi members, who relied on it to better understand the peculiar aspects of each person's unique egoic personality structure. Once they better understood it, they believed, they could relax its grip so that consciousness could unfold to higher levels of awareness. Helen Palmer, *The Enneagram: Understanding Yourself and the Others in Your Life* (San Francisco: Harper, 1975).

Mashid grinned. Even she would admit that she enjoyed her role as the hip spokeswoman for her generation. Of course, she paid a price for this role. She worried about the threatening phone calls, the hate mail, and the fact that she had to call the sheriff every time she received a suspicious or unsolicited package. There were those who hated Mashid's brand of Islam as much as Mashid detested the hatred and violence produced in the name of fundamentalism.

Angel knew that Mashid was a very busy woman, and she wanted to use their limited time together efficiently. She got right to work. "Ted has some general notions about Islam, but we need you to fill in some blanks. We have just begun to work together on the vertical levels and the introductory exercises. Ted is progressing very quickly. He's ready for the third level."

Mashid reached out and grasped Angel's hand. "I'll do my best to answer Ted's questions about Islam."

Ted interjected, "I tried to read the Koran and found it was, well, difficult."

Mashid looked sideways at Ted, and her green eyes were so luminous that for at least a moment he allowed that Angel was not the only woman in his universe. He was wondering what her hair would look like if she let it down, when he noticed that her eyes were turning red.

Ted reached across the table and offered Mashid his napkin. "Was it something I said?"

"Oh, Mashid," Angel gasped, "I'm so sorry." She clutched Mashid's arm.

"No. No. It's not Ted's fault. But now is such a troubled

time for Islam and for the world as a whole. We are, you see, at a pivotal point in human history. Christianity and Islam are both in chaos right now for the same reasons. Islam has so much potential for humanity, but that potential is not being realized. Still, I have hope."

Ted tried to reassure her. "Don't worry, Mashid. Father Chuck made the same apologies for Christianity. He said that both religions have moved away from the teachings of their founders."

"That sounds like Father Chuck!" Mashid said. "He's right. This is why a discussion of either Christianity or Islam can become so difficult right now. Depending on the individual and their progress along the spectrum of awareness, these religions can look unappealing to an outsider trying to peer inside a mosque or a cathedral."

"I read somewhere that Islam is the fasting-growing religion in the world," Ted said. "But there's all this extremism around the world and Islamophobia in the news. How does all that get reconciled?"

Mashid regained her composure and said, "Of course this is where I should begin. I'll try to make this simple. Christianity and Islam are both grounded in events that may or may not have occurred thousands of years ago. The more time passes, the more adept our archaeology and scholarship become, the more we come to realize that much of what is described in the Bible and the Koran simply cannot be historically accurate. Perhaps it made sense to describe spiritual events in this way two thousand years ago, but not now."

Ted offered his own explanation. "Or perhaps these stories

were never meant to be interpreted literally in the first place. It's not the ancients that were naive; it's us!" Ted turned to his own private spiritual consultant for affirmation. "The literalism of the first- and second-grade worshipers pushes the rest of us away from religion altogether. Maybe that's a shame."

Angel nodded. "I think you're almost right, Ted. Critically thinking and well-educated people, like yourself, too often throw out the baby with the proverbial bath water."

"Why?" Ted asked.

Angel rested her hand on Ted's wrist and said apologetically, "At the point of realizing that the Bible and the Koran cannot be literally true, it's tempting to reject the entire texts as a primitive waste of time. This is the tragic shortcoming of third- and fourth-level students: they fail to realize that the holy texts still point, like road signs, to life's great truths."

Ted raised his hand. "I plead guilty as charged. I often find myself wondering if it's even possible to be religious in a modern world. When someone starts talking to me about magical things that supposedly happened thousands of years ago, I check out. I find it impossible to believe that God would manifest once and only once for Jesus, Moses, Muhammad, or the Buddha—or anyone else for that matter—and turn a blind eye to the rest of humanity."

Mashid excitedly leaned forward, realizing that Ted had reached the crux of the problem. "What made these men great was not that God chose them over the rest of us but instead that these men found the path to open up and experience what is potentially available to all of us: the internal presence of God in life itself. We can be spiritual without disregarding science and eschewing rational thought. Thomas Jefferson, for example, created his own Bible by jettisoning the historical and magical-sounding material in the New Testament and focusing instead on the morality or the efficacy of the teachings of Jesus."*

Angel interrupted. "Sadly, Mashid, while I agree with you, it seems like this approach, as much as it makes sense to you and me, too often falls on deaf ears. In many ways the fundamentalists have won the battle for the soul of religion, and this is why young, educated people like my friend Ted here are leaving religion behind in droves. What remains of Christianity and Islam is therefore too often extreme and less acceptable to modern and more moderate thinkers."

Mashid was undaunted. "Ah, but Angel, the times they are changing again. I sense a great wave gathering. And that is what has me so excited. Literalism and fundamentalism have shackled the last thousand years or so of religion, and I feel in my heart that we are on the verge of shedding those chains."

Mashid looked warmly at Angel, took a sip of her tea, and continued. "Father Chuck, Angel, and many more of us are looking to a third alternative: something transcendent, beyond both the nonthinking approach of the fundamentalists

---

* Jefferson's Bible was a text that fascinated many of the coconuts. The entire Jefferson Bible can be viewed on the Web site of the Smithsonian Institution's National Museum of American History: http://americanhistory.si.edu/jeffersonbible/.

and the overthinking, intellectual approach championed by the secular world. The Buddhists call it awakening or enlightenment. Sometimes I think of it as realizing that our lives right now are every bit as much a manifestation of God as a burning bush was to Moses."

Angel brought her friend up to date on Ted's studies. "You're getting a little ahead of us, Mashid. So far, Ted and I have only explored the first and second levels."

"Oh yes, I see. Well, Ted, I'll be blunt with you. First- and second-grade Islam often has very little attraction to a Western intellectual like you or, for that matter, to a Sufi like myself."

Ted interrupted. "What is a Sufi?"

Angel knew that Mashid's modesty would get in the way of answering the question, so she did it for her. "Islam is very unique. Unlike Christianity, where the inhabitants of the upper levels are left to wander about alone, unable to support each other, the Sufis represent the most spiritually evolved Muslims, and they support each other and do the Work. If you have the pleasure of knowing a Sufi, you're probably meeting someone at a very high level of spiritual awareness."

Mashid tried to get to the bottom of Islam's plight. "Ted, fifth- and sixth-grade Islam, like the upper grades of Christianity or Buddhism, offer a transcendental awareness that can only be experienced and not described. Once you experience it, you will be changed forever. The paradox is that if you ask me to describe Islam, I must naturally begin with the Koran and first- and second-grade Islam."

Angel found another way to make Mashid's point. "Most of us are oblivious to the first-grade thinking in our own religious worldview, but *your* first-grade religious thinking will stand out like spilled milk on the countertop."

Mashid took a deep breath and dived in. "In many ways the story actually begins centuries before his birth, but nonetheless we'll start with Muhammad, the Messenger. He was born among the Bedouin people wandering around the desert near Medina and Mecca in the sixth century AD. They were a tough, resourceful, and practical people. To survive in the desert they could not be otherwise. They were also quite barbarous by our standards, and there was a tremendous amount of fighting and killing in their world."

Angel interjected, "As there was in the rest of the world in the sixth century."

Ted shrugged. "Pick up the newspaper. It hasn't gone away."

Mashid continued, "These Bedouin had no organized religion, but they had codes of honor and were generally animistic and pantheistic."

"Animistic?" Ted asked.

"Basically, the Bedouin projected human characteristics onto inanimate objects. If you stubbed your toe on a rock, it meant the rock was mad at you. Clouds formed shapes to offer us signs or portent."

Angel whispered across the table, "This was a very typical first-grade religious worldview. Remember, for the first grader the self and its surroundings are not yet fully separated or differentiated, and so religious thinking is still very much tied to the physical world of the worshipper. I can stick a pin in a voodoo doll and make you hurt."

"That's right," Mashid said. "These early nomadic peoples were classic first graders in their religious thinking: many gods and other spiritual beings called *jinn*—plus spirits existing in inanimate objects like rocks, mountains, or streams."

Ted stopped Mashid with a question. "By the sixth century, when Muhammad was born, both Christianity and Judaism were well established. Had the Judeo-Christian culture also made its way to Mecca?"

"Oh yes, a Christian and Jewish influence was definitely present and managed to exist side by side with these primitive Bedouin religions."

Ted smiled to show his appreciation and said, "Tell me more about Muhammad."

Mashid continued, "Shortly after his birth, Muhammad lost both of his parents, and he was raised by relatives. As a young man he went to work for a wealthy widow in the caravan trade, so here too he would have come into contact with Jews and Christians as part of his travels. The owner of the caravan was a woman named Khadija, and she was fifteen years his senior. They fell in love and she proposed to him. They married, and their relationship is looked upon as a model for marriage among the Muslim community."

Angel added, "He was no wimpy dude, you know. He screwed around a great deal, massacred entire tribes of people, and robbed his way to power. At times he was compassionate and loving and at times he was angry and jealous. In other words, a human."

Mashid glanced at Angel in a slightly dismissive way and said, "It is true, Muhammad was in many ways a regular guy, but nonetheless he is looked upon by Muslims as the most perfect man." She grinned and added, "Apparently, male role models have always been limited."

"Some things never change," Angel said. "Nonetheless, Muhammad was a natural to try to lead his followers from the first to the second level and beyond. He became the 'mythic other' that had direct access to God."

"Muhammad refused to attribute to himself any unusual power, yet he was selected by Allah to be the messenger of his word. After Muhammad's marriage to Khadija, he began wandering off to a nearby cave to meditate, and there he was approached by God and given the revelations that were to become the Koran. He was the scrivener of God's divine word. For Muslims the Bible is more like a history book and the Koran is more like the source. Miracles in the Bible are events, like the parting of the Red Sea. In the Koran the miracle is in the language of God: a direct conversation with God, unadulterated by human translations or memory."

Angel interjected, "Yes, but Ted is bothered by this. He wonders why God would limit the delivery of his message to one man alone."

Ted jumped in to elaborate. "Why did God choose to talk to Muhammad as opposed to someone else or, better yet, why not to a whole crowd of people or to all people simultaneously, so that there could be no disagreement about what he said? If God wanted to speak to man in this fashion, why not chisel his words on a mountainside where they could be read by anyone who walked by? All of these religious revelations are instead delivered privately, leaving the rest of us to take it on faith that nothing is lost in the translation."

Without any defensiveness in her voice, Mashid answered. "At these early levels, God is out there and separate from us, and so this description of communication makes sense for these worshippers. At the upper levels we no longer identify God as an object."

Ted wondered aloud, "So you're saying that Muhammad attributed the voice in his own mind to God because he had no other way to explain it?"

"Rather like Michelangelo believed that God moved through him when he sculpted." Angel added.

Mashid traced her fingers along the olive-skinned contours of her cheekbones and said, "This is a question that should be asked, but realize that the answer changes nothing. I would naturally question the assumption that God's mind and Muhammad's mind or, for that matter, your mind and my mind are properly seen as distinct and separate realms that communicate to each other from afar."

"You're saying the question is grounded in my left-brained, dualistic way of approaching a problem?" Ted asked.

Angel hesitated but decided that there would be no harm in saying it. "Ted, we're not quite there yet. We need to discuss the third level, the level of laws, but I promise you, we'll get to this."

Mashid knew this was the important point for Ted to grasp, so she spoke slowly. "Let me just say it this way to you, Ted.

Like the average Christian, the average Muslim does not question the truth in the Koran, even if there are historical inaccuracies. So whether or not God literally spoke to Muhammad while he was sitting in a cave is not what is important to us. Whatever the source—God or Muhammad's intuition—the miracle of the Koran and the Bible is the exploration of the relationship between man and God and eventually the collapsing of boundaries and separateness that we create in our own minds. The value is not always in the answers provided but in the way these questions inspire us to explore our true essence and to move away from our false self. Finally, as I think Angel is about to tell you, Islam is a good place to discuss the third level of awareness. You should appreciate this third level, Ted—Islam is very bound up in law and rules."

Angel picked up on that theme. "At the third level, worldview shifts away from the earlier emphasis on magic and mythological helpers. Consciousness evolves or unfolds one step at a time, but each step involves a partial letting go of what came before it. It's a process. It's not easy to move to this third level, and Islam is particularly good at encouraging that journey."

Ted tried to return the conversation to Islam, which he found interesting. "Well, I'm sorry I got you off track. Mashid, please return to Muhammad's history."

"Well, I was about to finish anyway. Islam took root in a bloody time and also quite an interesting time for me as a Sufi. For you see, Ted, when those crusaders were left to mingle among the Moors, as the Muslims of that time period are often called, some rather telling events began to unfold. It turns out, Ted, that at the higher grade levels, all of us—Christians, Buddhists, and Muslims—speak the same language and share the same experiences and truths."

Angel reached out and touched Mashid's forearm. "Thank you, Mashid. That's such an important point for Ted to grasp as we move forward. At the lower levels of awareness, spiritual traditions or religions seem very different; at the upper levels we essentially wake up, turn to each other, and realize we were all saying practically the same thing. Good religion is about finding a wisdom path. When we accomplish this task, we will come to better understand ourselves as divine, living participants in the flow of life and not as Protestants or Shiites."

Mashid's eyes flashed with a little embarrassment and she said, "I'm going too fast, aren't I? I'm sorry."

Ted wondered if he looked confused. "I understand. Please, continue."

"The Sufis and other upper-grade students," Mashid added, pointing at the ceiling, "like to say the finger that points at the moon is not the moon."

"Father Chuck means the same thing when he tells us that we must not confuse the boat with the journey," Angel interjected. "The first- and second-grade worshippers pitch their tents by these boats, call them churches or mosques, and form a religion of boat worshippers. At the upper grades we say, 'Yes, sir, that's a nice boat and a handy thing to have for a long journey, so let's climb in and start rowing.'"

"This goes back to your earlier point," Ted noted. "It isn't that the sign is wrong. It's just that there is a distinction between directions and destinations that is not well comprehended at the early spiritual levels. You're saying that people like me get frustrated with people worshipping the signposts, and as a result we ignore some pretty darn good directions." Ted took a last bite of his toast and rested his head on his elbow. His mind was trying to process too much new information on too little sleep. He pushed away from the table and asked, "Could we walk the dogs? They need to go outside and I'd like to get a quick tour of this Earthship community of yours."

Mashid stood up, swallowed the last gulp of her tea, and said, "Of course. Let's go walk your dogs and we can talk more as we stroll."

21

Mashid pointed out the distinguishing features of the homes in her unique subdivision while the dogs sniffed about and Angel continued with her tutorial. She wanted Mashid's assistance on what she considered to be the next important step.

"Let's dig deeper into the next level. The third grade is often defined as the level of rules or laws. At this level, Ted, we widen our awareness of others and we begin to comprehend the importance of rules in governing our relationship with others and God. As we move through the levels, you will see that each ascending level is less parochial and egocentric and more universal."

Ted found it invigorating to walk with his dog in the crisp early-morning desert air of northern New Mexico. He felt his energy returning. "Ah, I'm interested in this third level. We attorneys are all about rules and laws. Tell me more."

Angel smiled, suspecting that the third level was still where Ted spent a considerable part of his conscious awareness. "The third grader is an excellent rule follower, a conformist, that easily accepts traditional thinking and societal norms. The third grader is able to expand her universe of concern away from herself and give fully to others: her family, her group, her tribe, or her god, but her radius of awareness does not expand much wider than her field of vision."

"You're saying that Crossing Trails is not the universe?"

Mashid chimed in. "Mainstream Islam is dominated by a great deal of third-grade thinking. Like Jesus, Muhammad was trying to move his followers up to higher levels of awareness. To be Islamic you really have to believe in very little: there is no god but God and Muhammad is his messenger. But for Muslims there are a plethora of rules. Like Orthodox Judaism, Islam focuses on orthopraxy, or religious practices, more than orthodoxy, or religious beliefs. For the Muslim the path to God is daily prayers, fasting, pilgrimage, ritual cleansing, et cetera."

"All these rules—are they so bad?" Ted asked as they walked past one remarkable Earthship structure after another. Ted got out his phone and took a few pictures. He would have found it very difficult to describe these strange and awkward but somehow elegant structures. Then it hit him that the one person he wanted to text the photo to was Angel, and she was already standing beside him, so he put his phone back in his pocket.

Mashid answered his question as best she could. "You're right, Ted. Rules allow society to function. Political thinking is very third grade–oriented. If we just had the right law, rule, or regulation—and that usually means my party's or my religion's rules and not yours—then our problems would be solved. Third graders are tribal—they move from egocentric to sociocentric. If you can land in the right party and get the right rules, then not only will the universe add up but we can also influence or perhaps even control it."

Ted thought he got the point. "It's only logical that if rules are what makes the world work, then our spiritual relationship with God should also be governed by rules. Surely this is where the rituals of religion come into play? You know, if the pope doesn't wear the right robe, the Ayatollah doesn't pray in the right direction, then the world might crumble?"

Mashid nodded. "I think you're right. I think it's very tempting to believe that finding God is all about getting the recipe right."

Ted reached down and petted No Barks, then looked at Mashid. "I may have the best dog in the world, but this one is a close second." The she-wolf brushed against Ted affectionately and arched her back. Ted asked Angel, "It sounds to me like the logical-thinking left brain is still in charge of the third grader. Am I right?"

"I would say the left brain dominates the second, third, and fourth levels. The left hemisphere prefers to process information by using disjunctive thinking: everything is either X or Y, right or wrong, good or bad, black or white. The upper levels prefer the right brain's more nuanced, holistic, and conjunctive style of thinking: black and white exist both separately and together as gray. While fiercely loyal to her own tribe of rule makers, the third grader is not yet able to see herself as part of a more global community."

Mashid looked at Ted and her green eyes made him melt.

She added to Angel's point. "At the third level there is still a great deal of sneering at the United Nations—the ultimate group of others that are wrong, foreign, and invariably mis-guided. The third grader, although very adult and sophis-ticated in many ways, still harbors assumptions about the superiority of her worshipper's tribe, nation, political party, re-ligion, neighborhood, college fraternity, or profession and finds it difficult to listen to anyone that might have a different, and particularly a broader, view.

"On a purely psychological level, the thought processes of the first- and second-grade worshippers are dominated by what Freud described as the id: the egocentric and childlike aspects of our personality structure. The third grader is very motivated to follow the rules and do what is right, as reflected by the internalized voices of parents, church, teachers, and community leaders and her perception of God. The third grader's place in the world is primarily secured through con-formity to the provincial rules whispered in her ear by her hypervigilant superego."

"My rules are better than your rules?" Ted asked.

"Yes," Mashid answered. "Nonetheless, as long as she has a good rule book, the third grader is greatly advanced over her first- and second-grade cousins for the simple reason that social conformity and rule following have a lot of rewards. The more evolved third graders eventually move beyond their own clan as circumstances warrant and allow a more global set of rules to seep into their superego. This occurs as they become more aware that all rules are not created equal. They can become quite sophisticated when they allow that some big coach in the sky probably isn't going to give them life's playbook. They learn that unfortunately we sometimes have to write our own rules."

Angel chimed in, "Being a rule follower can have some adverse results, but in general it's a much more advanced way to see the world. It no longer hinges on magical or mythical thinking. It's a natural precursor to the next level, the fourth level, which is the rule of reason."

"So," Ted concluded, "a third grader sounds like most people I know. Maybe even me. Not such a bad place to be, is it?"

Angel elbowed Mashid knowingly.

"Well," Mashid said, "being a third grader is not the end of the trail, so a third-grade worldview must have its limitations. Right, Angel?"

"Good point, Mashid. First, the third grader will often follow the rules without understanding or even questioning and is too often indifferent to the purpose behind the rule."

Ted had been thinking the same thing. "This point reminds me of that awful experiment where people were told to keep applying more electric shock to actors who were screaming in fake agony. Rule followers tend to just do what they are told."

Mashid added, "For me this is a particular challenge for Islam. A blind rule-following mentality promotes rigid, maladaptive scripts like archaic gender roles and ancient dietary restrictions. These scripts can be very limiting, both spiritually and psychologically."

"For instance?" Ted asked.

Angel thought a bit and then elaborated. "Rules help us to understand the universe, but every so often we get the rules wrong. The rules we live by become habituated into our superego, and our superego can be a real brutal pain in the ass."

"The rhetoric of politicians and special interest groups seems to exploit our third-grade mind-set," Ted observed.

Mashid nodded but still asked, "How so?"

Ted collected his thoughts, hoping he had this one right. "Seductive 'It must be this or that' type rules and platitudes easily hook our left-brained logic. We've all heard them. 'You're either with us or against us' and 'People kill, not guns.' I've always thought that these little political aphorisms were designed not so much to encourage rational discussion as to shut it down." Neither Mashid nor Angel commented, so Ted continued, "Don't most rules need exceptions to work?" He paused to see if Angel was following his point and then asked, "As a percentage, how much of the world's population makes it to a third-grade worldview?"

Angel did her best to answer. "First, let me say that it's not quite that easy. Most of us slip in and out of our spiritual worldviews. In other words, on some issues I may think like a first or second grader and on other issues like a fifth or sixth grader. At Christmas, for example, I'm still very greedy and want everything to revolve around my needs and wishes, and I still want some magical being to deliver to me a perfect gift. So on that day I guess I'm thinking like a second grader, wanting a mythical intervener to make my life better. On other days my thinking might be, well, rather sophisticated, say, like a fifth grader. So the question is better posed as 'At what level does most of the adult world rest or seem anchored *most* of the time?' "

"That makes sense to me," Ted answered.

"We all have plenty of room to grow. I believe Jesus, Buddha, Muhammad, and all of the world's spiritual leaders address how to get humanity en masse to realize its spiritual potential and reach the sixth grade."

"Do some religions make it more difficult to . . ."

Before Ted could formulate the question, Angel supplied a hint of an answer. "Tomorrow, on the way to South Dakota to help Aunt Lilly, we're going to drive through Nebraska. You're in for a treat. You're going to meet one of most remarkable Buddhist scholars and bicycle repairmen, Stephen Singleton. When we talk about Buddhism, we're going to switch gears into a radically different type of religion than either Christianity or Islam. It is more a study of the mind and how our habitual thinking interferes with our own happiness. A very nice place, I might add, to talk about fourth grade, the level of reasoning, and the tendencies of various religions to either help or impede our spiritual journey."

Ted recognized that Angel would not allow him to move to the next level until she thought he was ready, so as they turned and made their way back to Mashid's Earthship, he allowed the conversation to rest, Lakota style, in silence. He stopped repeatedly to bend down and hold Argo close to him, watching the sun climb above the mountains that rose to the east of Taos. He commented to his dog, "Argo, it looks awfully nice up there in the mountains. Maybe you and I need to take another hike."

Argo wagged his tail, apparently concurring. The idea was a good one. Ted smiled at his host and they continued toward her house. He liked the way the early-morning sun reflected off the small sequins on Mashid's hijab. It was as if each one somehow captured the surrounding mountains, sky, and desert and reflected them back at him. Ted thought some more about the levels. This pilgrimage was the best thing he had done in a long time.

Mashid broke the silence. "It looks like we've worked our way back to my home. Why don't you let me pack a lunch for the road and then you can head for Nebraska with plenty of daylight driving time remaining?"

Ted showered and cleaned up, then pulled out his laptop and sent another inquiry to Legal Aid on the reservation. He'd already written and requested that someone contact him about Aunt Lilly, but he had gotten no response, so he wrote again and tried to provide more detail. He was a family friend, a lawyer, and willing to help out if he could, but he needed a copy of the file.

While Ted worked, Mashid and Angel spoke in the kitchen.

"I like Ted. He seems bright and sincere. You chose your student well."

Angel allowed herself to be vulnerable. "I felt so stupid driving around in Bertha for months, watching what little money I had dwindle away. My phone never rang. Not once. Now I realize how crazy this was. My father was right: no one was ever going to call me. I was just about to give up when I literally ran into Ted."

Mashid laughed, not at Angel but with her. "What in the world were you thinking?"

Angel giggled. "Don't laugh at me, Mashid! I already feel so stupid. I enjoy this man, but we are very different people."

"Isn't that what good partners do: bring out the best in each other?"

With his belongings all packed, Ted walked down the hall, collapsed onto the living room sofa, and waited patiently while Angel and Mashid spoke softly in the kitchen. He closed his tired eyes and relaxed. His leg twitched and soon he was dozing.

Looking over the half wall that separated the kitchen and living-room spaces, Mashid pointed to Ted and whispered to Angel, "Go and rest. I'll finish up in here."

At some point well into his nap, Ted's head fell forward awkwardly, and this jerked him back to consciousness. He was surprised to find Angel sitting next to him, also asleep. Apparently, the work of a spiritual consultant was as tiring as late-night legal research and brief drafting.

Even more surprising, Angel's head was resting on his shoulder. Mashid walked into the room and, seeing that Angel had fallen asleep, she looked at Ted, put her finger to her lips, and quietly retreated into the kitchen.

Ted tried to stay very still so as not disturb Angel. Having her snuggled up so close to him was comforting, and he was hoping it signaled a growing trust between them. Thankfully, No Barks wasn't on the sofa with them. She was on the floor beside Argo.

Ted wondered if Angel's resting position was an accident or a conscious choice. Was she growing more comfortable around him, or was his shoulder just a convenient headrest? Were they just friends, or was there something more? Surely teachers didn't rest their heads on the shoulders of students.

Ted wanted to savor this moment—really hold on to it and enjoy it. He could feel Angel's warm breath on his neck. He took a careful inventory of her so he could re-create her image in his mind later. It might have to last a lifetime. He wanted to know everything about her so he could recall this moment with precision.

He noticed the hairs in Angel's eyebrows and eyelashes. He pondered where the first wrinkles of age might appear on her warm face. He studied every nuance of her nose until he knew it like a skier knows his favorite run. He noticed the tightness of the skin over her cheekbones and the smell of her dog on her sweater. He noticed the soft, dark hairs that were barely visible on her upper lip.

After so carefully observing Angel, he shut his eyes and told himself that this was probably not appropriate, perhaps slightly prurient. He reminded himself that what made Angel Two Sparrow so special to him was not the hairs on her face. What he cared for resided deeper, much deeper. He was ad-equately versed in simple animal magnetism, but this more spiritual attraction he felt toward Angel was an entirely new experience. It occurred to Ted that falling in love with Angel would be like falling in love with the tour guide at the Taj Mahal. How could one separate the beautiful tour guide from the beautiful tour?

The sad thought also occurred to him that while most grown men and women spend every day of their lives snuggled up beside someone they love, perhaps to whom they even feel some spiritual connection, it had not been that way for him. He was nearly thirty years old. Why had he never felt this kind of connection before? With his eyes closed, he breathed in the subtle scent of her coconut shampoo and made a commitment to himself.

He and Argo would not spend the rest of their lives alone. He could never return to his same old life in Crossing Trails. Grandpa Raines had been right. It was empty and he now knew it.

Angel was slowly giving him the confidence to climb out of the hole where he been sequestered for too long. It was as if he had been on a long drunken bender and was slowly returning to sobriety. He was finding a great deal of value in Angel's instruction. He committed to double down on his efforts and be less cavalier about his course work with Angel.

Angel moved slightly, and he was concerned she might rouse from her slumber. Instinctively he moved closer to her, hoping that she would feel secure and safe beside him. He felt sincere affection for Angel, so why hide it? Why not act on how he felt?

Ted slowly put his arm around Angel and let it rest comfortably and confidently on her shoulders. Without waking, Angel nestled in even more closely, and Ted felt a strange merging of their bodily energies. Being a novice at such feelings, he knew he was speculating, but it felt like something was different between them. In some way Angel had permitted Ted into her space. It seemed important, but he wasn't sure why.

Ted thought he saw a slight smile on Angel's face, but he quickly concluded it was just her generally pleasant demeanor shining through. Basking in Angel's aura, Ted felt gratitude emerge. He wasn't sure exactly what to do with this feeling, but he knew he had to find a way to be as valuable to her as she was to him. How could he ever accomplish this? The answer seemed to be Aunt Lilly.

22

Angel and Ted navigated north from Taos and into Colorado. At I-70, they turned east toward Kansas. Ted was reluctant to leave the Chieftain behind and unattended in Pecos, but he was even more reluctant to travel separately in his own vehicle without Angel and No Barks by his side. Argo and the wolf dog had become inseparable.

Father Chuck assured Ted that his grandfather's beloved RV would be safe in the large monastery parking lot and that Ted could fly back to retrieve it when he was ready, presumably in the next week or two.

As Bertha chugged along, Angel gave Ted another meditation practice to add to his spiritual tool set. Angel claimed that she'd learned the practice from Father Chuck. This seemed strange to Ted, so he asked her, "I thought priests prayed. So Christians meditate too?"

"Christianity has a long history with meditation, particularly within the early church. There's been a considerable resurgence in the last fifty years or so. As you might suspect, prayer becomes more like meditation or contemplation when practiced by Christians at the upper grade levels."

Ted enjoyed doing the exercises with Angel. As she had predicted, he found them easier with her by his side. He closed his eyes and got comfortable in the passenger seat. But before she could start, Ted had to ask, "Do you think it's safe to do this meditation stuff while you're driving?"

"Are you saying that my preoccupation with spiritual matters might divert my attention away from the mundane task of piloting a two-ton bookmobile down I-70 at eighty miles per hour?"

"You do have a history here."

Angel grinned. "As long as no one pulls out right in front of me, totally failing to yield, we'll be fine."

"Promise to keep your eyes open and resist the impulse to levitate out of your seat to the beat of Lakota drum music?"

"For you, yes."

Angel continued, "Instead of just observing your mind and body, thoughts and feelings, I would like you to visualize a benevolent energy force hovering in a twelve-inch sphere directly above your forehead. If you see it larger or smaller, that's okay. After you visualize this energy source, allow it to expand gently and envelop your entire body. You might perceive this force to be something like a radio frequency or a ball of energy. But remember, the energy force is good: it is love and compassion. I want you to tune in to this energy frequency and allow it to resonate in your chest cavity—in the spaces around your heart. This is where it is best perceived. It will not enter without your consent. In fact, you must earnestly desire its presence within you. You are like the receiver, and you must consciously choose to flip on the switch and receive the signal. Form an intention to allow this presence of goodness, godliness, to rest within you."

Ted found that Angel's words once again had a nearly hyp-notic effect on him and, just as she had described it, he could immediately sense the orb of positive energy hovering above him, expanding, migrating, and eventually resonating within him.

"Some might call this benevolent force God stuff, but that label may not be helpful for you. So don't put a human per-sona on the energy field. You might refer to it as your *inborn divinity*. Simply try to experience this reverberating energy in your chest cavity. Can you invite it in and allow the signal to resonate and slowly increase in amplitude?"

Sitting in the high-backed passenger seat with his feet flat on the old vinyl-covered floorboard, Ted tried to open up his heart space to this energy that Angel described and let it ex-pand even further. Again, somewhat to his amazement, that was precisely what occurred. At first the reverberation was so mild that he thought he was just imagining it—sort of a spiritual placebo effect.

Angel continued the instruction. "You should welcome this energy to reside within you. Nurture it with your own positive energy. Imagine that this energy is awakening or act-ing as a catalyst for your own light, the energy of your higher or true self. Think of it as *love*. It's akin to the feeling you ex-perience when you hold Argo tight to your chest. Let it swell. Allow yourself to attune to this energy that now dwells within you. Sense it in your entire chest cavity. Come to know this space well. This is the real Ted Day, not just Ted Digit."

As he listened to Angel's words, Ted stayed with the energy sensation and it did seem to unfurl, to grow in intensity and become more focused in his heart and lungs. The energy force was palpable, and though he did not yet have the vocabulary to describe it precisely, it seemed to take on a physical dimension like a bright white light. The light seemed to possess a molecular density and even a temperature—it frightened him. He'd never felt anything like this before, and its unfamiliarity was making him uneasy, as if he had lost control of his mind. He opened his eyes and looked about nervously to get his bearings. He noted to himself that what he had experienced seemed quite strange and was now gone.

Angel called an end to the exercise. "That's enough for now, Ted."

Ted was slightly concerned. First there had been the finger trance and now there was this energy transfer. Where did Angel get these unusual skills? Hell, he told himself, all he could do was write a good legal brief.

That evening, as Bertha the Bookmobile made her way out of Kansas and into the lovely, low, rolling hills of western Nebraska, Angel slowed so they could take in the scenery along the highway. Ted was surprised by the landscape. He wasn't sure if it was beautiful or if his growing powers of awareness only made it seem that way.

"As a third-grade graduate," Ted quietly observed, "I don't

really believe in elves, fairies, or leprechauns. But if I did, this is where I would look for them. It's beautiful, isn't it?"

"I agree. The plains are magical. I can almost sense the buffalo and antelope grazing under the watchful eye of my ancestors."

As they traveled along a rural Nebraska highway in silence, a long list of questions wandered, uninvited, into Ted's mind. He wondered if he would reach the sixth level and get the full value of his Spirit Tech tuition. If his appreciation of beauty had changed so dramatically after a few meditation sessions, what could he expect at even higher levels of awareness? Or would it be like getting an improved eyeglass prescription—sure, his vision would be crisper, but nothing in his life would really change except his perception of it.

Ted thought more about Aunt Lilly and his future as a lawyer. He had promised himself not to think about it for at least six months, but with his rather sizable inheritance, he did not really have to work. If not work, though, then what? His mind raced, but in the end he found his growing connection to Angel the most troubling of all.

Ted wanted to reach over and rest his hand on Angel's wrist to bridge the space between them. He hesitated. Would the pursuit of the lesser goal of romance thwart the greater goal of enlightenment? There were doubts. It might not be a good idea to consider a future with Angel. He was a lawyer, grounded in the real world. As much as he adored her, Ted sensed that Angel's spiritual mooring made her less than practical—in the being-able-to-make-the-rent-payment kind of way. What would they be like together? Would they drive around in a bookmobile, saving souls? It couldn't work.

Ted figured it was unfair to make assumptions about Angel, to not even give her a chance, so he impulsively broke the silence and asked, "Angel, before you were a spiritual consultant, what did you do?"

If Angel didn't know better, she would have thought that Larsen was sitting beside her, insisting in his own kind way that she needed a different line of work. She made a conscious effort not to be defensive, but still, the question hurt. Ted couldn't know what a sensitive subject he had broached. She tried to be honest, but the recounting only made her feel worse.

"Well, I went to this school and then that school, sang, played my guitar, did artwork, helped my dad, taught yoga and meditation." She hesitated, looked over at him, and then added, "Does that sound irresponsible?"

Ted thought long and hard and decided to be honest. "It depends. I mean, how do you pay your bills? Where do you get your car and health insurance? Do you think about your future?"

Ted's questions felt oppressive to Angel and further out of bounds. "Ted, to be honest, I'm awful at that stuff. I never had a real job, can't save money, forget to buy insurance, and I am so moored in the spiritual *now* that I seem to be rather indifferent about the tangible problems of *tomorrows*. Maybe I'm irresponsible. I just have to believe that if I do my best to make the world a better place today, all of those tomorrows will work out."

Ted's heart sank. Her attitude sounded reckless and, indeed, irresponsible. It was just as he had suspected: Angel was clueless about the real world. Ted placed his hand on her wrist. He remembered something he had read in one of her books that he thought might gently drive home the point. "Angel, in some of the Sufi materials you gave me I read something that I really liked."

Angel's temperature was rising, but she tried her best to tolerate what she perceived as an assault on her self-worth. "Yes."

"Trust in Allah, but tie up your camel."

Angel considered pulling her hand away. She didn't want Ted's affectionate understanding of her shortcomings. It seemed patronizing. He wasn't Larsen. He wasn't paying her bills. Intentionally or not, Ted had crossed into one of Angel's verboten zones. The steam continued to accumulate, but Angel remained silent—and not the open and airy Lakota sort of silence. It was an oppressive, angry silence.

The heat in the cab flashed to red, and Ted removed his hand. "I guess that's none of my business." He looked around, wondering why Angel was slowing down.

Angel got in Ted's face. "It's a sensitive subject for me, and you're right: it's none of your business how I pay my bills."

The quiet persisted a bit longer before Ted said, "I'm sorry. I didn't mean to hurt your feelings. I was trying to be helpful. You can be spiritual and also have a real job. Right?"

"You mean like Mashid, Father Chuck, and everyone else but me?" Angel pulled off to the side of the road. She considered booting Argo and Ted. They could walk back to New

Mexico. She'd been a fool. What sane person would even try spiritual consulting? When she'd finally gotten a client, she'd tutored the man for free and bared her soul, and now he was humiliating her. Mashid had said it well: "What were you thinking?"

When Bertha was fully stopped, Angel stomped on the emergency brake pedal. "Screw you, Ted Day," she said. She put her head in her hands and started to sob. "Don't you see?" There were more sobs before she spat it all out. "I've lived in the spiritual realm because the real world wants nothing to do with me. I can't do anything right. This pilgrimage is a bust. Another avoidance." Her tone turned apologetic as she wailed, "I'm so sorry I got you involved in my ridiculous ideas. I'm going to go back to South Dakota and help my dad fix trucks. At least I can weld."

Ted took her hand again. "Wait a minute, Angel. You haven't failed. You're a wonderful spiritual consultant. I'm having the best vacation of my life with you and No Barks. Maybe you just need a little help getting your feet on the ground. That's all."

"Really?" she asked, her confidence desperate to be restored.

"You're a unique and wonderful person. Don't condemn yourself for being different. You're just ahead of your time. That's all. Maybe we ran into each other so I could help you with Aunt Lilly and your finances."

"You don't think I'm ridiculous for driving around in Bertha with signs painted on the sides?"

Ted laughed, leaned over, and hugged her. "It's the most ridiculous thing I've ever seen in my life and I love it."

She held him tightly. "I can take you back to Pecos if you want. We don't have to finish this."

"You've spent entirely too much time hanging out in the teacher's lounge doubting yourself. You've got work to do and you're not getting rid of me."

At a roadside stop on a lonely stretch of Nebraska highway, Angel and Ted shared the food that Mashid had packed. Angel was still teetering and Ted tried to reel her in. "Is it a good time to start on Buddhism and the fourth level?" He rested his hand on Argo's furry head and stretched his legs comfortably out in front of him. "I am at my desk, pen in hand, ready to go back to work."

Pushing down doubts about her value as a spiritual consultant, Angel dived back into the curriculum as if she had been carefully outlining it in her mind. If nothing else, she was resilient. Angel took a big bite of an apple, chewed it, and said, "I think it's good that we continue. It'll do us both some good. You've done so much hard work that it would be a shame not to finish up. Don't you think?"

"Agreed."

They finished their lunch and had traveled east a few miles before Angel resumed the lesson. "Buddhism is a good place for us to return to the Work. Like me"—her humor revived, Angel poked fun at herself—"it has a radically different view. But unlike me, it is grounded and practical. Good beliefs and good practices are measured by one test alone: do my actions, beliefs, and behaviors result in less suffering or more happiness in this lifetime? Like an ancient self-help system, Buddhism promises us a happier life. To believe in something or practice something that does not reduce suffering in this life would not make sense to a Buddhist." She glanced down at the gas gauge before continuing. "Buddhism moves more like a science than a religion: experiment and be open to many possibilities. Frankly, Ted, this could be right up your alley."

"Doesn't even sound much like a religion to me."

"Generally speaking, you're right; the core of the Buddha's teachings have little to do with what we traditionally describe as religion. Buddhism takes on this whole issue of how to wake us up."

"I thought Buddhists believed in reincarnation," Ted said.

"Well, Buddhism has institutionalized and adopted the beliefs of the indigenous peoples where its practice spread. But this has nothing to do with what the Buddha taught. In fact, Buddha was stalwart in his refusal to address metaphysical questions, including the biggest question of all: Is there a creator god?"

"Heaven and hell?"

"He wouldn't touch it."

"Life after death?"

"Ask anyone, but not me."

"I always thought that religion was all about metaphysical questions."

"You can ask Singleton when we arrive, but I suspect a Buddhist would say that trying to answer these questions will not move you down the path to happiness, nor eliminate suffering. Pursuit of these questions is therefore a distraction or diversion from the real business of life."

"Still, they are important questions."

"Are they, though? The Buddha offered the parable of the poisoned arrow to explain. Imagine that a man has been shot with a lethal poisoned arrow and his only chance of survival is to remove the arrow quickly, but instead he instructs his rescuers to not remove the arrow until they first tell him the name and clan of the person who shot it, whether it was shot from a longbow or a crossbow, and the nature of the arrowhead. What would you think of such a man?"

"He would be a fool."

"Yes, the Buddha taught that religion can be a foolish pastime when we preoccupy ourselves with questions that cannot be answered. By doing so, we waste our precious lives avoiding the hard work but significant gains that await us on the spiritual path the Buddha suggests we begin navigating. He called that spiritual path the dharma."

"I'll try to remember the parable the next time I discover an arrow in my backside." Ted looked down at the map he was using to help Angel navigate. "Turn at the next intersection. We're almost there. Only twenty more miles." Ostensibly to make sure he had her attention, he again touched her wrist.

"Nice, slow turn this time. There might be someone coming in the opposite direction, minding his own business and not interested in being broadsided."

Angel grinned. "Yes, Ted, I heard you." She slowed Bertha and made the turn. The road narrowed and was not well scaled to Bertha's wide girth, so Angel reduced her speed even further. "How about that? No one pulled out in front of me, failing to yield."

Ted removed his hand from her wrist and asked, "The Buddha's famous Four Noble Truths—are they about happiness and this dharma path?"

"Yes, the First Noble Truth is that suffering and unhappiness are part of the human condition. They are inevitable. It does not end well for us, and there is plenty to suffer through along the way: we get sick, we get old, we wither, and we die."

"Doesn't seem too cheery, this Buddha."

"Journeying down the hall to the upper-grade classrooms is not easy. By helping us to deny our true human condition, our Western culture is an impediment to our spiritual progress and psychological health. From the cradle to the grave, we are conditioned to avoid thinking about our inevitable illness, aging, and death. We want to live in a Peter Pan world, forever young and healthy. Or if we do die, it doesn't really matter—we'll just somehow continue our existing lives in heaven, except on better terms."

"Life of Ted, part two."

"Belief in an afterlife allows us to avoid dealing with our own mortality. What we don't understand is that denial di-

verts a great deal of energy away from healthy growth, acceptance, and moving down this path. Eastern cultures venerate
the wisdom and maturity that come with age. Western ones,
however, are ageist, denigrate maturity, and will go to any
lengths to avoid looking older."

Ted nodded. "Our economy seems to rely on us wanting to
avoid aging, sickness, and death. Cosmetics, hair dyes, plastic
surgery—the list goes on. I'm not sure why we find something
as natural as aging and death so terrifying. Toward the end,
my grandfather seemed to come to terms with dying. He liked
to say to me that not living was far sadder than dying."

"I think the Buddha was trying to say the same thing. He
emphasized that this life is a blessing, but a short one. We
have a limited amount of time to get it right. Institutionalized
Christianity and Islam both place a great deal of emphasis on
heaven and hell. Judaism is far more circumspect about such
claims. Father Chuck will tell you that most Christians ignore
or deemphasize that Jesus said heaven exists in the now and
not in an afterlife."

"I'm no shrink," Ted said, "but surely this fear of death is
part of our Mr. Digit self. I think, too, this gets back to the
second realization. We spend a great deal of energy creating a
thing called a self and then worrying about protecting it. So
what's the Second Noble Truth?"

"The Buddha's Second Noble Truth focuses on the gap between the way the world really exists and the way our minds
perceive it. As you just suggested, our ego and our Mr. Digit
personality get in the way of awareness about life's true condi-

tion. Much of our unhappiness stems from the ignorance of our true condition; our view of the world and how we fit into it is flawed on many levels."

"Don't all of us want to be happy and not suffer? What's so profound about this?"

Angel nodded approvingly. "I think these first two Noble Truths are the foundation for the most important point, which the Buddha describes as our 'ignorance.' Because we do not understand the true nature of causes and effects, we engage in avoidable habits and practices that make us miserable. Mr. Digit is convinced that having a gold ring on his finger is the path to nirvana. It's difficult to get Mr. Digit to see his higher purpose or true self."

"The Third Noble Truth?" Ted asked.

"Precisely. By following the dharma path, doing the Work, we can eliminate much of our ignorant, Mr. Digit worldview. Albert Einstein described it as the religion of the future. Some Catholic monks are also practicing Zen Buddhists, and plenty of people, if pushed, would describe themselves as Christian Buddhists. It's a more consistent belief system than you might think."

As they entered the outskirts of the small community where Singleton kept his bike shop, they drove over speed bumps in the road signaling free-ranging animals. Angel slowed Bertha to a crawl to avoid jostling her passengers. Ted asked, "So what's the Buddha's secret for making us happy?"

"That's where the dharma practice begins. It's the Eight-fold Path: the Buddha's Fourth Noble Truth—at bottom, a systematic process for disabling our Mr. Digit ego. It's the Buddhist's treasure map that leads us to the upper-grade classrooms. If we can understand these Four Noble Truths and incorporate them into our lives, then we can achieve a peace here on this earth, a nirvana. I think this is what Jesus was referring to as the Kingdom."

On a brick street lined with lush green grass, they came to a clapboard Victorian house with a sign in front, SINGLETON HOUSE. A BED & BREAKFAST, and beneath that, another sign read CYCLE RENTAL AND REPAIR.

Angel excitedly parked the bookmobile. They snapped the leashes on their dogs, gave them a few minutes to sniff about the yard, and approached the front of the bike shop.

23

When Stephen Singleton—bike repairman, innkeeper, and Buddhist teacher—heard that Angel and Ted were planning to sleep on the floor of old Bertha the Bookmobile and that they had been sustaining themselves primarily on granola bars and fruit for the last three days, he insisted on cooking them a warm meal and putting them up in his cozy inn. They offered no resistance. He wasn't sure whether to offer them two rooms or one, so he took the cautious approach and handed them each a room key. What they did afterward was their business. Each room in his bed-and-breakfast was named after a Nebraska-bred movie star. Angel was in the Marlon Brando room and Ted was in the Fred Astaire suite.

It was midweek and business was slow for both Singleton's bed-and-breakfast and his adjoining bike shop. Not being a die-hard capitalist motivated by money and money alone, Singleton enjoyed these occasional slow days. It gave him more time to study, meditate, visit with friends, and hike or bike along north central Nebraska's 321-mile Cowboy Trail, where he had anchored his business.

After an evening of getting acquainted but before retiring to bed on full stomachs, Ted and Angel put Argo and No Barks in the fenced-in dog run in the side yard—a space Singleton had created especially for his canine guests. They fed and watered the dogs, gave them good-night hugs, and headed up to their respective rooms for what they both hoped would be a good night's sleep.

Resisting the urge to immediately climb into bed, Ted moved about the room and inventoried all the Fred Astaire memorabilia that hung on the walls. The best part of the collection was a life-size movie poster of Astaire dancing with Cyd Charisse in Central Park. Beneath the poster Singleton had carefully typed and framed the lyrics to a melody Astaire had made famous.

> *Dancing in the dark 'til the tune ends*
> *We're dancing in the dark and it soon ends . . .*

Ted turned and thought a moment. He could see how, when read a particular way, the lyrics could be profound and very Buddhist. He tested the resistance of the mattress with his hands. It seemed firm and inviting. Ted kicked off his shoes, grabbed his phone, searched for Fred Astaire on iTunes, and listened to "Dancing in the Dark" until he fell asleep.

Having gone to bed early, Ted woke up at five thirty the next morning. Out of habit, he began sifting through his e-mails to find a response from John Shinn, Lilly Two Sparrow's Legal Aid lawyer. Ted had written three times to Shinn, and now there were three separate responses waiting for him to review.

In the first, Shinn apologized to Ted for taking a few days to get back to him, explaining that he'd first had to procure his client's permission to release the file or even discuss the case with Ted. With Aunt Lilly's permission, Shinn e-mailed the requested portions of the file to Ted. Shinn encouraged his fellow lawyer to double-check every detail of his work. He openly admitted that he was running out of options for Aunt Lilly. Perhaps some stone had been left unturned. "Who knows?" he remarked. "If you can find something I missed, great. Just let me know. I'm pleased to have your help."

Shinn followed up with a second e-mail a few hours later, where he elaborated further and responded to a couple of theories Ted was considering. Shinn told Ted that he felt sorry for Aunt Lilly. He added, "Although she might be a bit unhinged, unfortunately, as far as South Dakota law is concerned, she's not crazy enough to get away with murder."

Ted had mentioned that Uncle Harry might have physically abused Aunt Lilly and asked if this could bolster her self-defense claim. In a third and final e-mail, Shinn said that he did not believe this fact changed much about the case. He reminded Ted that there was no objective evidence that Uncle Harry had threatened her on the day of the shooting. Aunt Lilly had made no such statement to Shinn or to the police. When Ted asked Shinn about the state of mind necessary to claim self-defense, Shinn responded that while he also believed the law was a bit unsettled in South Dakota, any self-defense claim would be governed by a reasonable-person standard and not some murky subjective standard. Shinn's view was the same as Ted's: reasonable people don't listen to bears that speak to them in dreams and then shoot their husbands. Aunt Lilly's best option was to accept the manslaughter plea that Shinn was hoping the State of South Dakota would offer her. After that, they could only hope she was still alive after serving her ten-year sentence. A hearing was scheduled for October. Unless something earthshaking came up in the next week or two, Shinn would push ahead and try to plead Aunt Lilly to an amended charge of manslaughter. With time served, she might be out in eight years. No matter how hard Ted thought about it, Aunt Lilly's situation seemed desperate. Shinn was right. A bad dream simply couldn't be the sole basis for a murder defense. They needed something more to show reasonable fear.

Ted rested in bed waiting for sunrise. He closed his eyes and concentrated on several of the meditation exercises Angel taught him. He continued with these exercises for twenty minutes and found it easier than he had before to occasionally find the space behind the Ted chatter. Still, even twenty minutes was a long time to work at it, so he turned to one of the books on Buddhism that Angel had given him. He heard Argo bark and this broke his concentration. Argo was having quite an adventure of his own, palling around with No Barks. With all his preoccupation over leaving Angel in a week, it hadn't occurred to him until now that Argo might not be that happy back in Crossing Trails, alone all day while he worked. Ted would not be the only one regretting the end of their pilgrimage.

By six o'clock the sun was up and a cool breeze was com-

ing off the meadow behind Singleton's inn. Incongruent
sounds—distant car horns, music playing, sprinklers running,
and cattle lowing—passed unfiltered through the window and
diverted Ted's attention from another of the exercises Angel
had given him: Ted was to periodically take an inventory and
notice, really pay attention, to his surroundings.

He walked over to the window and stared at the cattle
grazing in their fields under the Nebraska sun, which was now
well above the horizon. The sun slipped out occasionally from
behind white clouds like a worried mother checking on her
earthly children. Outside the second-floor window were window boxes spilling over with red and blue pansies. Ted tried
next to notice the rich scents lingering in the air. The smell
of strong coffee and freshly baked scones came up the stairs
from the kitchen below, triggering hunger pangs in Ted's stomach. Suddenly it clicked: this was the smell of a very old house.
Over the years, many owners had scrubbed the old wood floors
and dusted the woodwork with a wide range of cleansing agents
that had lingered and coalesced into the old house's smell.
Ted imagined generations of housekeepers scrubbing floors—
vinegar and water giving way to Pine-Sol, Mr. Clean, and others. But the scent that hung in the air now was distinctive. It
reminded him of Angel. If Ted had asked Singleton, he would
have discovered that his host was using an old-fashioned, hand-
crafted natural antibacterial soap made from sodium laurate—
the by-product of lauric acid after it has been neutralized by
sodium hydroxide—or, put more simply, coconut oil and lemon
juice. The scent was sweet, clean, luscious, and inviting.

Ted could hear water running through the pipes from a nearby room and Singleton talking on the downstairs phone. He decided to end his noticing exercise and join his newest spiritual comrade at breakfast. Ted straightened the room and took a quick hot shower. As he dressed, Ted put at the top of his morning wish list some hot coffee.

Singleton was of medium build, his blond hair giving way to gray. Wearing a T-shirt that touted his own business, he leaned patiently against the frame of the kitchen door, discussing rental prices with a caller. "No, we only offer half-day or full-day rentals. That's right. No hourly . . . Yes, plenty of bikes available for this afternoon. You won't need a reservation."

He had a gentle smile and glowed in a way that suggested pleasure, or at least contentment, with life. Finished with his conversation, Singleton hung up the old landline phone, quickly crossed the galley-style kitchen, and extended his right hand. "Good morning, Ted. How are you? I trust you slept well?"

"Yes, thanks. I got up early this morning. I had to do some legal research and I also read through some of the Buddhist writings Angel gave me. I got halfway through your book, *The Biking Buddhist*,* before I realized that you wrote it. I was very impressed. It was excellent!"

---

* For a very similar book, see Stephen Batchelor, *Buddhism Without Beliefs: A Contemporary Guide to Awakening* (New York: Riverhead Books, 1997).

Singleton was also appropriately pleased with his book—he thought it was one of his best. He had poured his life energy into it in the hope that he could share with others the understanding he had worked so hard to achieve. "Good, I'm glad you enjoyed it."

"I thought that a little preparation would allow us to better use our time together." Ted hesitated. All at once it occurred to him that he was not sure why Singleton, Mashid, Father Chuck, or even Angel, for that matter, was bothering to guide him, show him how to do the Work. In today's world, who just gave things away? Was spiritual knowledge less valuable than tax, medical, or legal advice? "It's so kind of you to share your time with me," Ted stammered, "I don't mean to barge into your life like this."

"You needn't feel that way. Do you know what happens when the tide rises?"

Ted didn't offer an answer, just smiled and waited for Singleton to continue.

"When the tide rises, all ships come up with it. It may not seem logical to you, at least not yet, why we are generous with our time. You may feel like others are more deserving. You will feel this way only if you are approaching the situation from the third level, rather like a lawyer who wants to follow the rules or an accountant who wants the ledger to balance. Today we are going to suggest another outlook, but first sit, eat, and relax. Then we'll get to talk more about Buddhism."

Ted was pleased to be sitting in Singleton's kitchen on a late-summer morning. He filled his cereal bowl and poured in some milk. "The books Angel loaned me have all been good, but Buddhism is nothing like I expected. I see why all of those Hollywood types are so attracted to it."

"I'm honored to be your guide. We can't get too far in one morning, but we'll do what we can. I've devoted my attention to these teachings for most of my adult life. They have been richly rewarding for me and I hope, no matter how limited our time together, they will be for you." Singleton paused, refilled Ted's cup of coffee to the brim, and added, "Let me say first, Ted, that there will be no pressure to accept what I share with you. The Buddha taught that you should take what is of value from his teaching and leave the rest behind. Buddhism, at least the way I see it and the way I believe the Buddha originally conceived it, encourages its aspirants to evolve, grow, and not remain stagnant—locked into a centuries-old worldview."

In a nod to his other spiritual teachers, Ted wondered aloud, "Perhaps when properly read, Jesus and Muhammad had the same message?"

"Ah," Singleton playfully responded, "I can see you were listening when Father Chuck and Mashid spoke with you. They'll be pleased."

"I tried." Ted took a long sip of coffee. "I appreciate not being pressured into something just because it works for you or for the Dalai Lama."

Singleton pointed to a small side table against the west wall of his kitchen. "Grab some of those pastries if you like. We'll let Angel sleep awhile longer while we do some preliminary work. Once she's up—it's such a beautiful morning—

perhaps the three of us could walk along the Cowboy Trail and talk more about this ancient tradition from India."

In Ted's mind, Angel's idea of eating was more like fortuitous foraging. Happy to be sitting down to a real meal, he heaped food on his plate, sat down, and readied himself to do more of the Work, but this time with the luxury of a full stomach and a sizable dose of caffeine in his bloodstream.

Stephen watched Ted eat for a few minutes before he began. "Buddhist teachings, practices, and knowledge are sometimes all rolled up and described by one word: 'dharma.' It is said that the dharma has two wings, compassion and wisdom. Put another way, Buddhism cannot be realized—wisdom—unless it is also practiced—compassion."

"I think you're saying that it is interactive. You must experience it before it can truly make sense for you."

Singleton politely smiled and said, "Without the practice, without the walking on the path, the doing of the Work, Buddhism is just another set of beliefs or rules, and its practical impact on your life will be negligible. You'll end up just being another 'bookstore Buddhist.' Meditation and studying the mind are very important parts of this practice."

"Angel has started me on some meditations and other sensing exercises."

"This requirement to participate and practice has sometimes made Buddhism seem a bit esoteric, like a secret or tantric path, but the core teachings of Jesus, Muhammad, and the Buddha are all trying to deliver the same message: transformation of the self."

Ted thought about it for a minute and interjected, "Seems strange that three men so far apart in geography and in time would share similar ideas."

"Maybe not as strange as you think. Perhaps Mashid told you that Muhammad lived along an important trade route? Well, he wasn't alone."

"Jesus?" Ted asked, surprised.

"That's right. Some scholars believe Jesus may have also been influenced by the Buddhist travelers that made their way along the Silk Road and stopped to trade in Galilee. It's not far-fetched to envision Jesus coming into contact with Buddhist teachings. Likewise, Muhammad lived among Christians in Medina. But that's not important. What's important—for me, at least—is that the world's brightest and greatest spiritual minds seem to end up at a similar place."

"And the place, this spiritual path that you, Father Chuck, Mashid, and Angel work on, is what you are calling a tantric path?" Ted asked.

"Yes, the tantric path is where Angel, Father Chuck, Mashid, and many others of us are moving and what we believe the Buddha, Jesus, and most other spiritual seekers were trying to communicate. But before I describe this path to you, just like 'repent' is a lousy translation for 'metanoia,' as Father Chuck is so fond of explaining, please don't confuse New Age, or what some people describe as 'California tantra,' with this ancient practice. Tantra is not about enjoying our bodies and it is not about sex. Not that there's anything wrong with sex, but this is rather like equating French fries with French food."

"What does it really mean, then?"

"Tantra stands in contrast to asceticism—the renunciation of the world and all its pleasures and pains, which are seen as mere illusions and distractions from our godlier selves. The ascetic path is about the annihilation of the self and the denial of the importance of our humanity. Tantra goes the other way. It embraces life. To realize our humanity we must transcend our ordinary consciousness so we can get above and beyond our small, ego-bound self. Some people call this 'Christ consciousness' or 'Buddha mind.' There is a subtle but important difference between the two paths.

"Both the ascetic and the Buddha recognize that life is flawed in some fundamental way. We do suffer a great deal. The difference between the tantric path and the ascetic path is in the reaction to that suffering. The ascetic believes that we must exile ourselves from life and its pleasures as much as possible to obtain an ecstatic and mystical union with God. The hedonist seeks, during this brief time on earth, what pleasures he can. The Buddha taught what he called the *middle way*. By seeking pleasure, you never find happiness. Nor does self-mortification get you to nirvana. The middle way, the tantric path, is akin to letting go and becoming more attuned to what life is really all about."

"The Four Noble Truths?" Ted asked.

"Yes, but even more than that—the tantric path ushers us into the fourth, fifth, and sixth levels of awareness. At these higher levels of our development, there is no need to push life away, like the ascetic, or cling to its pleasures, like the hedo-

230 *•* Greg Kincaid

nist. The Buddha helped us to realize that it is our very cling-
ing to what we want and our aversion to what we detest that
cause much of our unhappiness. These very natural human
habits take us away from the realm of the now, where happiness resides, and either drag us back into the past or catapult
us into the future."

Angel moved quietly behind Ted and rested her hands on
his shoulders. Her long fingers gently massaged the muscles
along his spine. "Did you sleep well, Ted?"

Ted was delighted and somewhat surprised at Angel's
touch. He looked up at her and could think of nothing love-
lier to wake up to than Angel Two Sparrow. Whatever irritation she had been feeling toward him before had apparently
passed. "Yes, I did. And you?"

"Very well, thank you." Before Stephen had a chance to
greet her, she joined the conversation. "Have you talked yet
about the fourth level?"

"Not yet," Singleton answered, "but I believe we now have
a better context to do so."

Angel walked over to the kitchen window and pulled back
the simple white curtains to peer outside. "Let's eat. Then, if
the two of you are up to it, I'd like to get the dogs, take a walk,
and introduce Ted to the fourth grade. He's earned it, and
I want to explore this Cowboy Trail that Stephen has been
talking about for years."

24

There were other hikers and bikers on the Cowboy Trail that morning, so Ted and Angel put the dogs on their leashes. Neither dog seemed to mind. They trotted along with their humans enjoying all the scents that were floating in the still cool morning air. "Now that you're ready to leave the first three grades behind," Angel told Ted, "Spirit Tech will really get interesting! A certain amount of maturity, wisdom, and psychological health are required to move to the fourth level. It's not an everyday achievement. To get here, one must accept both the suffering in life and our inability to control it. Mr. Digit comes to know that he is more than a ring-bearing finger. He begins to sense what is beyond his puny self."

"Is this the higher self I've heard you refer to?" Ted asked.

"Yes," Angel answered. "At this level, we use more than just our minds and our language; we use our hearts, and we move through life with compassion or love toward self and others and resonating—or becoming united with—the beauty that exists in the universe above and beyond us—no matter the name we choose to assign it. Our life goal and purpose shift away from protection and toward integration."

Singleton cemented the concept. "We move away from our small selves and toward our unique divinity, our true selves. It is a very big step toward becoming a fully actualized human being."

"Father Chuck told me, while we were in divinity school together"—Angel winced, realizing that she had just confessed to another one of her failed attempts at a career—"that this movement to the fourth level is rare before we are thirty years old. He thinks this is why Jesus's ministry is mysteriously silent until Jesus reached that age."

Ted found it interesting that Angel was able to maintain all of these spiritual relationships—Father Chuck, Stephen, and Mashid. He regretted not having similar friends in his own life. He wondered too, for the first time, if—with a little effort—he could be initiated into Angel's little band of coconuts. Could he fit in? He quickly decided that a lawyer from Crossing Trails, Kansas, was not a likely candidate.

Angel noticed that Ted seemed to be losing focus, so she tried to dive deeper into the fourth level while his mind was still fresh. "Ted, for the first time, the fourth grader can say, 'The answers need to be my answers, and not your answers.' That is why we call it the level of reason. Using our intellect and logic is the first appropriate step in seeking the truth. The fourth grader is able to step away from her tribe or group and skeptically analyze conventional thinking, rules, and laws; she becomes postconventional. The fourth grader is capable of comparing the thinking of her group to the thinking of your group and allows that her group may not have all of the right answers. She either entirely lets go or at least disidentifies with her past affiliations. She realizes that where she went to high school or what church she attends or what neighborhood she lives in really says very little about her true self. She is no longer tribal but instead has a more global or worldcentric perspective. She becomes less concerned about her rights, fears, and causes and more concerned about humanity and the planet as a whole."

Singleton added a few more characteristics. "The fourth grader understands her microscopic coordinates in the universe. The most remarkable aspect of the fourth grader is that she can direct her rational scrutiny not only onto others and onto abstract ideas but, more important, onto herself. The fourth grader becomes introspective and psychologically insightful."

Ted listened to their footsteps as they strolled across a wood bridge that took them over a slow-moving creek. The cottonwood trees that flanked the brook blocked the warm morning sun, and for a few moments they walked together in the shade. When he had Stephen's attention, Ted asked, "Is meditation a fourth-grade activity?"

"Yes, very much so. Being able to take a step back to really think about how I am thinking and how my thinking affects my happiness is a very sophisticated step and requires the ability to think abstractly. That's why Angel and I associate Buddhism most closely with this level."

"And in the process," Angel added, "we find not so much the answers to the questions that have eluded us on the first three levels but more of a way of smiling at the very questions we ask."

Singleton concluded, "When you can reflect critically about your own thinking, your identity is no longer tied to thinking in a particular way or coming to a particular, often comforting, conclusion. At this stage something very important happens that is key for your understanding of the next two levels. A new part of consciousness is beginning to take shape, wake up, and have a voice."

"Is this good?" Ted asked Angel with a hint of worry.

"Yes. Very good," she answered. "You must listen carefully here. We're to the crux of this level and the two that succeed it."

"Go ahead," Ted said to Angel. "I'm awake . . . so to speak."

"What you found in meditation and what the fourth grader discovers within herself is that there is something beyond our lowercase 'self' or what we think of as 'me.'"

"You're referring to the higher self again?" Ted asked.

Singleton responded. "It's our uppercase 'Self' or, as some describe it, our observing self. It's the more subtle spiritual side of us that exists but that, until we attain this level of awareness, hibernates in the right side of the brain. It is a part of our soul or our being. The emergence of the essential or true self is the hallmark of the fourth-grade thinker."

Like an orchestra transitioning from the string section to the wind instruments, Angel returned to the refrain. "At this level, the sleeping psyche is starting to really wake up."

Singleton continued, "For many, this process begins in

college, where students are exposed to ideas, lifestyles, and levels of critical thinking they hadn't encountered in their own communities. The engaged student has the sensation that her brain is going to explode with awareness. Four years later she graduates with a remarkable new way of looking at the world—often to the consternation of her parents. For the lucky few, this is the final physiological stage of brain development and the launching pad for the fourth level. Some research indicates that without the stimulation of a safe, nurturing environment and good role-modeling by our parents, our brains lose the opportunity for this developmental movement to the higher levels."

Ted was surprised. "This could have some very sad consequences."

It was clear that Ted had touched a sensitive spot for Singleton. He seemed almost angry. "The most important course of study for any human should be what Angel is trying to teach you." His emotion shifted quickly and he reached over and clutched Angel's hand. "Nobody else is climbing into a bookmobile and spreading the dharma, trying to do the Work. These teachings should be part of the curriculum of every high school student in the world. We should all be so lucky as to find that someone who cares enough to show us the way."

Ted looked at Angel. "You're right. She's a gift on wheels."

They walked a bit farther, taking in the landscape and enjoying the dogs. Singleton pulled up his little party of travelers and said, "Let's rest for a while on the bank of the river. Sometimes ducks come along in the early morning." He reached into his backpack and pulled out some stale bread. "If they do, we can feed them."

While the two teachers and Ted fed the ducks that occasionally paddled by, the dogs tugged at their leashes. They looked up at Ted and Angel, dumfounded. Did humans not understand that God put ducks on the earth to be chased? With the ducks fed, the group started walking back.

Angel draped her left arm around Ted's waist and her right arm over Singleton's shoulder. Ted turned to Angel and said, "Thank you. It was a lovely morning."

When they were approaching the bed-and-breakfast again, Angel said, "What a gift, getting to hang out with my favorite Buddhist and my favorite student." She pulled Singleton closer for a warm hug. "It was good seeing you again, Stephen. I'm looking forward to our November get-together. Will you be there?"

"Wouldn't miss it."

While collecting her belongings, Angel stared out over the meadow from the window of the Marlon Brando room. She'd had a dream the night before that she was still trying to dissect. In the dream, Bertha had been restored to her former status as a functioning bookmobile. The walls were again filled with books. Bertha was parked somewhere on the reservation. Angel was sitting behind the librarian's desk, wearing glasses and reading to a circle of children. The door to the bookmobile was wide open so the sun could gush through. She kept looking up at the door, as if she were waiting for someone or something to arrive. No Barks was lying on the floor. Being skilled at dream interpretation, Angel probed behind the facts of the dream and tried to root out the feelings and sensations that the dream evoked. What she felt was grounded and at home.

Angel felt proud of her role as Ted's spiritual consultant. She wondered, however, if the dream was trying to tell her to get an entire classroom of new students—that Ted's time with her had ended. She wondered if the significance of the dream was in Ted's absence. She realized that she was going to miss him when he did leave. Still, she felt like something from the dream hadn't yet fully revealed itself.

Angel thought about the fifth and sixth levels. This terrain would be far more difficult, not just for Ted but for her too. Instruction is a didactic, left-brained operation. This approach would not suit the fifth and sixth levels. In fact, that would be the whole point—transcending that kind of thinking. One could not metabolize these materials, hang easy labels on them, and then warehouse them in the left brain for future access. The ineffable could only be sensed and imagined, not really known or defined. One could not uncover these truths in books. They have to find us as much as we have to find them. She would have to find a different way to instruct. The problem was simple, but she was not sure how to solve it.

As Angel looked out even farther over the fields and took in a wider view of the low-lying hills of the Nebraska countryside, she realized that what she needed to say to Ted next might be upsetting to both of them. Still, it was a necessary conversation.

25

With Bertha packed and Singleton thanked, Angel and Ted took a short walk on the path beside the inn. "I want to say something," Angel said.

Ted stepped closer to Angel. "Yes?" he asked.

She put her hand on his shoulder for a moment, quickly removed it, and spoke earnestly. "I want to congratulate you on your hard work. You've stuck with a curriculum that's not easy. You've been an amazing student." Her tone dropped as she said, "I want to warn you, however, that continued progress will require two things."

"Like?" Ted prompted.

"Thank goodness for Father Chuck, Mashid, and Stephen. Without their help, I never would have made it. The material gets harder from here on out. I can't lecture much anymore. It's not that kind of material, so I'm going to have to tell less and show more. This might be difficult for me. I don't know if I can do it."

"Angel, what are you talking about? Of course you can do it. You've been fantastic. You'll find a way. I have nothing but confidence in you."

"Hear me out. I have two concerns. The first is my ability and the second is your readiness to continue."

"I feel ready."

"Ted, slow down. Remember, I practically hijacked you to come along with me. It wasn't something you asked for. I was being selfish; I so wanted a student. You can have your diploma now, graduate early from Spirit Tech, summa cum laude, if you like. Take the remainder of the vacation doing what you and Argo want . . . and not what I think you need. If you're still interested, I can outline the next two levels for you while I take you back to your Winnebago."

"What would you do if I went back to Kansas?" Ted asked.

"Maybe you had the right idea: I should repaint Bertha— ANGEL TWO SPARROW: FIELD WELDER. It turns out that there's not much of a market for spiritual consultants." She sounded dejected. "Besides, welding metal pays better than fixing souls."

"I don't understand what you're saying. Why would you want to stop now? Angel, we're not finished. Not you and not me. Your spiritual-consulting practice is just getting ready to take off!"

"Ted, thanks, but we both know it's never going to work. Still, this time with you has been a real gift to me. It's helped me to do my own work, and I do hope I've also put you on a healthier path."

"You have, but am I finished?"

"There is no startling epiphany, blinding lights, clay tablets from God, or conversations with a burning bush. There is just living life better, with more awareness, and aligned with our truer selves."

Ted remained steadfast. "What good is half a curriculum? I want the whole course."

"There are unique opportunities in our lives when we can grow and move ahead, but there are times when we need to integrate what we've learned into our lives. If you want to continue to the next levels, I should warn you that what lies ahead will be far more difficult to grasp. I'm still struggling to become stable at these levels myself."

"Angel, I don't want to be a Spirit Tech dropout." Ted felt like he already had one foot off the pier and was about to fall into the ocean, so he just finished the thought. "And I don't want to say good-bye to you, either."

It had been a long time since someone had said something sweet like this to Angel, and it felt good to be valued. Particularly when she knew she felt the same way about him. "Thank you, and of course we can finish your vacation together, if that's what you want. But still, recess is an option."

"Our plan is fine. Let's just stick to it. You keep working with me, and I need to do some work for your aunt Lilly. It's the most interesting legal case I've had in years, so don't fire me before my first day of work."

"You're sure?" She held his elbow. "You don't have to do this unless you really want to. It probably won't work, unless you really want it."

Ted took a few steps backward on the path and then bent down and pulled Argo close to him for comfort. He realized that he was about to say something inauthentic, something that he thought he *should* say, but not what he really felt. He tried using one of the exercises Angel had taught him to dig deeper and be more truthful. He sensed into his stomach and heart spaces and investigated carefully what he was sensing and experiencing. What arose surprised him. It was the same fear that had manifested from his dream. It came to him rather suddenly, like a door slamming shut when you're alone in the house. Ted put his face in his hands and exhaled a long slow breath.

Angel sat down beside Ted and put her arm around him. "Is something wrong?"

"There was a frightening dream I had in Bertha. It was upsetting enough that I've tried not to think about it. It's been lingering in my mind, and for some reason it came back to me again out of nowhere, but it returned as an answer, an explanation. I think I get the dream."

"Tell me."

"In the dream, No Barks and Argo were sitting on a grave. Strangely, it was me that had died and been buried. That's not supposed to happen in dreams, is it? Seeing your own death? But it wasn't exactly me buried in that cemetery in Crossing Trails. It was my life. The point is that I can't go back to that life in Crossing Trails. It's dead and buried. There is nothing there for me, not anymore. Something needs to change. Somewhere, somehow, there has to be more for me."

"Sometimes when we experience incredible periods of growth in our life, there is sadness and it does feel like the death of our old universe."

"I'm not sure what any of it means, not yet. I just feel the need to go to South Dakota to help your aunt Lilly. You need to do your best to finish the job you started. We both need to figure out what this is all about. That's our pilgrimage."

"We?" Angel asked.

"If you don't finish your work, I'll spend the rest of my life looking over my shoulder hoping to see another bookmobile with mountains painted on the side and some crazy dark-haired woman driving to the distant beat of drum music. Where will I find someone else to finish the job of waking up Ted Day? No one can do it but you. You can't quit on me."

Angel smiled and her eyes shone. "Thank you, Ted. We're not wasting our time together, are we?"

"Far from it."

26

"Can I be blunt?" Angel asked as they neared the entrance to Custer State Park.

"My feathers don't ruffle easily."

"You're the poster child for the fourth level."

"And . . ."

"I'm not sure how to get you past it."

"I have total confidence in you, but just the same, why is being rational a problem for moving up and on?"

"The intelligence that has served you so well in the early stages of this journey won't be of any help to you now. In fact, it may be a hindrance. The fifth and sixth levels, you see, are transrational. For people like you, reaching the fifth and sixth levels can be very difficult. From here on out, transformation rests in the mind opening with questions and not closing with answers. Suzuki called it 'beginner's mind.'" Angel grabbed her necklace and showed the letters to Ted. "This is how I describe it."

The word "imagine" around her neck had initially irritated him. He remembered how he had wanted to carve his own moniker: "knowing." Maybe Angel was right. He was a fourth grader through and through. He lived by reason and logic. "How can I get beyond my need to know?"

Angel said nothing and instead formed an intention in her mind. *I promise to do my best for you.*

Angel missed the entrance to the park and had to back up to make the turn. Once they were parked, Ted impatiently threw open the passenger door and stumbled out. It had been hours since he'd had his feet under him for anything more than a quick restroom or gas stop. The door creaked and groaned as he got out with Argo at his heels. "Terra firma feels great."

As if the air were reparative, Angel inhaled deeply. "Oh, the pine scent is marvelous."

"This place is"—he spun around to take it all in—"beautiful." While he knew he had never been anywhere near the Black Hills, there was still something familiar. Finding no personal experience that might have created a memory, he concluded that it must be a picture or a movie that he was remembering. Perhaps it was that movie his grandfather liked to watch. Without much effort, the name of the movie came to him: *Dances with Wolves*. Ted tried to make clumsy horns with his fingers and asked Angel, "*Tatanka?*"

Angel laughed. "Yes. Many tatanka!"

The next two days were spent hiking, trout fishing, and relaxing about the campsite. When he could, Ted used this time to meditate, practice the exercises, and begin exploring the fifth level, the level of the emergent self, as revealed to him by Angel in bits and pieces when it felt right for both of them.

At the first four levels the self, not yet fully capable of monitoring and observing both mind and body, is progressively resuscitated from the ego's stranglehold. It is only when the student truly grasps that he is not his ego and has another voice or aspect of being that he reaches the fifth level. Angel's exercises both emptied or weakened Ted's ego and built or strengthened the voice of his higher self. At the fifth level they began to pay off for Ted.

Reaching the fifth level was not easy for Ted, nor is it easy for anyone else. He did sense that a whole new spiritual dimension was waiting for him, but like a rubber band, he was consistently snapped back to his comfort zone, the fourth level. Angel knew from Ted's cemetery dream and her own experience that the fifth level can be a painful, anxiety-ridden place to linger. She worked intently to help him move through it.

The morning after their arrival, Angel introduced a whole new set of exercises. At first Ted felt as if he had been sent back to kindergarten. The first exercise involved an easel and colored pencils. She had him draw things upside down. It was a fun exercise to help Ted dislodge his usual way of looking at things.* Then Angel dug out her guitar and asked Ted to sing

---

* Angel had been fortunate enough to spend an entire week learning the process herself, but she'd forgotten to bring along the bible on this subject: Betty Edwards, *Drawing on the Right Side of the Brain, The Definitive 4th Edition* (New York: Penguin, 2012). Fortunately, she remembered enough to give Ted a crash course.

along with her. Angel believed that, just as drawing introduces a different way of seeing, singing allows a different voice to arise. Finally she tossed pen and paper his way and asked him to craft a short story for a six-year-old boy. "If you can't think of anything else," she directed, "try something with Argo and bears. Boys like bears. Be silly and just have fun with it."

These and the other exercises she gave him engaged and empowered the right side of his brain. On the morning of their third day in the park resting and doing the Work, with her confidence restored, Angel decided to try a more advanced exercise to explore and probe levels of consciousness unknown to most of the world. She simply said, "Lie down on the blanket, Ted. We're going to try something again. This time it will go better."

Angel began by readying her own mind to enter into a clear, empty place: a place of transrational clarity. Although it certainly does not always work, Angel knew that it is possible for the trained teacher to invite the student to occupy a passenger seat on the teacher's journey into this space. The first step built on the previous exercises: she must get Ted to stop assessing, categorizing, analyzing, prioritizing, labeling, judging, discriminating, thinking, and knowing. Getting the superego to relax is no easy task, but by now Ted had the ability to at least relax its grip. Angel moved closer to Ted, took his hand in hers, and turned his palm upward. She began to massage his index finger from the palm to the root of his fingernail.

The first time Angel had put Ted in what he described as a trance, while rubbing his finger in the parking lot of the RV park, he had found it very frightening. Understandably, he was not eager to repeat the exercise. "Just relax and close your eyes," Angel again instructed. She sat by him quietly for a few more moments until she had fully activated her own awareness or uncluttered being. "What do you feel inside your body, Ted? What comes to mind? Suspend the critical voice. Tell your superego to leave you alone. Don't judge or analyze; just sense into your body and tell me what arises."

Ted tried to describe what he felt without assessing it or making it sound logical. "There is an expansion around the left lobe of my lung. There seems to be some energy there. A reverberation. Something is definitely happening, but I'm not sure what."

"Good, just stay with it. Try to go deeper and be more visual if you can. Instead of pushing it away or ignoring it, see if you can go into it, merge with it. What can you describe to me?"

"It's still very subtle. I'm not sure if it's anything." Ted's mind made an unprecedented shift. Because he now totally trusted Angel, he did not resist this shift into a seemingly hypnotic state. He continued, "What I am sensing is a movement of some kind of energy. At least in my mind, it has a structure, like a vortex. Now it is expanding and gathering more energy—something is passing through this vortex, in and out like a breath. It's almost like there has been an incision in my abdomen and I am breathing energy and life through this space and not through my mouth."

"Can you put your consciousness into that space? Really explore what's there. See if you can get inside it and look around. Let it take you where it will."

Ted's dreamy peacefulness went even deeper, but this time

instead of falling asleep, he tried to follow Angel's lead. He felt very aware. Awake. "I can imagine this space and I am sensing it growing, and in fact my entire self is expanding rapidly."

"How big are you now, Ted?"

"I am both expanding and diffusing." Ted's breathing was shallow, but his words were strong. "My sense of proportion is slipping away. But . . ."

"It's okay. Try to stay with it."

"I now find myself having expanded into the sky. Where the vortex of my lung was a few seconds ago is now a dark, star-clad universe and I'm just suspended there. I feel like one of those early cosmonauts, spacewalking in eternity. My relative size and proportion are lost—this territory is just too vast, too infinite."

"Does it feel like infinite space, Ted?"

"Yes, but there is nothing. Absolutely nothing but me and a luminous darkness. Yet I can somehow see."

"Are you alone!"

"I don't feel alone."

"In this space, Ted, are there any sensations available to you?"

"Yes. Tranquility, peace, and something primordial. It is so very empty. I sense the absence of time and all things physical."

Angel's voice was calm, soothing, loving, and accepting. "If you could put a word to where you are, what would it be?"

"The boundaries between me and the universe are collapsed. I don't know where I start and everything else ends. It's groundless. It's peaceful nothingness."

"Can you stay with that feeling?"

Ted teetered back into his normal state of being. He opened his eyes. "It's gone."

"Don't be disappointed, Ted. You've just experienced something powerful. It will live in you for the rest of your life. It is very much a part of you. No one can ever take it away. You will travel back to this place again and you'll get clearer about what you are experiencing."

"What was it?"

"Don't try to define it. If you do, it'll become stale. Just let it be whatever it is."

Ted sat up from the ground, where he was sprawled out on an old blanket, and looked up at Angel uneasily—wholly unsure if he should be committed or sainted. "What did it mean? Where was I? Was it a good thing?"

She gently encouraged him to lie back down. "Relax. It's always been there for you. There was just too much chatter and distraction in your mind before. Too much knowing. You'll come back to this space later. Don't grasp for it or try to hold on to it. Resist the urge to define it and own it. Just let it be like a dream from which you have now awakened. Your right brain can sense it, intuit it, and embrace it without knowing. Leave it there for now."

Ted kept his eyes closed and wondered what exactly he had just experienced. Was it God? Did some force or presence indeed underpin his existence? Was this some exhilarating mystical experience or just some bland, empty, and ordinary thing that had somehow eluded his consciousness for the last thirty years? He didn't know. He tried to follow Angel's advice and just accept it without labeling it.

"Just rest here, Ted, for about twenty minutes. With this exercise there are sometimes little aftershocks. I'm going to go to the river and bathe. I'll be back soon."

Ted closed his eyes. He wanted to enjoy the peaceful tranquility that had just passed over him, but soon thoughts of Angel bathing crossed his mind. Again he slipped into a near dream state, except he was totally conscious. He was able to *see* Angel in his mind. Her lithe, strong body was perched atop a large boulder. A strong afternoon sun kept her warm as she leaned over and let her long black hair float atop the icy-cold current. Her fingers moved through her hair like a comb, helping the shampoo to dissolve into little bubbles that floated down the river and disappeared. She sat up, bent her right leg and crossed it over the left, and twisted her hair to squeeze out the excess water. When it was dry enough, she stood and looked over the hills like a guardian, with her hands cupped to protect her eyes from the sun's glare.

Ted was unsure if he was just daydreaming or if he was somehow *seeing* Angel in his own mind. The prospect of some extrasensory experience frightened Ted, so he opened his eyes, got up, and sat in a chair, inviting the return of ordinary consciousness. With nothing else to do while he awaited Angel's return, and hoping the exercise he had just experienced might make it somehow easier, Ted tried to plunge deeper into the fifth level.

The fifth level, he decided, was the logical extension of

the formula that Father Chuck had introduced to him a week earlier. At some point there had to be a consequence of less self. Angel had told him that when enough of Mr. Digit's influence has been dismantled, the higher self emerges with its own unique voice. No longer a curious guest lingering on the front porch of his personality, the higher self moves in and becomes a functioning member of the psychic household. He wondered if that was what he had been experiencing the last few days: the growing emergence of a part of himself that he had lost somewhere along the way.

Lately he could almost feel himself cringing at his own Mr. Digit's ego chatter—a constant barrage of wants, wishes, aversions, feelings, and thoughts. Sometimes it was just laughable. At other times it was depressing to realize that such an unruly little tyrant had been running his life. He used another of Angel's exercises and tried to focus and welcome into his mind this new kid on the block—a calm, peaceful, and accepting presence.

Ted's ego was bruised and banged up from all of the Work. The relationship between the egoic or false self and the true self had devolved to the breaking point.* Around two fifteen,

---

* Father Chuck counted himself very lucky to live close to Richard Rohr and was heavily influenced by his Catholic brother. One weekend Angel and Father Chuck had been fortunate enough to attend a seminar that dealt entirely with the false self and the true self. Angel had a recording of the seminar and played it over and over—loving it almost as much as her Lakota drum music. See Richard Rohr, *True Self, False Self* (Cincinnati: St. Anthony Messenger Press, 2003) (audio recording).

Ted closed his eyes and let out a long, sweet sigh. Finally, it just happened: the pieces fell into place. Ted woke up.

He knew nothing but experienced everything. He opened his eyes and was able to locate the sensation, truly feel, the presence within himself that was not Mr. Digit. An almost overwhelming sense of love and gratitude flowed over and through him. He recognized that this space within him was the real Ted, his true self. He simply rested there, as if he had finally come home to peace. Still, it was somehow also frightening.

Angel returned from the river and sat down beside him. She sensed his awakening and his fear. "Ted," she said, "I know your head is probably spinning right now. I warned you that this would be hard. You've come much farther along than you realize in a very short period of time. You now recognize clearly that Mr. Digit and his entire worldview are off target. The problem is that his software has been running your life for so long that without it you will feel lost. Even though you sense the presence of your higher self, you have not yet fully attuned to this new operating system within you. It may seem like you're floating in spiritual no-man's-land for a while. Trust me: eventually you will be standing on firm ground."

Ted recognized some of what Angel was saying but did not entirely agree. "I am disoriented, Angel, but I'm also committed to this idea of sifting through the disparate parts of my personality structure and electing a new chairman of the board. I never realized I had this option. It's exciting."

"My mother called it something different. She said that alcoholics must turn their lives over to a higher power. I think she meant that her Mrs. Digit personality was literally killing her and she had to learn to tune in to a different voice in her head. She was saying the same thing you are saying. She wanted to find the voice and turn her life over to it."

"This higher power still seems like a small, whispering voice that I have to strain to hear."

"Yes, Ted, our purpose in life, the Work, is to amplify that voice and learn to deeply respect it."

"It's always been there, but for some reason I stopped listening to it. I don't know why I stopped hearing it."

Angel only smiled. "You're not alone—we all become very adept at ignoring this aspect of ourselves. The fifth level is about reclaiming your true self. Strange as it may sound, it's not just alcoholics that struggle to hear the voice of their true self. Deeply religious people struggle at the fifth level just like everyone else. No one is exempt from doing the Work."

Ted sat there for a moment and tried to let everything they had talked about over the last few days coalesce. He was anxious, so he stood up and began to pace around the fire. He realized that this shifting, waking feeling was vaguely familiar; it was like the shift from studying a foreign language to actually speaking it.

"You know, Angel, the tumbler on a safe is an interesting mechanism. All the parts have to be set at just the right spot. When that happens, the lock clicks and the safe door can swing wide open." Ted thought a bit more and continued, "Randomly, it would take many lifetimes to come across the right combination of numbers that allows the tumbler to fall into place. However, you've been giving me hints at the combination. It's quite an amazing feeling to find yourself standing in front of an open door—suddenly aware of the entire contents of the safe. It's an exhilarating rush. That's how I feel right now. Everything you told me and what Father Chuck and the other coconuts provided has all come together for me."

What was in that safe was a grand discovery. Ted felt as if he suddenly understood everything. Not just the levels but everything: the grand big picture of Angel Two Sparrow, Ted Day, and their journey together.

He realized who she was, why she was here with him, and what his vacation was all about. Ted was a smart guy but still, at the end of the day, like the rest of us, he'd had so many nagging little questions. Not one of them bothered him now. He'd had a blinding flash of intuition. Now it was up to him to slow that flash down and put the pieces together. The right side of his brain had given him the answer. Now he needed to learn to use the left side to slowly put the answers into words and explain himself as best he could. "Angel, I could be wrong, but I think I've got it."

Ted continued to pace about their campsite testing his theory in his mind. He wanted to rehearse it to himself before he said it to her.

Angel, being a full-blooded Lakota, respected his need for silence. She retrieved an old dog brush from Bertha and sat down and groomed No Barks. The wolf dog enjoyed the attention. Angel hummed quietly to herself while Ted paced and pondered.

As he circumambulated the fire faster and faster, his excitement grew. He knew that he was onto something important, but he still couldn't quite get it to tumble out of his mind in words. Angel herself might not be aware of the importance of what she was doing. Maybe it was a long shot and he had it all wrong. He needed to articulate this theory. This was not knowing.

Finally Ted sat down next to Angel and No Barks. Angel smiled generously but still said nothing.

27

"My vacation is coming to an end," Ted told Angel. "Only a few days left. What you, Mashid, Stephen, and Father Chuck have taught me has been turning around in my head and is finally all coming together. When I add it all up and then break it back down, I keep landing at the same spot. It might sound strange to you, but from an entirely objective stand-point, being the little agnostic fellow that I am, this is my take on the essence of religion and spiritual development and everything you've taught me."

"Well, there are no tests at Spirit Tech, but if it's helpful for you to have a final exam, I'll listen."

Ted started. "Two thousand years ago, give or take a few centuries, three very spiritually advanced sages, all men, walked the earth. They all preached and taught a similar lesson about the possibility and the methodology of human transformation. Their vocabularies were different, but they all believed that a life without awareness was deficient. They came from different cultures and different times and, on the surface at least, they are remembered in different ways. One was a savior. Another was a messenger. The third was an awakened one. Each of these men was born into a community that recognized his exceptional nature and appreciated his unique message of hope through human spiritual transformation. Naturally, each culture placed around the neck of its hero the highest honor it could bestow—its own unique epitaph of greatness. In those days they didn't hand out medals or Nobel Prizes; instead they bestowed titles: king, savior, son of god, angel, and enlightened one. All the same thing."

"Ted, it's a sound enough theory. But remember, too, that it's the nature of most religious followers to firmly believe that their brand of religion is the only authentic flavor and the other brands are just watered-down, quaint versions of the truth practiced by a few billion people on the other side of the planet."

"You mean a Christian would say that what I said is a fair enough analysis of Muhammad and the Buddha but not of Jesus, who is truly the holy one?"

"Yes, and a Jew might say 'right on' about Muhammad but not Moses. Or a Lakota, 'You sure nailed the Buddha. He was just a regular guy, but have I ever told you about Buffalo Woman?'"

"That's my point, Angel. That's just the third level. When we let go of knowing, we have to let go of thinking that our way is the only way—or necessarily even the best way. You were right. This part was easy for me because I was never sold on any one program to start out with. I don't for a minute believe that any one religion has the right and only answers. Instead I believe that each religion uses the best metaphors and signposts that exist for them in their culture to try to explain that which is entirely inexplicable."

Angel nodded. "Ted, many people might argue with you, but I'm not one of them. I will say this. It may be fair to say that religion is in large part metaphor, but it is also fair to say that some metaphors work better than others, depending on our cultural differences."

"So much for background. Now let me take my final exam from Spirit Tech."

Angel held up her hand. "I have my red pencil."

"It's quite clear to me, Angel, that the first realization is accurate: to varying degrees we are unawake. It's also clear that the second realization is equally on target. Our lack of awareness is tightly linked to our Mr. Digit personality. Finally, as the third realization dictates, we are resting at different stops along the way, and by doing the Work we have the capacity to evolve and wake up."

Angel clapped her hands. "Bravo, Ted. I'm already confident you have the first five levels of awareness down, so skip those and get right to the sixth level. If you get that one right, I am giving you a diploma."

Ted moved closer to Angel and began. "First, imagine if you can that these great men we've talked about so much for the last few days—the Buddha, Muhammad, and Jesus—were all born not thousands of years ago but, let's say, thirty or forty years ago and in the Western world, maybe Cleveland or Cincinnati. So now Jesus, Muhammad, and the Buddha are out there somewhere wandering around the Midwest with the exact same abilities and gifts they were wandering around with a few thousand years ago in the Old World. They have essentially the same message of personal transformation to deliver to this now totally different, modern audience. Imagine too that instead of the Buddha, Jesus, or Muhammad, it's one of their equally talented sisters. What would this feminine savior look like, and what would she say today? In this more modern world, with a millennium or two of human development and understanding behind us, would she be a carpenter, the leader of a caravan, the son of a prince?" Ted waited for Angel to answer, and when she didn't, he supplied some more likely options. "A minister, a doctor, or a poet?"

"It's your exam. You tell me."

Ted continued. "All right, then. Here's my theory. I don't think anyone would believe Muhammad's sister if she said she'd wandered down from some cave with her laptop after capturing this really catchy prose, word for word, that God delivered to her."

"Maybe not."

"The Buddha's twin sister, starving herself half to death beneath the bodhi tree, wouldn't get much of an audience on the five o'clock news."

"Just another lost, homeless soul."

"Jesus's female alter ego, claiming to be the by-product of an immaculate conception, would likely find herself in a straitjacket."

Angel wrapped her arms around herself and gave a little fake struggle.

"In fact, in today's world these men or their sisters would have a hard time getting airtime and would have to find a different way to communicate."

"It was hard enough then. You're right; it might even be harder today. Maybe that's why no spiritual giants have emerged in the last two thousand years or so."

Ted continued his line of questioning. "Yes, it would have to be very different. So let's think about it. What would a savior sound like today? How would she think? How would she deliver her message?"

"All good questions. Do you have answers?" Angel asked.

"Yes, I do, and I think you gave them to me. The only way you could recognize a teacher like that today—and this is a crucial point of your Spirit Tech teachings—would be by grasping the levels. No matter the epoch within which these men or women were born, they would have to be at the sixth level of awareness."

"Makes sense to me," Angel said. "So you're saying today we wouldn't assess their credibility by the magic they performed or by some physical attribute like a halo; we would simply expect them to be the most highly evolved spiritual beings on the planet."

"It also seems fair to assume that however difficult it is to reach the sixth level today, it would have been harder and therefore far more unusual to have evolved to this level one or two thousand years ago. We can pretty safely assume that it was so unusual that anyone who reached the sixth level would have been enshrined in near godlike status—as in fact occurred with each of these three men whose lives we have examined at Spirit Tech. Whole religions grew up around them.

"So here's my hypothesis, Angel. What if making the sixth level, while still rare, is much more doable today? We have more resources and we've had a few thousand years to practice. Our entire world culture has been profoundly influenced by the teachings of Jesus, the Buddha, Muhammad, and most likely many more sixth-level graduates that came after them. We have more time on our hands to study and ponder. It makes sense to me that in many ways these men successfully transformed the world. Today making the sixth level may not be such a cosmic accomplishment. This could explain why, with the exception of the Mormons, no new religions have come into being in modern times as the result of God choosing to communicate to one man alone. It just seems implausible in the modern world. Today's sixth graders have to settle for a Nobel Prize, an occasional beatification, or maybe a lucrative publishing contract. That's about it."

Angel wanted to make sure she was following Ted's point. "Are you're saying that because we create no new gods, it is very difficult to let go of the few old ones we still have hanging around in the public consciousness?"

"I think it's a reasonable theory. Okay, Angel, I'm going for extra credit now."

"I'm listening."

"Let me turn to the sixth level. Father Chuck set it up for me last week. Progressing through the levels is a continual process of emptying of the false self. As we empty the ego, the higher self moves into the vacated spaces. The fifth level, as you have been explaining to me over the last few days, is about the emergence of the higher self as a now-audible part of the psyche. To some extent, through all of the exercises you've been giving me, I've experienced something that I suspect is indeed this higher self, or what your mother might have described as a higher power. I understand that it was not something you could describe to me; it was something I had to literally experience myself. Thank you."

"Yes, the fifth level is of the emergent self, and I too believe you have seen and experienced this part of yourself."

"The sixth level can only be one thing. The higher self finally eclipses Mr. Digit. The right brain is restored to dominance, or at least balance." Ted waited for Angel to correct him if she thought he was headed the wrong way. She didn't, so he continued. "You opened up an unusual space for me in one of our exercises together. My Mr. Digit personality relaxed its grip for a few moments and I lost my separateness. I was able to merge with something vast and mysterious—it was simultaneously everything and nothing. For myself, I can't define this awakened state any better than that, but I was able to experience it. If I lived in a different time, I might have run into the village with clay tablets in my hand and claimed that God showed himself to me. Today we have to be more circumspect. I simply remain curious and open to the experience, whatever it might have been, and see it not so much as a unitized experience with God as a symptom of my own unfettered consciousness. I may never achieve this state again. That's okay."

"Do you think this state was indicative of your transformation?" Angel asked.

"Maybe, but I don't know. It doesn't matter. Like Father Chuck said, and the Buddha too, I'm no longer interested in sitting on the shore debating the characteristics of the boat. I'm just rowing. I know I may not be there myself—Mr. Digit may still have a firm grasp on me—but still I suspect I might recognize a modern-day sixth grader if she was staring me in the face."

"Try it," Angel encouraged.

"At the sixth level the false self still hangs around. I suspect none of us can totally rid ourselves of this aspect of our personality. I'm not convinced that it would even be a good idea to be totally unselfish."

"If you give all your money to feed the starving masses, you might starve yourself. You're making the logical distinction between self-preservation and the Mr. Digit worldview or personality. That's an important distinction."

"Here's how I see it. By doing the Work we can at least dethrone the ego as the master and commander of our lives. The same is true with the superego. The sixth grader is not going to allow archaic rules, tribal norms, or even plain old logical thinking to run her life. She is grounded in and operates to the highest extent possible from her core, true, or higher self. As a practical matter, her concerns are more global and less provincial. She is not a dualistic thinker. She is more interested in putting things together than breaking things apart—cohesion and not conquest; cooperation and not competition. Her world is anchored more by 'ands' and less by 'ors.' This is her calling. Being postconventional and transrational in her thinking, she will probably have a hard time fitting into a conventional lifestyle. She will seek out others to support her in her convictions."

"You're heading the right way. What else can you tell me about the sixth level?"

"Being less mired in left-brained thinking, she finds that the world opens up to her in seemingly magical or at least paranormal ways. She is so rich in spirit that others experience her as a healer and a nurturer of souls. She sees and observes things with her right-brain, heart-anchored mind that others might ignore as, for example, in dreams. She is the substantive embodiment of love and compassion. She thinks in images and feelings and is highly artistic and creative. She is kind and accepting and approaches life with love and not fear."

"I think, too . . ." Ted hesitated. What he said next came from an emotional place. "She will be the very best human being any of us could ever want to know." He took Angel's hand in his own. "She only has two flaws."

"Yes?" Angel innocently asked.

"Not being fully of this selfish world, I would not expect her to excel in selfish pursuits. The world might seem like a very confusing place for her."

"You said two things were wrong with her."

He took Angel in his arms. "She would have a hard time

knowing how to reach out to the ones she so desperately wants to heal. She might be reduced to rather strange methods of transmitting her message."

"For example?"

"Well, she might have to drive around in a beat-up bookmobile with advertising signs painted on the side. None of which would be that bad except for the fact that she can't drive worth a damn!"

Angel held Ted tightly. She was not sure if Ted had really grasped the sixth level, but he'd made a very decent stab at it. She was sure of this: what Ted had said was a sweet declaration of love. She whispered in his ear, "Thank you."

28

The next morning, Angel suggested that they take the dogs on an overnight hike. When they got back, they could leave for Pierre to visit Aunt Lilly. Ted had no problem extending his vacation for a few more days. Still, he offered a few conditions of his own. "I'd like to fly-fish. Also, I'm still hoping to catch sight of . . ." He wiggled his index fingers above his head.

"*Tatanka?*" Angel asked.

Ted nodded, pleased that Angel had followed his Lakota so well.

She pointed to the trailhead. "The best way to find buffalo is to look for them.

Angel had spent many hours in Custer State Park with Larsen, her mother, and her brother when she was young. Less than one hundred miles from her childhood home near the reservation, it was the largest state park in South Dakota and boasted not only the beauty of the Black Hills but also one thousand head of free-ranging buffalo.

The reservation lands and the adjoining park grounds were not heavily trafficked by human feet. There were still trout in the streams and it was not unusual to come across ancient bones and arrowheads unearthed by a heavy rain. There was a strange harmony between the meadows and the forest-clad hills. It was as if grass and trees took turns dominating the landscape of the Black Hills, each providing a captivating backdrop for the other.

Ted exited Bertha with a pack on his back and Argo by his side. "I'm ready."

"There's a swimming spot by the river where my father took me when I was a little girl. I'd like to try to find it. Absent a buffalo stampede, we should be able to make it well before dark. It would be the perfect spot for camping and fishing."

"I'd like that very much."

With their packs slung over their shoulders and their dogs tagging along, Angel and Ted set out on their hike in the early-morning sun. Although the hiking was not strenuous, Ted found a sturdy pine branch resting on the ground and quickly fashioned a walking stick. As they proceeded along the barely trodden trail, Angel sang familiar tunes and Ted joined in on the choruses when he could. Periodically Angel would stop, position herself toward the east, and tilt her head back so the sun was on her face. "Ahh, how nice is that?"

Ted believed that for each human being there is a moment, or perhaps several moments for the particularly lucky ones, where life simply gets no better. On that day everything was aligned for joy. He too tilted his head back and reiterated her sentiment. "Perfect sun! Perfect day. Perfect spiritual consultant. What else could I ask for?"

Angel took Ted's hand and held it close to her chest, asking, "Me?" With that small gesture, she suggested that things could hypothetically get even better for Ted Day.

Several hawks circled high above them in the sky. The sight of two humans and two dogs walking across their hunting grounds was disturbing enough to send the birds gliding away to range elsewhere. The path slanted to the west, in the direction where the elevation and timber increased. In another quarter of a mile the trail intersected a creek. Angel and Ted walked along the creek for about thirty more minutes. The trail generally followed the water and then turned north, where, after several more miles, they came to an even larger stream. Angel hesitated but turned right and followed the river back to the east. After an hour of hiking, she was concerned that her memory of the clear lagoon was faulty, perhaps an amalgamation of several different trips. She was about to give up on finding it when Ted did something strange. He stopped, looked about, and set his pack on the ground.

"I've been here before. I can sense it."

"You've never been to South Dakota."

Ted looked at Angel. "That's true, but still I feel like I've been here before."

"Let's stop, then. It's as good a place as any."

"Are you sure? You don't want to find that place?"

"This is better." Angel was excited for Ted. He was tapping into something intuitive, transrational, and more than that, he was trusting that his world might not always add up. He was letting go of his need to know. His reality was not fixed. "Do you want to fish?" Angel asked.

"Yes, but first I want to gather firewood. We'll need a fire to cook."

There had not been much rain. The stream was running low and Angel doubted very much that Ted would need the fire to cook. It was not a good time for fishing. Still, she had plenty of granola bars and that was good enough for her.

Ted undid his pack and carefully set out his fly reel. "Come on, Argo, let's get a pile of wood together."

While Ted found firewood near the shore, Angel set up the rest of their camp. From the first armload of wood Ted brought to her she decided to get a small fire going. She rummaged through her pack for matches and went to work.

Angel had the fire well established when Ted began to fish. To her surprise, he got not one quick hit but three. In fact, as sunset approached, Angel and Ted were lying on the ground laughing. The fish seemed to be jumping onto his hook. It was one of those days.

Angel stared at the stringer. "I don't get it. This is not how fly-fishing works. You spend an entire day slapping at the water and, if you're lucky, you catch one or two. What's going on here?"

"I'm a natural—what else can I say?" Ted couldn't figure it out, either. He looked about and knew only that there was something magical about this spot.

Angel grabbed the rod from Ted. "Enough fishing. Let's eat."

Ted cleaned the four largest fish and released the rest of his catch. The fish, roasted over the flames from pine boughs, made a nice meal—slightly bland but, after the hike, fine dining.

Ted ate both of his fish, but Angel pulled off pieces of her second trout to add to the dried dog food they had carried in for No Barks and Argo.

When the sun was fully set and the meal was behind them, Ted had no desire to speak further of spiritual matters. It had been such a delightfully carefree day that he just wanted to continue in the flow. They had no cards, so Ted just lay down on his bedroll, stared up at the emerging stars, and tried to let whatever was welling up inside him bubble to the surface. A barely perceptible grin came across his face as the idea emerged—from where, he did not yet realize.

He had never once uttered these words, not once in his life. Maybe the ghost of Astaire forced him to do it. Ted leaped up from the ground, grabbed Angel's wrist, and said, "Let's dance!" He waited for her to respond.

She looked at him, rather surprised. "Ted Day dances?"

"He does now!"

Angel was hesitating, so Ted pulled her up into his arms. They both closed their eyes and swayed to the rhythm of nature: the wind, the stream, the distant cry of the coyote. They were all part of the band. Angel started dancing in a very free and rhythmic swaying motion. Ted did his best to imitate her moves. The lighting was just poor enough that neither of them needed to feel self-conscious about their movements. The dogs sensed the excitement and began jumping up and down, wanting in on the action. Ted allowed No Barks to jump up and place her front paws on his chest. He led her around the fire prancing about on her hind legs. Ted tried a quick two-step with the wolf dog. He looked at Angel and said, "Two-legged moon dancing!"

Angel laughed. "My dog is jealous! She wants you all to herself."

Ted let go of the wolf's paws. "You can cut in if you'd like."

"No. I think you two make a nice couple." Angel couldn't resist the urge to dance around the campfire like an elated Lakota. Like a Lakota in love. Like a Lakota in her element. Like a Lakota who enjoyed life down to its sugary fruit-cocktail core, along with her sweet place within it. She shuffled her feet in small, quick steps and danced around the fire pit, tipping her head first down and then back up again. Both dogs followed behind Angel, apparently equally in the moment. The pine logs popped and crackled and the scent was life itself. Angel began a Lakota chant.

Angel's song stirred something within Ted. It was as if her notes were plucking the strings of his heart. He watched the red embers pop, rise, and disappear into the starry night sky. Angel stood and looked at Ted. She was quivering, but it was not cold.

Ted snuggled in close to Angel. He found his hands reaching behind her head, which she gently tilted back, but this time not to accept the warm rays of the sun. Ted smelled everything good on Angel. Coconut soap in her hair, the pine scent from the fire on her shirt, and the fresh stream water on her lips as their mouths found each other, first softly and gently and then excitedly. As the lyrics of the moon slowly fell silent, they fell to the ground, wrapped in each other's arms. Angel's space and Ted's space was now their space.

When the moon was high in the night sky, Angel interrupted Ted's bliss to describe her dream from a few nights past. "I was reading to the children on the floor of Bertha, but she had been restored to a bookmobile. What do you think?"

"Even I know what that means."

"Really?" she asked without hiding her surprise.

"Sure, don't you remember what Singleton said?" She didn't answer, so he continued. "He said that our schools desperately need a spiritual curriculum. That must have triggered your dream."

"Did I ever tell you how Bertha came to Aunt Lilly?" Angel asked.

"No, but now that you mention it, I was wondering."

"The children on the reservation are very spread out. Many parents don't have cars or other transportation, so they can't drive their young ones to a library, and there is certainly no money for books. Years ago there was a grant for the bookmobile, but the money went away and the school district had to sell the bookmobile for scrap. Lilly bought it to live in, and one of her husbands helped her to convert it into a residence. That's where it came from."

"Good for Aunt Lilly, bad for the children on the reservation."

"The reservation desperately needs teachers. I only need one more semester to get a degree. Perhaps Bertha was trying to tell me I should be a different kind of teacher."

"I think you would make an excellent teacher, but what about the other part of the dream—restoring Bertha to her former glory?"

"Restoring Bertha would be impossible. It would cost too much money."

"How much is too much?"

Angel rolled her eyes in exasperation. "Maybe twenty or thirty thousand dollars? On the reservation that would be a fortune; might as well be five million."

Ted tugged on Angel's ɪ-ᴍ-ᴀ-ɢ-ɪ-ɴ-ᴇ necklace. "What better teacher than you . . . the ultimate spiritual consultant? When you get home, you should check into this. Remember . . ."

"Yes?" Angel asked.

"Bertha knows best!"

There were quiet whispers under the moonlit South Dakota sky. A mile west, six hundred head of buffalo bedded down on the prairie. Angel and Ted sensed that their experience together was as rare and valuable and natural as buffalo bedding down for the night.

Angel held Ted like she never wanted to let him go. Ted held Angel just as tightly. He was certain that nothing on the face of the earth could possibly compare to this day and now this night. His life now seemed like a long march with a sweet ending. Both dogs rested close to the fire, equally content and in their element. As far as they were concerned, each day was the best day.

Angel fell asleep quickly. As usual, Ted struggled. Instead

of the pesky bolt on the floor of Bertha, he was now dealing with several poorly positioned rocks. Just after midnight, when he should have been falling asleep, he was watching the embers from the dying fire rise into the sky. Ted sat up and nudged Angel until she opened her eyes. "We need to talk. Now."

29

"What's wrong?" Angel asked.

"I figured it out."

"You've figured out enough for one day. Go back to sleep."

"No, you have to listen. It's important." When he was confident he had her waking attention, he continued. "Bertha has given another message! When you put me in that finger-rubbing trance at the campground back at Perfect Prairie, I had a dream while I was resting in Bertha. It had you and me dancing around the campfire with the dogs. It had these woods. Everything was just like what happened tonight. Nothing like this has ever happened to me. Dreams cannot predict the future."

"Lots of people have these experiences. My mother came to me the night before she died and said good-bye to me in a dream. She hadn't even been sick. Go back to sleep. Have more good dreams."

Ted became very frustrated. "No, you don't understand. It's not that. I'm not frightened. I'm thrilled."

"Okay, Ted, take it easy."

"Don't you see?" Ted waited for Angel to connect the dots,

to see what was now so obvious to him. When she still didn't answer, he did it for her. "We need to go to Pierre first thing in the morning. I'm quite sure of it now."

"What, Ted? You're sure of what?"

"Aunt Lilly. She's innocent. I think I know what happened."

Angel's sounded surprised. "Of course she's innocent. That's why I asked you to help her."

30

Early the next morning, Ted insisted that they hike back to Bertha and get on the road to the South Dakota Women's Prison. It occurred to him that he was not going to look very lawyerly in his hiking clothes, and his grandfather had always told him that, when it came to clients, first impressions are important. Once in Pierre, he and Angel located the town's only shopping center, the Pierre Mall. There was not a huge selection of men's clothing, but Ted was pretty sure he could put together something decent. None of the suits in JCPenney seemed to appeal to Angel, though, and Ted was beginning to get frustrated. "It's just an hour interview. As long as I look professional, it doesn't matter that much if Aunt Lilly doesn't approve of my outfit."

Each time Ted would pull something off the rack, Angel would say, "I don't know. . . . We've got to get her to trust you."

Finally, Ted said, "Angel, just pick something out for me. I want to get there before dark."

Angel decided to disclose some more details of her early-morning phone call to the lawyer, John Shinn, and her conversation with her father to make the arrangements for visiting Aunt Lilly. "Ted, I think my father is going to be at the prison too. He wants to meet you. He's afraid if you're not careful, you'll get Aunt Lilly the electric chair."

"Well, that changes everything."

Angel nodded slowly. "I want you to make such a good impression. Ted, you should know that he doesn't particularly like white men."

"Oh, that's just fantastic. Is there anything else you want to tell me?"

Again Angel nodded. She slowly looked down. "He hates lawyers."

"Is that all?"

"I'm worried that he won't see what a good man you are."

Ted paced about practicing the Lakota silent treatment and then came back to Angel in a near panic. "What should we do?"

"I don't know."

She took Ted's hand and said, "Come with me. I have an idea. I told my dad you work for farmers and ranchers in Kansas. He thinks you're a cowboy."

"No wonder he hates me. I hope you set him straight."

"No, that was the one thing he seemed to like about you."

"I thought Indians hated cowboys."

"No, they sympathize. The cowboys got kicked off the range, just like the Indians."

They walked out of JCPenney, and Angel found a bench and made Ted sit on it. "Wait here. I'll be back in ten minutes."

Angel scurried around the corner to the Rancher's Outlet.

Fifteen minutes later, she came out and found Ted still waiting on the bench. "Come on. I've got it all picked out. You just
have to help with the sizes."

Ted and Angel parked Bertha, walked the dogs briefly, and
entered the main door of the prison. Once inside, they sat in
the waiting room for ten minutes until Larsen arrived.

Larsen came in the front door and looked around until
he saw his daughter and the lawyer from Kansas. He had not
been expecting a tall, lanky lawyer-dressed-like-a-cowboy. He
wondered where Angel had found this man. At least this one
had a job.

Larsen did his best to not show his suspicions. On more
than one occasion since Angel had told him about this man
he had wondered what a cattle lawyer knew about criminal
defense. Still, Angel had said he was smart and wanted to
help. The Legal Aid lawyer, John Shinn, had said the same
thing. "Larsen," Shinn had told him, "if the man wants to
help, let him." He'd said that Ted had written an entire memo-
randum on self-defense and something called the castle doctrine and e-mailed it to him, and that it was well written.

The way Shinn had explained it to Larsen, Ted had a
pretty decent argument and some case law to back it up, but
there were lots of gaps that needed filling in. Shinn doubted
Ted could find those pieces. Still, if he wanted to work on the
case, Shinn had no objection.

"Could you send me the memo he did?" Larsen had asked. "I'd like to read it."

"Sure," Shinn had said. "Knock yourself out."

Angel ran over and hugged Larsen. It was one of those lingering hugs that demonstrated sincere affection more than just a polite greeting. Ted could feel the connection between them. He heard Angel say, "*Age*, I'm so happy to see you. Come meet Ted."

Larsen held out his hand. "Larsen Two Sparrow. Lilly is my aunt." He got right to business. "Do you think you can help her?"

Ted thought about all the legal theories that he might throw at Larsen in an attempt to impress him but decided that none of that mattered much. Larsen looked like a worn-out man, with long graying-to-white braids dangling over the edge of grease-soaked overalls. He doubted Larsen cared much for legal theories. "Even if she is not entirely innocent, we may be able to avoid a conviction. There are several things from the police reports that bother me. That's why I wanted to meet her, talk to her myself."

"Aunt Lilly does not always speak in a way that makes a great deal of sense. I hope you have better luck than the others did, that she trusts you."

"We'll try."

"Let us talk to her first." Larsen handed Ted a bag he had carried in with him. "While Angel and I talk to her, put this on. If she asks, you may tell her that I loaned it to you. It will restore your energy."

Larsen walked out of the waiting room and into the visiting area. Ted found a chair and opened up the sack. Inside was a very strange piece of clothing. It appeared to be an orange hunting vest with some bizarre ornamentation attached to it. Ted looked at the vest in confusion, shrugged, and put it on. If Angel's father wanted him to look like a fool, he guessed he would look like a fool.

A uniformed guard entered the room. "Attorney Ted Day."

Ted walked as confidently as he could in his new shiny black boots and bright orange hunting vest. After being screened by the metal detector, he passed through two locked doors that buzzed and opened. The guard sat him down in what looked like a concrete-block cafeteria in a middle school. The seal of the State of South Dakota was painted on one wall. The linoleum floors were polished to a bright sheen. Angel, Lilly, and Larsen waited quietly at a table.

Angel wanted to jump up and hold Ted's hand, but she was afraid he might not approve. Larsen wanted to hold Angel's hand but was afraid Ted would not approve. Ted wished Argo were there, but he was pretty sure the warden would not approve. The door on the other side of the room buzzed and the guard stood silently by the now-locked door.

Aunt Lilly ignored Larsen and Angel and spoke straight to Ted in what could only be described as the gentlest voice he had ever heard. "Tell me, Ted, has Mother Earth been generous with her energy? Are you fully charged today?"

Ted looked to Larsen for guidance. He could see Larsen

slowly nod his head up and down. "Yes, Aunt Lilly, I am fully charged today."

"Good. Then we can get to work on my defense."

"Yes, I am ready." Ted looked over his legal pad, where he had carefully crafted and organized questions while they drove from the state park.

Before he could start, Aunt Lilly said, "Let me ask you, Ted Day. Is it murder to shoot someone that wants to steal your money and your house and kill your dog?"

Larsen did not wait for Ted to answer. "Please, Aunt Lilly, let Ted ask the questions. Ted has written a memo. It's like this. You can use deadly force to protect yourself or your property, but only if it is reasonable. The police asked you if you feared for your life and you told them . . ."

Lilly interrupted her nephew. "Not after I shot the bastard. Why would I be scared of a dead man?"

Larsen continued, "You have to show that the reasonable fear existed at the time you shot him. So why did you shoot him?"

"I told you. There was no meaner man on the face of the earth than your uncle Harry when he was drinking. The bear in my dream told me he was coming for me. That was good enough."

Ted was impressed by the way Larsen handled Aunt Lilly, but she was not answering what he believed to be the crucial question. Angel apparently agreed. "*Age*, let Ted ask the questions."

Ted was attuned to Aunt Lilly's fear and anxiety. He could

tell that she was very scared. He had never done it before, and it almost seemed unprofessional for a lawyer, but he reached out and took the old woman's hand in his own. "May I call you Aunt Lilly?"

She only smiled, so Ted continued. "I have a few questions. In your dream, exactly what did the bear tell you?"

"I already told the police and the other lawyer, Shinn. They say dreams don't matter in court."

"I believe that truth can come in dreams. So let's find the truth in the dream. Would you tell us again?"

"It's a short dream. Not much to tell. I was sleeping in a cave. My spirit bear comes to me in many dreams. This night he came and said that I was in great danger. That Harry wanted my money, my dog, and my home. The bear said that either Harry would shoot me or I would shoot Harry. It was my choice."

Ted thought a moment. "That's just like you told it before and how the police wrote it down in their report. It's good that you remembered the dream so well." Ted paused. "How do you think the bear knew this was going to happen?"

"You believe that the bear talks to me in my dreams?" Aunt Lilly asked.

"Yes, I think the mind finds many ways to talk to us; sometimes it uses words; sometimes it uses dreams. What's so crazy about that?"

"You're a smart lawyer, Ted Day."

"Let me ask you, what does the bear know? How could he know this bad thing was going to happen?"

"The bear knows everything I know. We are like one."

"If I asked the bear how he knew Uncle Harry was going to threaten you, what do you think the bear would tell me?"

"I'm not sure. Tonight when I sleep, I will ask him how he knew." She thought a bit longer and then continued. "The bear knows that Harry threatened me many times before. The bear knows that Harry said he would come out with his gun and shoot me. The bear knows that Harry sneaks around my house and breaks in when I'm gone doing my laundry at the creek. The bear knows that Harry likes to shoot his gun when he is drunk. The bear knows all of these things."

"Does the bear know if they are all true?" Ted asked.

"Of course. Bears never lie."

"Was Harry drunk the day you shot him?"

"Harry was always drunk."

"Did Harry have a gun like the bear said he would?" Lilly didn't answer right away, so he asked again. "Was he carrying a gun?"

"Harry always carried his gun. That's why I always had to wear mine."

"The police report didn't mention a gun being found anywhere on or near Harry's body. Aunt Lilly, are you sure he had one that day?"

"Of course I'm sure. It's dangerous having a loaded gun lying around like that. I picked it up."

"Where is it?"

"I put it in a safe place in Bertha."

"I need that gun."

"It's easy enough to get. Just take a half-inch wrench and undo the bolt on the floor. It's under the floor."

It did not give Ted any great comfort knowing that he had spent the last two weeks sleeping on top of a loaded gun and a crucial piece of evidence in a murder trial. He motioned to the guard that he was ready to leave.

"Aunt Lilly, thank you for your time. Mr. Shinn and I must go straight to the police station with the gun. This is very important evidence that needs to be added to the file." He started to walk toward the door, stopped, and turned around. "Angel, stay with your dad. I'll call you when I'm finished." He then looked to Aunt Lilly. "Thank you for allowing me to wear your vest. It has good energy."

Three days later the additional evidence had been logged into the official police report and Uncle Harry's fingerprints on the weapon were confirmed. Ted and John Shinn filed their motion and supporting brief seeking the dismissal of all charges against Aunt Lilly. They asked to be heard immediately on the motion. Over the prosecution's objection, the judge allowed that it was an urgent matter and deserved to be taken up promptly at 9:00 a.m. the following Monday.

31

Ted summarized his arguments while Lilly sat at the defense table. Larsen and Angel waited at the back of the courtroom. Ted and John Shinn had worked the rest of the week and through the entire weekend on their arguments. Shinn was impressed by Ted's legal analysis. He didn't have a brief writer like Ted on staff. He could have used one. Most lawyers were eager to try cases and were lazy with the research and the writing. Shinn listened patiently while Ted methodically walked the judge through the arguments. When there were only two minutes left for summation, Ted shifted gears.

"Your Honor, the castle doctrine allows a resident of this state to use deadly force to defend herself or her property from an intruder. I understand that the court may be reluctant to define the legal perimeter of Ms. Two Sparrow's residence as reaching beyond the walls of her bookmobile, but several courts have extended the doctrine to the surrounding yard." Ted handed copies of cases he had located from other jurisdictions to both the judge and the prosecutor, then continued. "Extending the doctrine past the walls of her home seems particularly reasonable in this case. The bounds of her fear had likewise been extended. We're not dealing with just with any intruder but with an intruder who had a history of abusing the defendant, who was intoxicated and was carrying a loaded weapon."

After Ted completed his arguments, he sat down next to Lilly and John Shinn. Aunt Lilly reached over and shook his hand. "Your energy is good today, Ted Day."

The prosecutor rose and made her arguments. About an hour later the judge returned to the courtroom and issued his ruling: The newly discovered evidence was compelling. Aunt Lilly had been acting in self-defense. He slammed down the gavel. He had always thought Aunt Lilly was innocent. For himself, he always thought dreams mattered. "Motion granted. The defendant is released and all charges are dismissed."

One Year Later

The gorge was about 450 feet deep, and a raging river carried the melting snow from K2, the second-highest mountain in the Himalayas, beneath them. The Pakistani village generally known as Two Forks could be accessed only via a wooden box that ran on pulleys on a cable suspended across the gorge. As they approached the cage, they slowed down and debated the next step.

"You go first," Angel said. "This doesn't look safe."

"You want to go on vacation with Ted Day, this is what you get. You can't just stay on the reservation, driving around in your new bookmobile, reading to those little reservation rug rats and hoping that adventure will find you. Life doesn't work that way. Now come on, you can do it."

She pointed to the crate and said, "My children need me. Your life insurance is paid up. Get on board, buddy."

Ted looked down. The pass did look considerably more frightening than he had expected. He might have overdone this one a bit. "We could draw straws."

Angel shook her head and said, "We don't have a straw. How about we flip a coin?"

Ted thought a moment and offered, "Rock, paper, scissors?" Angel put her hands on her hips and played her trump card. "Ted, you're the man; just go first."

Ted removed his cowboy hat and wiped the sweat from his brow. "We're short-staffed at Legal Aid. The pay on the reservation is lousy. They can't afford to lose me. You know that. Remember what Shinn said. How valuable I've been."

"That may be, but you can't afford to lose your wife, either. It took you thirty years to find a good one. Remember? The dogs love me more than they love you. You go first."

Ted leaned over and kissed Angel on the forehead. "You win." He tentatively put one foot in the crate and tested his weight. It seemed solid enough. Two tooth-challenged men pulled him across from the other side of the gorge. The wind blew, causing the wooden container to sway back and forth. Ted closed his eyes and grinned. It was a rush. When he got to the other side, he fell out of the crate, wide-eyed and excited.

He brushed off his pants—waterproof, of course, as recommended in *The Complete Idiot's Guide to Trekking in the Himalayas*. He had secretly checked out the book and planned the whole wedding trip in advance. So far, so good.

The Sherpas pulled the crate back across the gorge and opened the door so Angel could climb in and cross. She hesitated and then backed away from the crate. Perhaps she should just let him go see the monastery by himself. If you've seen one mountain monastery, you've seen them all. The sun streamed through the valley and illuminated the rushing river below. The water was pristine and reflected dazzling beams of light that danced on the canyon walls. Angel told herself that the crate had made it across the gorge thousands of times and would make it again. Still, it just didn't look safe.

The wind pulled the cooler air down from the mountain-top and brushed her long black hair from her face. Ted glanced at Angel. She was as beautiful, as wild, and as enchanting to him as she had been that first day they smashed into each other. He knew she could do it. She just needed to savor the adventure. He yelled across the gorge, "You can do it!"

Angel looked at the crate and yelled back, "Go ahead without me. I'll wait here."

"Angel!"

"Yes?"

Ted directed that the crate be pulled back to his side of the gorge. He then took out a small notebook and pencil that he kept stashed in one of his vest pockets and scribbled a note. He put the note in the crate and they pulled it back to Angel's side of the gorge.

Ted cupped his hands around his mouth and yelled out one word at a time, "Read. The. Note!"

Angel leaned into the crate and picked up the note. After reading it, she could not help laughing. Ted looked so ridiculous standing over there in Aunt Lilly's orange vest. Still, his energy was good. It was a nice wedding gift from Aunt Lilly, but he should have left it at home. She climbed into the crate as if she were climbing onto her bike for a ride around the block. The Sherpa gave the signal and the crate slowly traveled back across the gorge. She closed her eyes at first and then decided to look around her. How often does one get an opportunity to view life from this perspective? When the crate slowed for a second, she threw Ted's note over the side and watched it slowly flutter to the bottom of the gorge.

When she closed her eyes, the printed letters from Ted's note were seared in the black spaces of her mind where she could still easily retrieve them.

IMAGINE.